Why hadn't he asked her to stay the night?

He must have felt that tonight she had been ready to put aside her sensibility and make love, except he hadn't asked her. He had withdrawn, instead.

Being the gentleman that I am... Susan surrendered to an amazed laugh as she recalled what Chris had said the evening they'd first gotten to know each other. He was a gentleman. Just as he had been a gentleman in removing her from a bar when she was making a fool of herself and in making sure that she was unattached before he asked her on a date, so he was now being a gentleman in not pushing her beyond her limits. Regardless of their attraction, regardless of the heat that tore through them whenever they kissed, he was holding back, protecting her.

ABOUT THE AUTHOR

Judith Arnold can't remember ever not being a writer. She wrote her first story at age six and pursued a successful career as a playwright after getting a master's degree from Brown University. Judith, who now devotes herself to writing full-time, also pens novels under the pseudonym Ariel Berk. She and her husband and two sons live in Connecticut.

Books by Judith Arnold

HARLEQUIN AMERICAN ROMANCE

*KEEPING THE FAITH SUBSERIES

HARLEQUIN TEMPTATION

Don't miss any of our special offers. Write to us at the following address for information on our newest releases.

Harlequin Reader Service
901 Fuhrmann Blvd., P.O. Box 1397, Buffalo, NY 14240
Canadian address: P.O. Box 603,
Fort Erie, Ont. L2A 5X3

Twilight
Judith Arnold

Harlequin Books

TORONTO • NEW YORK • LONDON
AMSTERDAM • PARIS • SYDNEY • HAMBURG
STOCKHOLM • ATHENS • TOKYO • MILAN

Published March 1988

First printing January 1988

ISBN 0-373-16240-5

Chapter One

At the ripe old age of thirty, Susan Duvall got crocked for the first time in her life.

She wasn't aware of how drunk she was until she settled herself behind the wheel of her car and tried unsuccessfully to stick the key into the ignition switch. When it didn't slide into place after three jerky attempts, she lifted the key and inspected it, squinting in the glaring early-evening sunlight that poured through her windshield. Once she'd ascertained that she had the correct key pinched between her thumb and index finger, she tried again to poke it into the ignition. She missed by a good half inch.

If she couldn't find the damned slot with the key, she reasoned, she probably wouldn't be able to find the road with her car.

She had consumed only two vodka sours, ordinarily not enough to have such an effect on her. But she'd never patronized that particular watering hole before. To be sure, she rarely ventured inside bars at all, and for all she knew, the bartender might have made her drinks stronger than she was used to. She'd drunk the cocktails quickly, too, and on an empty stomach. She hadn't eaten anything since breakfast; by noon, she'd been too upset to face the prospect of eating lunch.

She let her key ring drop into her lap and gazed through her windshield at the tavern. It was a tasteful upscale establishment, decorated with wood paneling, greenhouse glass, leather-upholstered seating and too many potted ferns to count, and it catered to the professionals who worked for companies situated within the Cheshire Industrial Park a short drive away. At least sixteen people from Schenk Chemicals' corporate headquarters had been inside the bar with Susan, celebrating the big Pentagon rocket-fuel contract Schenk had just landed. The contract would bring millions of dollars to the company over the next several years. Those millions of dollars would translate to new jobs and to job security for current employees. Raises for the hourly workers in the plants, perhaps, and whopping year-end bonuses for those who, like Susan, worked at corporate headquarters. It was no wonder everyone was hoisting up drinks in toasts to themselves, to one another, to Schenk and to John Langers.

Susan had hoisted her glass along with her colleagues, but more in desperation than in revelry. She had worked with John in formulating Schenk's bid for the Pentagon. But not until that morning, after the announcement that the bid had been accepted, had John revealed to her exactly what he'd done to win such a lucrative contract for the company.

Thinking about it didn't make Susan feel like partying; it made her feel like gulping down enough vodka sours to anesthetize herself into unconsciousness. She hadn't passed out, however. All she'd accomplished was to wind up too muddled to drive herself home.

The front door of the tavern opened. John Langers and two other Schenk people emerged, blinking in the fading sunshine. Seeing Susan slouched inside her car, John frowned, exchanged a few words with his companions and jogged across the lot to her. He bent over so his head was level with the open driver's window. "Hey, Susan—is everything all right?"

If her morale was an acceptable measure, nothing was even remotely all right. But what to do, other than seeking temporary relief in the mind-numbing power of vodka, eluded her. "Everything's fine," she mumbled.

"You left the bar five minutes ago. You said you were heading straight home."

Susan studied John's familiar face: the thinning brown hair, the dark, earnest eyes, the disproportionately small nose and the deep lines bracketing his mouth. Because he was no longer at the office, and because the early August heat bordered on oppressive, he had removed his tie and unbuttoned the collar of his wilted yellow shirt.

John had always seemed gentle to Susan, sincere and honest in an avuncular sort of way. He didn't look half as shrewd as he was; Susan suspected that his ability to present himself as affable and folksy rather than cunning contributed in a large way to his success. Competing for Pentagon contracts wasn't for the faint of heart; John was as clever as he was intelligent, as manipulative as he was knowledgeable. But Susan had always trusted him.

Today, she had discovered that this man, her mentor, the person from whom she'd learned everything she knew about procuring major government contracts, was a crook. For the past forty-five minutes she'd sat beside him inside a bar, watching as their associates sang his praises and slapped him on the back. He'd accepted their congratulations, and she'd guzzled liquor and wondered if she would ever be able to trust him again.

She certainly wasn't going to trust him with the news that she was too inebriated to get herself home safely. "It's just a little car trouble," she muttered, uncomfortable about having to lie but unable to think of a better excuse. "I think I flooded the engine. It should be all right in a couple of minutes."

"Do you want me to wait?"

"No, thanks," she declined. "It does this all the time. I'm sure it'll start any minute now."

"Okay," John said. "Have a good weekend, Susan. And thanks again for all your help. You deserve a lot of the credit for the contract, you know—the background work, the support, the trip to Washington with me—"

"Yes, I know," she cut him off. She didn't want any of the credit, even if she had done a great deal of the work entailed in preparing and submitting Schenk Chemicals' bid. As John's assistant, she helped him in all his projects. Providing him with support was her job, and until today she was completely satisfied with it. She had enjoyed being his second in command, letting him show her the ropes and guide her through the corporate mine fields.

"I know I was the one getting all the kudos in there," he persisted, gesturing toward the tavern behind him, "but when it comes time for handing out bonuses, honey, I'm not going to let them overlook you. I couldn't have done this without you."

"Uh-huh." Attempting to hold up her end of this conversation was extremely difficult when her head was spinning and her vision kept fuzzing up. "You really don't have to wait, John," she asserted, eager to get rid of him before she started slurring her words. "Go on home and take Margaret out to dinner. I'll see you Monday."

"Sure thing." He leaned through the open window, kissed Susan's cheek, then waved and sauntered across the lot to his own car.

Suppressing a shudder, Susan watched him back out of his parking space and drive away. She and John had worked together for over two years—ever since she'd come to Schenk from the low-key entry-level position she'd had in the marketing department of a small chemical company in northern New Jersey. That had been an excellent job for Susan when she was fresh out of business school, but after a couple of years she'd outgrown it. She had been looking for greater challenges, greater responsibilities, and John Langers had been looking for a gung-ho assistant. Theirs had been a perfect professional match, and it didn't take them long to become close friends, as well. When Susan had bought her condominium, John and Margaret had showered her with housewarming gifts. When their daughter had gotten married, Susan had attended the reception. For John to kiss her didn't signify anything other than friendship.

Today, however, she was repulsed by his kiss. The man was a criminal, after all. If and when she ever got home, she vowed, the first thing she'd do would be to wash her cheek.

She noticed a few more company people leaving the tavern, dispersing outside the door and climbing into their cars. Perhaps her best strategy would be to hide in her car until the last of her co-workers vanished, so nobody from work would have to know how pickled she was. Then she would emerge, return to the bar and call a cab to take her home.

She folded her arms over the steering wheel and used them to cushion her aching head. Closing her eyes, she replayed mentally the discussion she'd had with John that morning, shortly after the broadcast on the building's public address system that the Pentagon had chosen Schenk's bid over all the others it had received.

As soon as Susan had heard the announcement, she'd raced across the hall to John's office, given him an exuberant hug, and shrieked, "You did it, John! You did it!"

"I couldn't have done it if the brass down in Washington hadn't been so greedy," he had scoffed modestly. "All it takes is knowing how to read the other guy, knowing how to get him to see things your way." Then John had told her precisely what he'd done to get the Pentagon purchasing agents to see things Schenk's way: he had engineered a convoluted, virtually untraceable scheme of kickbacks and payoffs.

"That's illegal," she'd blurted out.

"Don't be so naïve, Susan," John had chided her. "This is the way people do business with the Pentagon. You want to learn, and that's why I'm telling you. All's fair in love and war—especially in war. When it comes to the big deals, the big profits, your motto has to be: Better Schenk Than Our Competitors."

The air inside Susan's car was hot and stagnant. Sighing, she shoved open the car door, fluffed her shoulder-length brown hair out from underneath the collar of her blue silk-blend blazer, wiped the beads of perspiration from her brow with her hand and trudged across the gravel parking lot to the tavern. Whether or not there were still Schenk people inside, she had to get out of the sultry heat and into an air-conditioned environment.

Swinging open the door, she was accosted by a gust of refreshingly cool air and a babble of jovial, animated voices. Compared to the pre-dusk brightness outside, the tavern's interior was gloomy, and it took a few seconds for her eyes to adjust and come into focus on the customers lined up along the bar and clustered around the cocktail tables.

A quick survey of the room informed Susan that all the Schenk employees had left. All but two, she amended, recognizing a couple of men at the far end of the bar. Richard and Dave worked in the purchasing department, and they frequently sat together for lunch in the dining room. They had just finished settling their bill, and as they swung off their stools they glimpsed Susan hovering near the door. She responded to their smiles with an impassive nod and then pretended to be engrossed in the contents of her purse until they'd both left.

Taking a deep breath, she crossed to the bar and beckoned to the bartender. "Excuse me," she whispered. "Is there a telephone here?"

"There's a pay phone in back, by the rest rooms," he told her. "Anything I can help you with, miss? Car trouble?"

She stared mutely at him, suddenly finding herself unable to shape a coherent thought. The bartender's smile hurt her eyes; his teeth seemed too big and bright, his hand too large as he swabbed the polished surface of the bar with a towel. He was only being polite, offering his assistance, yet his kindness seemed sorely inadequate. Her world was falling apart, her good friend and mentor had broken the law—and there was no way this beefy bartender, who might or might not have put too much vodka in her drinks, could help her.

She sank onto the nearest bar stool, holding her shoulders proudly erect and her posture ramrod straight. Then she covered her face with her hands and began to sob.

"It's all right." She heard the voice behind her, low and gravelly, stretched by a subtle Southwestern drawl. "It's all right, I'll take care of her. I know her, I work with her."

Oh no. Someone from Schenk was still inside the tavern, someone from work was there to witness her blubbering. Someone who claimed that he knew her—and whom she herself didn't know. No matter how intoxicated she might be, she wouldn't have forgotten such a distinctive voice if she'd ever heard it before.

She leaned back, expecting to feel the upholstered back of the bar stool supporting her. Instead she felt a man's chest, solid and warm against her shoulders and spine. His arms arched around her, and she realized that she hadn't leaned back at all; this man, this twangy-voiced stranger had pulled her to himself. He gently pried her hands from her face and stuffed a linen handkerchief into her clenched fingers. "Dry your eyes, darlin'," he murmured. "It's all right."

"I'm not drunk," she sniffled, then berated herself for resorting to so many lies in such a brief expanse of time. She'd lied about her car to John, and now she was lying about her blood alcohol level to an utter stranger. For someone who prided herself on her honesty, this was not good.

"Nobody said you were drunk," he assured her, his voice a rumbly purr, vibrating inside her skull in an inexplicably soothing way. "This just doesn't seem like the most appropriate place in the world for you to be doing what you're doing. Why don't we take a little stroll?''

She inspected his arm, which he had somehow managed to loop around her shoulders. Whoever he was, he was wearing a well-made summer-weight suit of beige.He was also wearing a wafer-thin watch on a brown leather strap, and his long, thick fingers were ringless.

Without bothering to wipe her eyes, she spun around on the stool to confront him. Her gaze instantly sharpened on his face.

It wasn't that he was obviously handsome. He was, but that wasn't what clarified Susan's vision and held it, what drew her attention from his mussed honey-colored hair to his high brow, the straight nose, the square jaw and sun-burnished complexion, the hazel eyes peering at her from beneath slightly drooping lids...The smile. His lips were thin and strong, and they were twisted into an ironic smile, somewhat bemused and somewhat mocking. Combined with the sparkle in his sleepy-lidded eyes, his smile gave Susan the distinct impression that this man, whom she was positive she had never seen before, was far too amused by her current plight.

Whoever he was, declaring that he knew her made him an even worse liar than Susan. "I will *not* take a little stroll with you," she rasped, her tongue moving with all the agility of a stick of wood. "And *don't* call me darling. Take your hands off me."

His eyebrows rose in response to her adamantly stated demands, but his smile lingered, cool and just mischievous enough to annoy the hell out of her. Still, he repossessed his handkerchief and obediently withdrew his arm. "I'm not saying you're drunk, Susan," he said calmly, returning the handkerchief to his pocket. "But in your condition, you ought to think twice about issuing orders."

How did he know her name? "Who are you?" she asked, finding the entire encounter strangely sobering.

"Chris Kelso. Personnel."

Chris Kelso? She'd been working at Schenk for a long time, and while she didn't pal around with anyone in the personnel department, she knew most of the department's staff by name. She shook her head. "You must be mistaken," she said. "I have no idea who you are. We certainly don't work together."

"Of course we do," he insisted. "There were more than twenty employees in here, you and me among them, drinking to John Langers's good health for the better part of an hour. Not that you're drunk, of course," he hastened to add. Susan was finding the sly glint in his eyes progressively more irritating. "Now, do you want to sit here sniffling and arguing with me in front of all these people?"

Susan tore her attention from Chris Kelso to scan her surroundings. The bartender was leaning on the bar near her, his face registering deep concern. The rest of her audience—a handful of onlookers seated along the bar on either side of her—appeared gleeful, some maliciously so. Susan closed her eyes and cursed quietly.

"You're catching on," Chris whispered, his lips seductively close to Susan's ear so the gawking bar patrons couldn't eavesdrop. "Now, darlin', with your permission, I'm going to escort you out of here."

She wavered. She did wish to get out of there, and as far away as possible. Yet to waltz off with a total stranger... "You work in personnel?" she asked dubiously. "At Schenk?" She wanted to believe him, but she didn't think she should. The fact that he knew her name and John's didn't prove anything. He might simply have overheard their names mentioned by the crowd when everybody had been making toasts.

He obligingly pulled his wallet from his hip pocket, flipped it open and handed her a laminated Schenk ID card. She read the tiny print: "Kelso, Christopher E.," followed by a Social Security number and an employee number. Then she studied the inch-square mug shot filling the left half of the card. It was a typically awful photograph, the print underexposed and the subject's expression glowering, but there was no doubt that the man in the picture and the man standing next to her were one and the same.

She returned his card and gave him a final dubious perusal. "I'll go outside with you," she muttered reluctantly. Just because he worked for Schenk didn't mean he wasn't a creep. Look at John Langers—he worked for the company, broke laws in the course of his job and was toasted for it.

Chris Kelso grinned and helped her off the stool. He stood only an inch or so taller than her, a fact that made her grateful. She didn't think she could have borne it if he'd turned out to be a huge he-man rescuing a damsel in distress, ready to fling her over his shoulder and tote her away. He curled his fingers around her elbow, nodded quietly to her nosy audience, shoved open the door and ushered her outside. "There," he said once the door swung shut. "Isn't that better?"

Susan took a few bracing breaths. The sky had darkened to a lovely pink color, leeching some of the sticky heat out of the air. Shrugging free of Chris's clasp, she folded her arms across her chest and stalked the length of the parking lot, hoping against hope that fresh air and a brisk walk would sober her up enough for her to feel safe driving home.

At the end of the lot she pivoted and found Chris close behind her. He had shoved his hands into his trouser pockets, and his arms held back the flaps of his jacket to reveal the fine proportions of his chest—the chest against which she'd briefly rested inside the bar. Despite the heat, his white oxford shirt wasn't wrinkled, although he'd loosened the knot of his tie. Maybe he wasn't very tall, but he had a wonderful build, trim and athletic, powerful in an understated fashion that Susan found extremely attractive.

He was laughing, and her attraction to him was quickly overtaken by a healthy surge of anger. "What the hell do you think is so funny?" she snapped, dismayed to discover that he had dimples.

He made a half-hearted attempt to stifle his laughter, then gave up. "Well," he drawled between chuckles, "I'm sure if you thought about it for a bit, you might find something comical about the past few minutes."

"I would not," she argued peevishly. "I've got the world's biggest headache, I'm afraid to drive home, I don't know who you are and you're embarrassing me. Forgive me for failing to see the humor in that."

"I don't mean to embarrass you," he swore, tempering his smile. "I only meant to help. Going back into the bar after you'd left wasn't your best line of action—and bursting into tears was even worse."

"I don't need you to enumerate my mistakes," Susan huffed, trying not to overreact to the news that Chris had been following her movements closely enough to have noticed her initial departure. Apparently he'd had his eye on her for some time before she'd returned to the bar and done her impression of Niagara Falls.

"Why did you come back inside, anyway?" he asked.

Even without his smile he had faint dimples. And his voice, low and husky, his accent neither deep Southern nor hillbilly...Susan almost wished that she *did* know him.

She was in no mood to be meeting a new man, however. Besides, the impression she was making on him had to be abominable. "It's none of your business why I went back inside," she mumbled.

"You were in trouble in there, darlin'," he said, once again dropping the final *g*. She couldn't imagine why that sexist word sounded so alluring coming from him. "Why didn't you stay outside, or go somewhere else where nobody would recognize you?"

"I thought all the Schenk people had left," she explained. "And I wanted to call a cab."

"A cab? Here in Cheshire?" He succumbed to another brief laugh. "I've only lived here a couple of months, and even I know that the nearest taxi service must be down in New Haven, a good fifteen miles away."

"They've got cabs in Wallingford," Susan informed him.

"Have they?" He arched one eyebrow in spurious shock. "Do you mean to tell me you get drunk so often you've gotten to know all the local cab companies?"

"I have not—I have *never*—" Susan bit her lip to silence herself. She didn't owe this man any explanations. Choosing to take the offensive, she said, "I thought you believed me when I said I wasn't drunk."

"I'm a gentleman," he rationalized, his solemn expression belied by the playful glint in his eyes. "And I don't think you're going to find a cab tonight, Susan. So, being the gentleman that I am, I will drive you home."

"You will not," she said firmly.

His eyes momentarily locked onto hers. She was astonished by the strength in his gaze, the challenge. There was something undefinably aggressive about the way he looked at her, something disconcertingly sexual about it. Not that he was leering, not that he was directing his vision to the scooped neckline of her silk blouse or the modest slit rising from the hem of her straight skirt. Perhaps what made his stare so charged was that he was an uncommonly good-looking man; perhaps Susan was reading her own feelings in his glittering hazel eyes.

"I'm not going to get into a car with you," she declared, as much to herself as to him. "You're a complete stranger—"

"Come on, Susan. I showed you my ID."

"Just because we work for the same company doesn't mean I know you."

"Bob DeGraff introduced us," Chris reminded her. "In the dining room, over a month ago. You were eating lunch with Langers. He asked me something about dental insurance."

That rang a bell. Susan vaguely recalled a brief lunchtime conversation among John, Bob DeGraff from personnel and Bob's new colleague. But the meeting hadn't really registered on Susan. Just before Bob had approached their table, John had invited her to accompany him to Washington for negotiations with several Pentagon purchasing agents. She'd been immensely flattered that he wanted her with him on such an important business trip, and she'd been too busy daydreaming about what she'd pack and how impressively she'd perform to give more than a cursory nod to the new man from the personnel department.

She should have paid attention. A man who looked—and talked—like Chris Kelso was definitely worth paying attention to.

Even so, she wasn't going to get into a car with him. That he worked with Bob DeGraff, that he and Susan had been formally, if superficially, introduced, that he'd shown her his ID and claimed to be a gentleman . . . none of it erased the fact that Susan's brain was currently operating at less than full capacity. She'd heard too many scary stories about men taking advantage of disoriented women to shut herself up inside a car with someone she hardly knew. "Date rape," she said aloud.

Chris looked stunned. "I beg your pardon?"

Realizing that she'd inadvertently given voice to her half-baked meditations, Susan colored slightly and lowered her eyes. "Nothing," she mumbled, then contradicted herself. "Just because we've met doesn't mean I should trust you. You've heard of date rape, haven't you? The woman knows the man, maybe they're even friends, and then when they're all alone he attacks her, and—"

Chris erupted in laughter again. "I'm going to drive you home, Susan. That's not my idea of a date. Or, for that matter, rape."

She glanced at him, chagrin and resentment contributing to the rosy blush spreading along her cheekbones. Given what a total jerk she'd made of herself in front of this man, first inside the bar and now in the parking lot, she didn't have the nerve to get into a car with him. It no longer had anything to do with a fear of assault; it was simply a matter of having behaved stupidly enough not to want to inflict herself further on him.

"I don't think I'm drunk anymore," she said, meaning it. If she were drunk, she wouldn't be feeling her em-

barrassment so acutely. "I'll get myself home. Thanks."
She offered Chris a timid smile, then ducked her head
and tried to walk past him in the direction of her car.

He reached out, snagged her arm and halted her.
"Don't push your luck, Susan," he said. "At least let me
pour some coffee down your throat. Then we'll run a
Breathalyzer on you."

"Like hell you will," she protested, although she didn't
sound particularly resistant anymore. The notion of
sharing a cup of coffee with Chris had a certain appeal to
it.

Ignoring her token objection, he slipped her hand
through the bend in his arm. "There's a Dairy Queen just
down the road," he remarked. "If you're really afraid to
get into a car with me, we can walk."

Susan considered her mid-heeled leather pumps, her
headache and the residual mugginess in the evening air.
"Which car is yours?" she asked in resignation, survey-
ing the parking lot and trying to guess what kind of ve-
hicle Chris would own. She spotted a sporty two-seater,
one of those hot Japanese models, and she wasn't surprised when he led her toward it.

"Right over here," he said, unlocking not the sports
car but an aged brown station wagon parked next to it.
The body had rusted through near the bumper, and a
strip of chrome trim was missing from one of the side
panels. When Chris opened the passenger door for Susan, she automatically peeked into the back seat. It was
strewn with baseball cards, a ponytail barrette, a tat-
tered issue of *Mad* magazine, a pair of pink rubber beach
slippers and numerous crumpled napkins imprinted with
the logos of various purveyors of fast food. The classy
leather attaché case stowed on the floor seemed wildly out
of place.

Chris noticed Susan's bemusement. "Sorry about the mess," he said, helping her onto the seat. "I try to keep the front neat, at least."

What had startled her wasn't the mess but the realization that Chris was a father. Scrambling through her thoughts in the few seconds it took him to shut her door, lope around the car to the driver's side and climb in next to her, Susan came to the conclusion that her supply of embarrassment knew no bounds.

The man was a father, and she had all but accused him of plotting to rape her. He was a father, and she'd berated herself for having failed to take note of his striking good looks the first time they'd met. She had idiotically experienced all sorts of ill-defined but erotic sensations when he'd gazed into her eyes . . . and he was a *father*.

"You have children," she announced unnecessarily as he started the engine.

He grinned and shook his head. "I used to think so, but not anymore. What I have are beasts," he corrected her.

"How many?"

"Two." He glanced over his shoulder as he backed out of the parking space and chuckled as he caught a glimpse of the disorder in the back seat. "The evidence might lead you to assume I had more than that."

Susan didn't speak for a minute. She was still reeling from the understanding that Chris was a family man. "Why are you doing this?" she asked sharply. "Why are you taking me out for coffee instead of going home?"

"I told the kids I'd be home later than usual tonight," he said calmly. "It isn't every day Schenk picks up a multimillion-dollar contract. I felt the occasion called for a celebratory beer after work."

"Yes, but—"

"And I'll call them again from the Dairy Queen," he assured her. "They're undoubtedly just as happy to be rid of me for an extra hour."

"What about your wife?" Susan asked cautiously. "Doesn't she want you home?"

Chris shot her a quick look, then smiled. "I'm divorced, Susan. At large and unattached—except for my two beasts."

"They're visiting for the summer?" she hazarded.

"Nope. They're all mine, full-time."

Before she could question him further, he steered into the parking lot of the Dairy Queen. He climbed out and ambled around to Susan's side. The door squeaked when he opened it, and the chivalrous offer of his hand to help her out seemed anomalous given the dilapidated condition of the car.

Still, Susan didn't refuse his assistance. His hand was warm and dry around hers, the skin of his palm hard and smooth. And knowing that he was divorced, at large and unattached, left her once again free to appreciate his attractive build and his sensual smile.

Inside the glass-enclosed eatery, Chris headed straight for the exposed pay phone attached to a wall near the entry. Susan loitered by the door, but she couldn't help overhearing his end of the conversation. "Well, Emma, I'm having some coffee now," he said patiently. "It'll be a while yet. Did you—Emma, I don't really care if he dumped mayonnaise on his jeans. We'll just—oh, *your* jeans? Well, babe, if you put 'em away instead of leaving them on the kitchen counter... All right, put Newt on...."

"Are they okay?" Susan asked once he'd hung up. From what she'd overheard, it sounded as if Chris's children were wreaking havoc at home. She wondered why Chris hadn't asked to speak to the baby-sitter.

"Just the usual," he said, ushering Susan to the counter and ordering two cups of coffee. "You want a hamburger?"

"No, thank you."

"I don't know if I should bring some burgers home for them," Chris said, musing. "I tried to find out whether they'd eaten yet, but they wouldn't talk about anything but whose fault it was that Newt spilled mayonnaise on a pair of Emma's jeans."

"Newt?"

"My son. James Newton Kelso. We've been calling him Newt all his life."

"How old is he?"

"Ten and a half. Emma's thirteen." Chris gestured toward an empty table and they sat facing each other.

Susan stirred two packets of sugar into the waxed cardboard cup and studied the man across from her, wondering if she appeared as astonished as she felt. Chris Kelso was full of surprises—not the least of them that his children were too old for babysitters. "You don't look old enough to have a teenage daughter," she commented.

"I'm not," he joked. "I was twenty-two when she was born—definitely too young. But Mother Nature works these things out. Raising two children—or two beasts, if you'd rather—has a way of aging a man, so I'm very nearly old enough now."

Susan shaped a faint smile at Chris's joke, then lapsed into a contemplative silence. He was only five years older than her—and he had two children with double-digit ages, while she wasn't even close to marrying, let alone becoming a mother. She had designed her youth around

obtaining a superior education, including a degree from
one of the top business schools, and then clawing her way
up the corporate ladder in the hope that finally, perhaps, her father would say, "Yes, you've made it, you're
a success and I'm proud of you." Finding a husband and
raising children—or beasts—had never been part of Susan's game plan.

Yet here was a man, an executive like her, who at the
age of twenty-two had been cradling a newborn daughter to himself instead of cramming for his finals or bon-
ing up for the Graduate Record Exams. She'd never met
anyone like him before. "I'm sorry," she said quietly.

"Sorry? About what?"

She continued to stir her coffee, afraid that if she hesitated long enough to take a sip she'd lose her momen-
tum. "I'm sorry about the way I acted with you before,
when you were trying to help me."

"You mean, taking me for a rapist?" He smiled gently,
his dimples curving down his cheeks. "Susan, I'm the
father of a girl. I understand that in this imperfect world
of ours, women have to be paranoid. I'd die a thousand
deaths if Emma ever accepted a ride from a man she
didn't know."

"But that's just it, Chris," Susan went on. "I should
have known who you were. I shouldn't have been so rude
the day Bob DeGraff introduced us. But I was so busy
thinking about a trip John and I were going to be taking..." A trip where, unbeknownst to her, deals were
dealt and souls were sold. A trip where a man she'd re-
vered for the past two years had sidestepped laws, turned
his back on ethics and bribed federal employees.

It was because of what John had done on that trip to
Washington that Susan had fallen apart today. It was
because of what she'd learned about John's manner of

conducting business that she'd needed Chris's help at the bar less than a half hour ago. She was stung by the irony that, at the moment she could have been getting to know Chris, she had instead been dreaming about her good fortune in working for a man as brilliant as John Langers.

"He's a talented guy," Chris opined before taking a long sip of coffee.

"Who?"

"Your boss. He reeled in a mighty big one for Schenk."

Susan pressed her lips together to keep herself from exploding in rage. Anyone willing to bribe buyers, as John had, could reel in a big contract. It had nothing to do with talent.

But she couldn't discuss that with Chris. She couldn't discuss with anyone what John had told her about the Pentagon contract. Not yet, not until she'd figured out what she ought to do about it.

"For someone who hasn't worked at Schenk very long, you certainly seem loyal," she said dryly.

Chris shook his head. "I've been with the company for twelve years," he told her. "I got my start in the personnel office at the Tulsa plant. I was running the department there when they decided to ship me up here to headquarters."

"Tulsa," she echoed. "Is that where your accent comes from?"

"What accent?" he teased, lowering his cup. "I haven't got an accent. It's all you Connecticut Yankees that talk funny."

Susan laughed. For the first time since the announcement that morning, she was genuinely laughing, and it felt wonderful. "How do you like Cheshire?" she asked.

"It's beginning to grow on me," he admitted. "I only wish the kids liked it better. Actually, Newt seems to be adapting. Emma...well, if we'd moved during the school term, she could have made some friends in her classes, so she'd have people to spend the summer vacation with. She's met a couple of girls, but she misses Tulsa something fierce."

"Thirteen is a hard age for a girl to get through," Susan commented, although she suspected that Chris had more up-to-date knowledge about that than she herself did.

"She'll survive," Chris predicted. "She's sturdy. Would you like some more coffee?" he asked, eyeing Susan's cup.

"No. I'm feeling fine," she assured him. "I think I could even pass a Breathalyzer test."

Chris gave her a probing stare. "I'll tell you something, Susan," he drawled, leaning back in his chair and shoving a misplaced lock of hair off his brow. "I bet you could have passed a Breathalyzer test before you drank that coffee. I bet you could have passed one even when you were sitting at the bar and weeping. You weren't crying from the booze, darlin'. Those were tears of pain."

Stunned, she gaped at him. He was right, of course. Two vodka sours hadn't been what had driven her to tears, what had made her queasy and distraught and longing for oblivion. It had been the pain of learning that John had bribed people to win a contract, the betrayal of it, the discovery that a man she adored, a man who treated her with more respect than her own father ever had, was a crook. For money, for advancement, for whatever reason, John had committed an illegal act, and Susan was heartbroken about it.

"I've got to go," she said tersely. She was grateful to Chris for having extricated her from the bar and for helping her to regain her wits, but his statement proved that he was too perceptive. She had been crying from pain, yes, but she wasn't about to expose that pain to a man she scarcely knew.

As it was, she couldn't shake the unsettling thought that Chris Kelso's gentle hazel eyes had already seen far too much.

Chapter Two

Why was he even thinking about it? Why was he eating himself up over her?

So he'd overstepped a little, so he'd stated what had seemed obvious to him. He'd told her he knew she hadn't been drunk when she'd dropped onto the bar stool and wept until those beautiful brown eyes of hers were drained dry. He'd said something she didn't want to hear, revealed that he knew something she didn't want him to know. And he'd scared her off.

"I'll be fine," she said loftily when he dropped her off at her car in the lot outside the bar. "Thanks for...the coffee." She wasn't about to thank him for having spirited her out of the bar, or for having gone on record with the news that he was aware of her pain. Especially not for that.

"Would you like me to follow you in my car?" he asked. "Just to make sure you get home safely."

"That won't be necessary," she said, and of course it wouldn't be. They had already established that she was sober.

She seemed nervous to Chris, shooting him one final, searching look before she started her engine and drove away. He didn't sense anger in her, as he had earlier, but rather torment and confusion. Fear. Loss.

Damn. He had resolved weeks ago that he wasn't going to try anything with her. It was all too obvious to Chris that she had a romance going with John Langers. They were always together, always conferring, sharing lunch, taking off on business trips. After Bob DeGraff had introduced Chris to Susan that June day in the dining room, Chris had asked Bob who she was and what she did. "She's a junior exec in the marketing department," Bob had informed Chris. "And what she does is whatever Langers asks her to do."

Ever since that one superficial encounter with Susan—an encounter that apparently hadn't made the slightest impression on her, Chris pointedly reminded himself—he had wasted far too much time daydreaming about the sleek fall of her dark hair, the delicate structure of her face, those fine, high cheekbones and soft lips and wondrous light brown eyes. Much too often, he'd found himself imagining the slender body hidden beneath her broad-shouldered blazers and straight skirts, the curves barely hinted at by her loose-fitting silk blouses. He'd meditated on the graceful line of her throat, the peach tint of her skin, the understated sway of her hips when she walked . . .

The woman was a looker, no doubt about it. And she was throwing herself away on John Langers, of all people, a married man old enough to be her father. There could be only one reason, as Chris analyzed it: Langers was her boss. He was a major player in the company, a powerful man, and Susan Duvall was ambitious. So she did whatever Langers asked of her.

Chris shouldn't have rushed to her rescue at the bar. He had just telephoned Emma, told her he was on his way home and started toward the exit when he discovered Susan sobbing at the front of the bar. The revelries had wound to a close before he'd called home; as far as he knew, he was the only employee still there. His logic told him to keep walking, to leave Susan alone, to leave her to Langers and whatever affair they were embroiled in.

But he was unable to strand her when she looked so needy and forlorn, so unspeakably vulnerable. Susan Duvall, he had deduced from occasional glimpses of her and from office gossip, did not make it her habit to exude vulnerability. In all the time Chris had spent thinking about her, it had never occurred to him that she was capable of shedding tears.

Yet there she was, in an extremely public place, crying, her shoulders heaving and her cheeks streaked with moisture. Chris couldn't abandon her.

Something must have happened in the parking lot, he concluded, mentally reviewing the entire episode as he steered onto the road and lowered the visor against the glare of the setting sun. Susan had left the bar, then Langers had left, and then, fifteen minutes later, she'd returned alone and started to bawl. Maybe they'd had a fight, maybe she was ready to break off with Langers and take up with someone new.

"Forget it," Chris muttered beneath his breath. Her haunting beauty notwithstanding, he wasn't interested in the sort of woman who would have an affair with her married boss just to get ahead in the company. He could help a despairing business associate, certainly, and buy her a cup of coffee... It had been an act of mercy, nothing more.

So why couldn't he rid his mind of her? He navigated along the snaking, pitted back road that led to his house, feeling the lengthening evening shadows swallow his car and wishing that they could swallow all his thoughts of Susan, as well. But they couldn't. Her voice still echoed inside his skull, as cool and clear as a mountain brook. He still saw those wide, heavily lashed eyes and that fragile blush of embarrassment staining her cheeks. He still sensed the warmth he'd felt when he had urged her trembling body against his.

He hadn't experienced this kind of adolescent lust for a woman in a long, long time.

Adolescence was a transient condition, he reassured himself. At least once a week, after he and Emma argued over some nonsense, he would watch her storm to her room and slam the door and he'd think, "This shall pass." So it was with him, he supposed. He'd been living in Cheshire for only two months, settling in, establishing a new home for Emma and Newt, learning his new responsibilities in the corporate personnel department. Eventually he would start socializing, making friends outside work, meeting available women. Once that happened, Susan Duvall would fade from center stage in his fantasies.

Emma was reading a magazine in the lounge chair on the porch when Chris cruised up the driveway and stopped outside the detached garage. His house was essentially a log cabin with two additions constructed of brick, nestled into a hilly, heavily treed lot. The broker had done her best to discourage Chris from buying the place. "With what you'll be earning at Schenk, Mr. Kelso," she had asserted, "you can afford a much nicer home."

No argument there. The transfer had come with an enormous raise, enough to enable him to purchase one of the newer, more elegant homes in the developments, even though they were overpriced. Naturally, Emma had loved all those luxurious homes with their built-in microwave ovens and professionally landscaped yards. "This house is weird," she'd declared when the broker reluctantly brought him and the children to see the cabin. "It's a shack, Dad. Everyone's gonna think we're Okies or something if we live here."

But Chris liked the house. He liked the fact that the property abutted a semiprivate pond, which the broad porch overlooked, and the fact that, with all the trees on the lot, there wasn't much grass to mow. He liked the spaciousness of the kitchen, even if it lacked some of the amenities. Best of all he liked the room arrangement: Emma's and Newt's bedrooms were on the main floor, down the hall from the living room, and Chris's bedroom was downstairs next to the den, with its own door opening onto a slate back patio and a path leading to the pond. More than once, after the kids were asleep, Chris had sneaked out of the house and down to the pond, stripped off his clothes and skinny-dipped in the moonlight.

He might be an assistant vice-president at a major chemicals and petroleum products company, and he might be earning enough money to buy one of those fancy microwave-oven-equipped houses. But deep in his heart, Chris Kelso was still a country boy.

"The long lost father returns," Emma greeted him with a desultory sniff, slumping deep into the cushions of the lounge chair and stretching her lanky legs, which protruded from the cuffed ends of a pair of absurdly short shorts.

"Home from the wars," Chris responded as he climbed out of the car and strode up the slope to the porch. For not the first time, he was struck by how much

Emma resembled her mother. Like Elysse, Emma was fair, with straight blond hair, pale gray eyes and a milky complexion. Like Elysse she was disturbingly pretty, and Chris anticipated with dread the day she realized exactly how pretty she was and exploited her looks to make hapless boys fall for her. He hoped that would never happen. He had raised Emma single-handedly for the past nine years; he wanted to think he'd imparted some of his values to her.

He knew better than to take her sarcastic welcome personally. "I was going to bring you hamburgers," he said, pulling off his jacket, "but I figured you'd probably eaten already."

"We did," Emma reported, closing her magazine. "We sliced up some of that leftover roast beef for sandwiches. Newt's inside, doing something disgusting with the mayonnaise jar he emptied onto my jeans. How come you were so late tonight?"

"I told you when I called—there was a party of sorts after work this evening," Chris answered, sitting on the edge of the lounge chair once Emma shifted her legs to make room for him. "Schenk just won a huge contract to supply rocket fuel to the Pentagon."

"Rocket fuel," Emma repeated. "Isn't that what they were making at the Tulsa plant?"

"That's right. And this contract means that a lot of those folks the company had to lay off at the plant last February are going to get their jobs back. Other folks at other plants, too, but especially at the Tulsa plant. And that, Emma, is definitely cause for celebration. So I went out for a beer with a few of my friends from work."

"At least you've got friends," Emma complained with a self-pitying sigh. "All I've got is Newt."

"And those sisters who live down the road—Andrea and what was the other one's name?"

"Lisa. They're dips."

"Life stinks, babe," Chris said with a compassionate smile. "You're just going to have to tough it out." He stood, scooped up his jacket and started for the front door. "After I change my clothes, perhaps you'd be willing to move your carcass and keep me company while I scrounge up some dinner for myself."

What Newt was doing with the empty mayonnaise jar, Chris learned once he entered the house, was driving a nail repeatedly through the lid, puncturing air holes. "Tomorrow I'm gonna catch some toads down by the lake," Newt declared happily. "I'm figuring I can keep 'em in here."

Newt clearly favored his father over his mother in appearance, with his broad face, reddish-brown hair and multicolored irises. Newt also favored Chris's personality over his mother's. Unlike his mother and sister, he wasn't complicated or mysterious. He was right there, out in front, direct and unaffected.

Or maybe it had nothing to do with inheritance; maybe it was simply a measure of the difference between males and females.

Chris still hadn't managed to figure women out. Why, for instance, would a woman with so much on the ball, with a career on the fast track and a face that could launch a million X-rated dreams, let her married boss work her over to such a degree that she'd fall apart in public?

"You're obsessing, Kelso," he reproached himself, neatly arranging his suit on a hanger and hooking it over the closet rod. As soon as the kids started school, he promised himself, as soon as their social lives perked up, he would feel free to resuscitate his own social life. Cheshire was a small town, but Susan Duvall couldn't be the only single woman living within its borders. He had known some fine women in Tulsa, and he was sure he'd meet some women here, too.

Over a dinner of roast beef on rye—Newt devoured a second sandwich with his father, and Emma daintily nibbled on slivers of meat—Chris assessed the feasibility of Newt's toad-catching plan. "I can see where you're coming from, Newt," he conceded, "but supposing you were born to jump, and someone sealed you up inside an empty jar. How would you feel?"

"It's got lots of air holes," Newt claimed. "And I'd put in bugs for the toads to eat."

"Air holes aren't the same thing as air," Chris opined. "If you really want, maybe we could catch some toads tomorrow, play with them for a while and then let them go. That seems more humane, don't you think?"

"And what am I supposed to do while you two are playing with toads?" Emma sulked.

"You could find bugs to feed 'em," Newt suggested. Emma gave him a withering look.

"You can stretch out on a blanket by the water and listen to your Walkman," Chris said gently. It was hard being the only female in the family, being thirteen, being so far from one's hometown friends. More often than not Emma seemed incomprehensible to Chris, but he loved her and sympathized with her feelings of dislocation. "Or, if you're truly desperate," he continued, "you can visit the Dip Sisters." That provoked a reluctant smile from her.

After dinner, Chris made three chocolate ice-cream cones, and he and his children ate them out on the porch. He told Newt and Emma a little bit more about the rocket-fuel contract Schenk had landed, and when he mentioned to Newt that the contract might mean that the father of Newt's best friend in Tulsa could get his job back at the plant, Newt declared that he definitely believed the contract to be worthy of a celebration at a bar after work hours. "You can go out and celebrate some more while we're asleep," Newt offered. "We won't mind."

"One beer is plenty," Chris insisted. "But I appreciate the thought, Newt."

As soon as the kids were done with their ice cream, they went back into the house to watch TV. Chris remained on the porch, gazing through the silhouetted trees toward the pond. Its motionless surface reflected the lights of other houses lining the shore. Closer to him, he saw the brighter, sharper lights of fireflies dancing through the air, streaking like tiny comets across his vision and evanescing in the gathering darkness.

The Pentagon contract was worth celebrating. But all Chris could think of was a lovely woman, dark-haired, doe-eyed, staring at him in panic, in pain, in a moment of crying need.

SUSAN DREW IN a deep breath, straightened her blazer with a shrug, and knocked on his door. It had been a hellish weekend, hours upon hours spent in contemplation, soul searching, self-recrimination. She had no idea of what to say when she saw Chris. All she knew was that, given her appalling behavior on Friday evening, she had to see him, had to say something.

What she wasn't going to say was that her boss was a criminal. She recognized that going public with John's transgressions was one of her options, possibly the most ethical one. Not that telling Chris Kelso of the personnel department about John's wheeling and dealing with the Pentagon was going to accomplish anything. But she could tell John's boss, or the president of the company, or the C.E.O. She could tell them that one of their most successful employees, a man who had served Schenk diligently and profitably for over eighteen years, had bribed federal officers with kickbacks in order to win a contract.

At which point, she assumed, John's boss, the president and the C.E.O would argue fiercely over which one of them most deserved the privilege of firing Susan.

She might have been innocent about the way contracts were negotiated with the Pentagon, but she was savvy enough to know that as the messenger bearing bad news, she risked her own job if she informed John's superiors of the kickback scheme. It might be something they didn't want to know about; it might be something they already *did* know about, and they'd resent her for having deprived them of their pretense of ignorance. Or they might choose to fire her simply because she wasn't a loyal team player.

Loyalty was another concept she had pondered at length during the weekend. John Langers had been good to her. He had taken her under his wing, tutored her, opened doors for her. He had taught her the proper way to do things, the legitimate way to accomplish her goals at work. He'd taught her never to misrepresent herself or Schenk Chemicals, never to overstate the company's position. He'd taught her that clients preferred to do business with people they could trust, people who were true to their word.

His generosity had extended beyond work. John had provided Susan with emotional support. Choosing to accept the job at Schenk had meant leaving New Jer-

sey—and leaving New Jersey had meant saying goodbye
to the man she'd been dating for two and a half years.
The relationship hadn't survived the separation, and
whenever Susan became depressed about it, whenever she
found herself questioning whether she had been right to
pursue her career at the expense of her love life, John had
consoled her and cheered her up. She had confided in
him, and he'd bolstered her with words of wisdom. "If
it wasn't meant to be, it wasn't," he'd tell her over a cold
drink after one of their lopsided racquetball games, or
during their frequent lunches in the dining room at work.
"You're a terrific lady, Susan. You'll fall in love again."
He'd even arranged a few blind dates for her, none of
which ever developed into anything, but all of which
helped to restore Susan's spirits.

She'd taken enough psychology courses in college to
understand that John had become a surrogate father to
her. There was nothing wrong with that; it just so happened that Susan needed a surrogate father. Susan's
mother had died when she was nine, and her father, always aloof and judgmental, had reacted to the loss by
burying himself in his career. Susan had grown up be-
lieving that the only way she could catch her father's attention—and earn his love—was to dedicate herself to an
equally impressive career.

Her father rarely expressed his approval of her, but
he'd been pleased about her job at Schenk. "It's about
time you found a position worthy of you," he had said.
"This is your big opportunity—a chance to move up in
a major company. Stick with it, and you'll start rising."
Coming from a man as distant and undemonstrative as
Thomas Duvall, those were extraordinary words of
praise.

John was more accessible, more affectionate. He treated Susan with the warmth she had always craved and never received from her own father. She couldn't very well march into the office of the company president and announce that this kind, devoted father figure had committed a crime.

Yet, if she didn't speak up, she would in effect be his accomplice. She didn't think she could live with the guilt of protecting a lawbreaker.

What a choice: to be a tattletale, risking John's career and her own, or to be his partner in crime. Her mind told her she had to turn John in; her heart told her she couldn't. She had spent the entire weekend shut up inside her home, sipping herbal tea—after her debacle in the bar, she wasn't going to drink anything stronger—and analyzing the situation. The only conclusion she had reached by Monday morning was that she was a long way from reaching any conclusions.

Except one: she had to see Chris.

At a few minutes before noon, Susan took the elevator down to his floor, marched into the personnel department reception area and asked one of the secretaries to buzz him on the intercom phone. When the secretary informed him that "Ms. Duvall from marketing" wished to meet with him, he told the secretary to send her in. "Third door on the right," the secretary directed Susan, pointing to the back corridor linking the department's suite of offices.

"Come in," his voice filtered out to her in response to her knock.

Susan turned the knob and pushed the door open. As a rule she prepared herself well for meetings. If necessary, she wasn't above shutting herself up in the ladies' room for a few minutes before a meeting and rehearsing her presentation inside a locked toilet stall. She hadn't rehearsed anything for this meeting with Chris, however. She clung to the vague notion that seeing him would somehow inspire her.

He stood at her entrance. In her high-heeled shoes, she was nearly at eye level with him, and the searing radiance of his eyes inspired her to nothing but silence. She had noticed on Friday that he was handsome, but now, after two and a half grim days in isolation, she could look at him objectively, not through a blur of vodka and tears, but with poise and self-control.

To her amazement, he was even better looking than she'd remembered.

She absorbed the unnerving brilliance of his eyes, his dimples, the firm set of his mouth, the lean economy of his physique and his voice, slightly husky as he drawled, "Hello, Susan. To what do I owe the honor?"

"I'm here to say I'm sorry," she answered, deciding that that was as good a place to start as any.

The corners of his mouth twitched upward in a bemused smile. He circled his broad desk and crossed the room to close the door behind her, his loafers soundless against the plush carpeting. "Would you care to sit down?" he asked, gesturing toward the two upholstered chairs facing his desk.

Susan took a seat and wondered what to say next. As Chris resumed his place behind the desk, her gaze wandered from his leather-trimmed blotter and brass-and-maple nameplate to the two framed photographs adorning one corner of the desk. They appeared to be school photos, rigidly posed, one of a pretty blond girl seated primly, her hands folded in front of her and her hair held back from her face with a blue ribbon, and the other of a grinning boy with flopping auburn hair, deep dimples and glittering eyes. "Are those your beasts?" Susan asked.

Chris glanced at the photos and nodded.

"They're beautiful."

"Especially when you can look at them with the volume turned off," he agreed. He leaned back in his chair, his eyes never leaving Susan, and tapped his fingertips together. For a long moment, the only sound in the room was the whisper of the ventilation system. "Can we explore that 'I'm sorry'?" he asked. "I'm not quite clear about what it refers to."

His slow, delicious drawl made his meticulously phrased request come across as teasing. Susan let her gaze wander to his striped silk tie, his gray suit, the arms that had briefly closed around her while she'd wept, the strong, slightly callused hands that had held her. Then she lifted her eyes to his face again, bravely meeting his unwavering stare. "I was rude last Friday evening," she said, the words finally beginning to flow. "I was upset and I took it out on you. I'm sorry."

He chuckled, a low, smoky sound rising from deep in his throat. "No need," he assured her. "It was my pleasure."

"Your pleasure to haul a blubbering idiot out of a tavern, dose her with coffee and then have her leave you standing in a cloud of exhaust fumes as she tore away? I'm not usually like that, Chris. I'm a well-bred woman, and I've been thinking about this all weekend, and no matter what was going on inside my head, I had no right to take it out on you. No, don't stop me," she silenced him as he opened his mouth to refute her. "I'd like to make it up to you. Will you let me take you to lunch?"

Her invitation took her by surprise. She hadn't planned it. Yet it seemed like a perfect idea. Whatever shenanigans were going on in John's little corner of the marketing department, she saw no reason to deprive herself of the opportunity to get to know Chris better.

Her invitation evidently surprised him, too. His eyebrows rose and he tapped his fingers together again. "Here in the dining room, or out at a restaurant?" he asked.

"Whatever you want. As long as you understand that you're my guest."

He gave the question a great deal of thought. "Won't you mind if people see us eating together?"

"Mind?" She laughed. "Why should I mind?"

"Well..." He reflected for a minute, flexing his mouth as he considered and discarded several statements. "You usually eat lunch with John Langers, don't you?"

She wondered if her face registered the keen discomfort she suffered simply from hearing John's name. It had been fairly easy to avoid her boss all morning, since he was spending most of his time hurrying from meeting to meeting. At one point he'd asked Susan if she wanted to participate in one of the meetings, but she had said no. Until she made up her mind regarding what to do about him, she preferred to spend as little time with him as possible.

"John Langers doesn't own me," she declared quietly and firmly.

"He doesn't, huh," Chris murmured.

His skeptical tone sent a quiver of uneasiness up her spine. "Of course he doesn't," she retorted. "Just because I work for him doesn't mean he has any hold on me."

"Other than his ability to fire you—or promote you," Chris noted, then shook his head as if to stifle himself. "It's none of my business, Susan."

"What's none of your business?" she asked, wondering if Chris already knew about John's scam, if everyone at Schenk already knew, if Susan was the only person in the entire company who reacted to what he'd done with horror and indignation.

Chris swiveled his chair to face the window and squinted into the midday sun. He seemed troubled by something, at a loss for words. He rubbed his index finger thoughtfully along the edge of his jaw, silent.

"What?" she prodded him.

"If you're going to take me out to lunch," he said, shaping each word carefully, "I'd like to take you out to dinner. But before we get that far, Susan, I'd like to make sure I'm not ... trespassing." He swiveled back and examined her face, his expression enigmatic.

"Trespassing?" Chris might have a bizarre way of phrasing his thoughts, but it didn't take long for Susan to figure out what he was getting at. Her immediate impulse was to laugh at the absurdity of her sharing anything other than a close working relationship with John— although, at the present, she didn't even want to have that. Her second impulse was to reach across the desk and slap Chris's face for implying what he had.

She waited until the second impulse waned before shaping her response. "That is an incredibly offensive insinuation," she snapped in a constrained voice. "Do you honestly think the only way a woman can get ahead in the business world is to fool around with her boss?"

"I'm not speaking in generalizations, Susan," he explained. "We're addressing specifics here. If you're involved in anything personal with Langers, I would rather keep my hands off."

"And if I'm not, you'd rather put your hands on?" she countered furiously.

His eyes met hers and he began to laugh, that low, luscious laugh of his. "Only with your permission, darlin'," he promised.

Susan laughed, too. She ought to have been insulted; she ought to have retracted her invitation, her apology, everything she'd ever said to Chris after peering at him from a bar stool and saying, "Don't call me darling." But for some reason, she wasn't insulted, and she wouldn't retract anything.

"That permission," she warned him as her laughter ebbed, "will never come. I happen to think it's a bad idea to date people you work with."

"That seems like a wise policy if you're talking about Langers," Chris countered amiably. "But a very foolish policy if you're talking about me. What night are you free for dinner?"

If she truly believed that it was a bad idea to date someone from work, this was her chance to say no, to back off before Chris's seductive smile got the better of her. She could treat him to a sandwich in the company's dining room, consider him a friend, and leave it at that.

But she didn't want to.

Susan knew that now was the worst possible time to enter into something new with a man. She had too many profound questions to wrestle with, questions concerning her ethics, her professional future, her relationship with her boss, her life. She faced some overwhelming decisions, some frightening eventualities. She wouldn't have the energy to pursue a romance, to play getting-to-know-you games with a handsome man over dinner at a restaurant, to decide whether she ought to let him kiss her, whether she wanted to kiss him, whether she wanted his hands off or on. If she wasn't already an emotional wreck, she anticipated that she would be one before long.

Yet she couldn't bring herself to turn Chris away. She liked his smile too much, and his quiet confidence. She liked the way he had accepted her apology, without reminding her of her embarrassment. She even liked his old-fashioned gentility in asking whether she was involved with another man before he pursued a friendship with her. Looked at one way, his remarks may have seemed offensive, but looked at another way they were refreshingly sweet. Too many men these days didn't care whether a woman was seeing anyone else, since they were looking only for sex, not a commitment.

That Chris wanted to know Susan was unattached indicated, however obliquely, that he might be interested in a genuine relationship. And for reasons she wasn't about to analyze, she was elated by such an interest on his part.

"Friday night," she told him, figuring that would give her five days to come to her senses and back out.

"Friday night it is," he confirmed, standing and approaching her. "I'll cash in my lunch chit today, if that's all right with you. But since I've got a one-thirty appointment with some folks from an insurance company, we'd better use the dining room downstairs."

He helped her to her feet, then started toward the door. She remained by the desk, observing him, contemplating his lustrous hair, his long-legged stride, the flattering fit of his suit. The attraction she felt toward him was real enough, but...she didn't trust herself. She was confused, and she didn't trust herself not to let her confusion undermine her as it had the last time she'd been with him. "Chris..."

He halted and turned back to her. "Hmm?"

"I can't..." She inhaled, then forced out the words, knowing that she owed him her honesty. "I can't promise that I won't freak out on you again. The fact is, I'm going through something kind of rough at the moment, and . . ."

"I know, Susan," he said gently.

She gazed across the room at him. He knew she was in difficult straits; he had already seen her freak out once. He wasn't running away, though. He wasn't retreating.

"It's nothing I can talk about," she said hesitantly.

"Then we won't talk about it."

As simple as that. His respect for her feelings transcended any curiosity he might entertain about her problems. What had he said outside the bar the other night? *"Being the gentleman that I am . . ."*

He was a gentleman. Someone who, as he'd already demonstrated, would let her lean on him and cry when she had to. Someone willing to offer his help, no questions asked.

He took a step toward her and reached for her hand. Smiling shyly, she wove her fingers through his and let him escort her out of the office.

Chapter Three

"How does Associate Manager of Marketing and a ten percent raise sound?"

Susan lifted her eyes from the two-month-old "F.Y.I." newsletter she'd located inside the bottom drawer of her desk to find John Langers lurking in her office doorway, a smug grin splitting his face. Her first impulse was to tell him that nothing he could say in his characterless voice, not even an announcement of a promotion and raise, could sound as interesting as something, *anything*, spoken with an Oklahoma drawl. Her second impulse was to order John out of her office—out of her life, while she was at it—and, once she was alone again, to reread the blurb about Chris in the newsletter.

She had been meaning to do something about her slovenly habit of stuffing all the bulletins and flyers that crossed her desk into the bottom drawer until, every couple of months, the drawer became so jammed with papers it refused to roll shut. At that point she'd empty the drawer's contents, sort through the crinkled papers in search of any memos worth saving and dump the rest into her wastepaper basket. It was without question an inefficient system, and at least once a year Susan resolved to amend her ways by filing the important memos the day she received them, and discarding the junk with equal promptness.

Today, however, she was delighted by the chaotic accumulation of papers in her bottom drawer, because among them was the June issue of the monthly "F.Y.I." newsletter published by the personnel department. The Summer Preview edition of "F.Y.I.," which Susan had exhumed from the depths of her drawer, featured such scintillating items as "Fun in the Sun: Don't Get Burned," "Safety Tips for Barbecues," "Great Vacation Getaways for the Whole Family," and, on the last page, the regular "Who's News" column listing promotions, retirements, individual honors and new additions to the staff at corporate headquarters.

If Susan sorted through her interoffice mail more expeditiously, she wouldn't have saved this back issue, and thus she wouldn't have gotten to read: "Cheshire welcomes Christopher E. Kelso to the personnel department as an assistant vice-president. Chris comes to us from Schenk's Tulsa plant, where he worked for twelve years, the last four as head of plant personnel...." The brief essay also mentioned that Chris was a graduate of the University of Oklahoma with a degree in English literature, that he had a master's degree from the University of Tulsa, that he was a father of two and that his hobbies included swimming, boating and rereading for pleasure all the novels he was required to read in college. 'Our warmest welcome to Chris and his family,' the article concluded.

Susan already knew about Chris's children. As for the rest, the essay proved more informative than her lunch with him had been. Over sandwiches and coffee, Chris had managed to tell Susan a little bit about his house, which he described as a log cabin by a pond in the

underdeveloped western end of Cheshire. He'd told her
about the canoe he had purchased after he and his kids
moved in, and about how much Newt loved the water and
how blasé Emma pretended to be about the house's
lakeside location, although she'd recently bought two
new swimsuits, which, at the risk of sounding like an
overprotective father, Chris swore were much too skimpy
for any daughter of his.

But his conversation with Susan was disjointed. They
endured one interruption after another. People kept
wandering over to their table to ask Chris about the new
stock-option program the pension department was setting up, or about the possibility of a clerical position for
their daughter-in-law, or about rumors of union strife at
the Gary, Indiana plant. Chris would answer each of their
inquiries politely, and then, after the intruder departed,
he would smile apologetically at Susan and say, "It seems
I'm in demand today, for some reason."

Susan wasn't terribly bothered by all the interrup-
tions. She knew that she and Chris would be having dinner together on Friday; she would have the opportunity
to learn more about him then. In the meantime, she could
admire his richly hued hair, his easy smile and his sparkling eyes, and she could listen to his exotically twangy
pronunciations. Once they'd finished their sandwiches,
she supplied him with her address and confirmed that
seven o'clock Friday night would be fine with her. Then
she returned to her office, rummaged through her desk
in search of the outdated "F.Y.I." newsletter and used it
to answer at least a few of the questions she'd been unable to ask him in the dining room.

With John's sudden invasion of her office, however,
Susan immediately shoved thoughts of Chris from her
mind. John bounded into the tiny room, bristling with

energy. Lately, Susan had discovered that the happier John appeared, the uneasier she felt. "Associate marketing manager is a step down," she pointed out noncommittally.

"For me, yes. Not for *you*," John crowed, planting his hands on the edge of her desk and bearing down on her. "You're getting a promotion too, Susan. And a ten percent raise. Say, 'Thank you, John.'"

Susan shook her head, bewildered. "Why am *I* getting a promotion? I thought you were the big hero around here."

"I'm being promoted, too," John boasted. "Assistant V.P. Also a fat raise, of course."

"Of course," she echoed dully.

"When Pantella told me about my promotion and raise, I told him that there had better be something in it for Susan Duvall, too. Because you were instrumental in the Pentagon bid. I couldn't have done it without you, and I certainly wasn't going to let them overlook you."

Susan was tempted to cover her ears with her hands. She didn't want to hear that she was instrumental in the bid; she didn't want to hear that John couldn't have done it without her. Sure, a promotion and a raise were nice. But not when they came as a result of John's chicanery.

John straightened up and frowned, apparently noticing for the first time since his entrance that Susan didn't share his elation. "What's wrong, honey? You wanted a twenty percent raise? I got the best I could for you."

"I'm..." She sighed and averted her eyes. "I'm not sure I want a raise at all."

"Don't be an idiot. Of course you want a raise," John chided her.

"John." She sighed again and returned her gaze to him. He looked perturbed, aware that something was seriously wrong between them. Susan was relieved that he was finally catching on. Maybe he'd figure out what was troubling her and spare her the need to spell it out for him.

No such luck. His frown deepening, he said, "Fill me in, Susan. We've just landed one of the biggest contracts in the history of Schenk Chemicals. Some of the glory is reflecting on you, and you look like you're on your way to your own funeral." When Susan didn't speak, he sat on the corner of her desk and gathered her hand in his. "Talk to me, Susan. Tell me what's bugging you."

"The kickbacks," she whispered brokenly.

It had taken a considerable effort for her to force out those two words, and she anticipated some sort of reaction from John: chagrin, perhaps, or mortification, or fear that she might expose him. But all he did was to twitch his shoulders in an unconcerned shrug. "Don't talk about it that way," he said placidly. "I'd rather you didn't call them kickbacks. I myself prefer to think of them as financial incentives...agents' fees, or purchasers' commissions."

"Agents' fees?" Susan snorted. "Commissions? John, you bribed those men to accept our bid!"

"First of all," John explained, his tone even and mildly paternalistic, "our bid was valid. We'll deliver the product the Pentagon needs on time and at a fair price." He patted Susan's hand, then released it and stood. Pacing the length of the office, he sorted his thoughts. "Secondly, the amount these men are personally going to pocket is infinitesimal compared to the amount of money the contract will be bringing in to Schenk."

"Oh, well," Susan grunted. "Call it a commission instead of a kickback and keep the numbers relatively small, and that makes it legal."

"The law is hazy about this, Susan," John argued. "There's nothing outright illegal about giving bonuses to a few men—"

"Federal employees," Susan corrected him. "It's their job to decide on bids. That's what they do to earn their salaries—which are paid for by your taxes and mine, John. Schenk isn't supposed to be paying them extra just for doing their jobs."

"Whether or not Schenk is supposed to pay them extra is irrelevant. This is the system, Susan, this is the way things get done. I felt it was a reasonable cost of doing business. Schenk can certainly absorb the cost."

"Dollars and cents!" she erupted, clinging to the arms of her chair to keep from hurling herself at John and punching him senseless. "Where's the morality in it? And don't tell me the law is hazy. When it comes to kickbacks, I don't think there's anything hazy about the law. Ten'll get you twenty those Pentagon finks aren't going to declare their 'commissions' and 'agent fees' on their 1040 forms next April."

"Then *they'll* be breaking the law," John said with another shrug. "I'm not going to worry about their morality, Susan. All that matters is the bottom line. We got the contract."

"And you and I got promotions. For God's sake, John..." She bit back a curse and closed her eyes. "I can't accept a promotion based on this thing. My integrity isn't for sale."

"Oh, spare me," John groaned. "Aren't we getting a bit melodramatic now? You're blowing this whole thing out of proportion, Susan."

"No," she argued, her voice soft but steady. "You're the one who's got your proportions wrong, thinking the ends justify the means. I wanted us to win that contract, too, but not at the expense of my principles.''

John appraised her with a quizzical stare. When he took a step toward her desk, she shrank back perceptibly, and he halted. ''Don't do anything precipitous, honey,'' he cautioned her. ''You obviously feel uncomfortable about this, but I'm sure that if you think about it long enough, you'll agree that my strategy was sound.''

''A thousand years won't be long enough,'' she muttered.

John mulled over her statement, then smiled optimistically. ''Don't take a thousand years, then. Why don't you take the afternoon? Go home, go for a walk, buy yourself a new dress.... You'll feel better about the whole thing soon.''

Doubtful, Susan pondered, glowering at his back as he left her office. *Highly doubtful.*

She did take the afternoon off. She left work early, drove home and took a long walk, in spite of the fact that John had recommended it and she didn't want to do anything he recommended. After changing from her business suit into a pair of shorts and a sweatshirt with the sleeves cropped off, she took a leisurely stroll around the condominium complex, following the meandering roadways, gazing with a detached appreciation at the graceful mimosa and stark white birch trees, the lingering pink blossoms of the azaleas, the lawns cultivated as meticulously as a golf course fairway. As condominium developments went, Susan's was well planned and well maintained. Expensive, too. A ten percent raise wouldn't hurt ...

''Blood money,'' she grumbled. She could think of plenty of things she could do with a raise, but not *this* raise. No way.

In retrospect, she was surprised by how much she'd revealed to John, how much of her rage she'd let him see. As in her meeting that morning with Chris, she hadn't rehearsed what she would say to John. It had simply poured out, unpracticed and unprepared. She'd spoken her mind, and spoken from her heart.

Yet exposing her feelings to John didn't clarify matters much. Susan still faced the same options: reporting him to his higher-ups, reporting him to someone outside the company, keeping her mouth shut and quitting the company... or keeping her mouth shut and staying.

She decided to take a day off on Tuesday, too. She went to the library and took out every book she could find on the subject of whistle blowers. Other people in similar situations had called their superiors to account; other people had refused to condone underhanded business activities. Susan wanted to know how they dealt with it, what price they'd had to pay to ransom their souls.

After reading a book on Frank Serpico, the New York City policeman who exposed corruption in the police department, Susan hardly felt reassured. In fact, she felt a whole lot queasier. Serpico, it seemed, had maintained his integrity and acted ethically by reporting wrongdoing within the force... and he'd gotten himself shot and nearly killed for it.

"WHAT'S THE MATTER, Susan?" Lorraine asked. "Is something wrong?"

Susan shifted the telephone receiver to her left ear, freeing her right hand to stir an extra teaspoon of sugar into the steaming mug in front of her. After the quantity of herbal tea she'd drunk in the past four days, she could now say with absolute certainty that tea was no more effective than vodka sours in helping one to solve one's troubles. About the only thing tea seemed to be good for was flushing one's kidneys.

"What makes you think something's wrong?" Susan hedged.

"Every day this week, you've gotten home from work before me. I'm a banker, Susan, I'm supposed to get home early. Your car has been in the lot at four-thirty every day. How come you aren't at work?"

Lorraine's town house was three doors down from Susan's, and they parked in the same lot. Although Susan ought to have objected to her friend's nosiness, she was touched that Lorraine cared enough to check up on her. "I think I'm coming down with something," she said. "I've called in sick for the past few days."

"Maybe it's hay fever," Lorraine opined. "I hear it's going to be a killer season for hay fever this year. Something about the rain last April—"

"I've never had hay fever in my life," Susan informed her. "I'm sure it isn't that."

"Well, whatever it is, is there any chance you might recover by tomorrow night?" Lorraine asked. "Doris Kenner is having a sexy lingerie party at her house, and I thought you might like to come along. It's going to be a riot."

Susan could think of few things less appetizing than spending a Friday night in her neighbor Doris's living room, sipping wine and watching a group of giggly ladies trying on tiger-skin negligees. "If I recover by tomorrow night," Susan informed Lorraine, "I'm supposed to go out for dinner with a new guy from work. But I don't think I'm going to recover so quickly," she concluded morosely.

"What is it?" Lorraine asked, obviously concerned. "Are you running a fever? Is there anything I can get you?"

A new job, Susan answered silently. *A new life. A bullet-proof vest.* "No," she said aloud. "This is just one of those things that has to work itself out." That wasn't a lie, she assured herself. She hadn't exactly told Lorraine that she was ailing physically. Her nerves were a mess, that was all.

After reading the book about Serpico, she had returned to the library on Wednesday and Thursday to pore over every microfilmed newspaper article on the man, every fifteen-year-old story about the corruption he'd uncovered. After her day's quota of research, she had gone home, drunk some herbal tea, gone to bed and had nightmares. When she woke up she'd had more nightmares, ghastly projections about standing up for one's principles, doing the right thing and getting shot.

She had nightmares about ratting on John, destroying a man who had done more for her, both professionally and personally, than she could ever thank him for. She had nightmares about turning on her friend, turning him in. Stabbing him in the back and getting shot...

"Susan? You still there?"

"Yes," Susan said, snapping out of her reverie.

"You want me to come over?" Lorraine offered. "How about this evening? I could bring over some popcorn, and we can watch *The Way We Were* and go through a box of Kleenex. I think one of the Boston stations is broadcasting it on cable tonight."

Susan chuckled. She and Lorraine had already watched *The Way We Were* on television together countless times—and each time, by the movie's end, they'd be surrounded by mounds of soggy tissues. As tearjerkers went, that film was one of the finest. But at the present, Susan was miserable enough without having to view a depressing movie. "I'll pass, Lorraine."

"How about if I just bring over some popcorn and we'll talk?" Lorraine suggested.

Susan was tempted. She was dying to talk to someone about her predicament, but... "No," she heard herself say. "I think I'm just going to crawl into bed and rest."

"You want to get your strength up for your big date tomorrow," Lorraine said. "I understand." She paused. "You sure you don't want me to get you anything? Chicken soup? Cough syrup?"

"No, thanks," Susan swore. "Really, Lorraine—I'll be all right."

Lorraine subsided. "Okay. I'll let you get your rest. Maybe I'll stop by tomorrow before the lingerie party to see how you're doing."

"If you want," Susan capitulated. "Hopefully, I'll be all better by then."

She bade Lorraine goodbye, hung up and took a sip of her tea. Life used to be a lot simpler, she ruminated. It used to be simple to spend an evening wolfing down popcorn with Lorraine and wallowing in a pointless but entertaining debate about whether they were too old to wear bikinis or listen to rock and roll, or whether by choosing to become professionals they had sacrificed too much in their personal lives. The perfect conclusion for such a debate would be to turn on *The Way We Were*, to watch Barbra Streisand walk out on Robert Redford while she fought for all those noble principles she believed in.

During her many viewings of that movie, Susan had often asked herself whether she'd have the guts to walk out on a man like Robert Redford. Now that question

was no longer academic. Could Susan "walk out" on
John? Could she reject a friend for the sake of her principles?

Why couldn't it be simple?

"YOU LOOK LIKE HELL," Lorraine announced when, at
a quarter to seven on Friday night, she swept into Susan's foyer on her way to the party at Doris's house.

Susan couldn't dispute her. She hadn't eaten a proper
meal or slept well in days. Her complexion was wan, her
hair limp and lackluster, her lips bitten raw and her body
wrapped inside a loose-fitting silk kimono. Her eyes were
bloodshot, circled with gray shadows.

Lorraine followed her into the kitchen, where Susan
flopped onto a chair next to the breakfast table and
fussed with the mug of tea she'd just prepared. "I
thought you had a hot date tonight with some new guy at
work."

"I broke it," Susan said dully.

"What do you mean, you broke it?"

"I called him at work to tell him I didn't feel up to
going out," Susan explained. "I had to leave a message
with one of the secretaries. He was at an all-day conference in Waterbury."

"You don't sound terribly disappointed," Lorraine
observed.

Susan shrugged listlessly. Her luncheon with Chris
seemed far away and long ago, a pleasant, fading memory. She couldn't imagine herself making chitchat with
him over dinner at some restaurant tonight, engaging in
breezy small talk, welcoming a good-night kiss. What if,
in the middle of their meal, she suffered from one of her
chronic waking nightmares? What if she burst into tears?

Chris Kelso had seen her fall apart once. She had too much pride to let him see her fall apart again.

Lorraine noticed the soggy tea bag lying on the edge of the sink. She carried it to the trash can, lifted the lid and gasped at the sight of dozens of used ones heaped inside. "Maybe what's wrong with you is an overdose of tea," she proposed.

"The diagnosis doesn't matter," Susan countered. Actually, her diagnosis was rather simple. The proper treatment eluded her, however.

"Around here, if you're older than high school age, dates are not easy to come by," Lorraine pointed out. "Last night you said you were hoping you'd feel good enough today to go out with this guy from work."

"His name is Chris, not 'this guy from work.'" Susan took another sip of her tea and decided it had too much sugar in it. Grimacing, she shoved the cup away. "I know exactly how difficult dates are to come by, Lorraine, but I just don't feel up to it tonight. If Chris is genuinely interested in me, he'll ask me out again when I'm feeling better. And if he isn't, then who cares about him?"

Lorraine had drifted to the living room window, which overlooked the parking lot. "I don't know if he's genuinely interested or not, Susan, but does he drive a cruddy looking brown station wagon?"

Susan blanched. She bolted from her chair and raced to the window in time to see Chris climb out of his battered car. He was dressed in khaki slacks and a white shirt open at the collar. In deference to the August heat, he had rolled the shirtsleeves up to his elbows, revealing his strong, suntanned forearms. He reached into the car to pull a blazer from the front seat, then straightened up and shut the door. He scanned the row of shingled town houses, searching for Susan's number.

"Oh, no," she moaned, reflexively clutching the lapels of her robe and backing away from the window. "What's he doing here?"

"That's him?" Lorraine asked, her gaze riveted to the stranger in the parking lot. "He's cute."

"Lorraine—do me a favor and get rid of him, okay?" Susan pleaded, darting up the stairs to her bedroom. "I don't know why he didn't get my message, but he obviously didn't. Please—will you tell him I can't see him?"

"I can't do that!" Lorraine protested.

"Tell him I've got a contagious disease," Susan recommended, gathering the hem of her robe away from her bare feet and hurrying up the stairs.

"I'll tell him he can take me out for dinner instead," Lorraine suggested, absentmindedy running her hands over the curly black mane of hair that framed her heart-shaped face. "He looks more interesting than lingerie."

Susan shut herself inside her bedroom. She pressed her ear to the door long enough to hear the front doorbell chime. Then she flung herself across her bed and decided with a moan that refusing a date with Chris Kelso was absolute proof that she was suffering from a severe mental unbalance.

She listened to his and Lorraine's muffled voices in the foyer, unable to make out what they were saying. After several minutes, she heard the front door open and close, and then the sound of someone ascending the stairs. She exhaled shakily and sat up in bed, crossing her legs squaw-style beneath the voluminous folds of her robe.

The gentle tapping on her bedroom door made her jump. Lorraine wouldn't have bothered to knock before barging into the bedroom to provide a full report on her dialogue with Chris. Susan knew before she heard Chris's husky voice through the door that her supposedly reliable friend had gone off to Doris's stupid lingerie party and stranded Susan with Chris.

"Susan?" he called. "Can I come in?"

She fumed. How could Lorraine have done this to her? It wasn't that Susan didn't trust Chris to enter her bedroom, but that—as Lorraine herself had observed—she looked like hell.

She had also looked like hell the evening she'd wept like a baby in front of a rapt audience at the bar. She hadn't frightened Chris off then; she didn't suppose she would frighten him off now. She fluffed her fingers through her hair a few times, as if that small, futile gesture could salvage her appearance, and then exhaled. "All right," she acquiesced.

The door opened. Chris hovered on the threshold for a few seconds, simply gazing at the nervous, disheveled woman seated on the unmade double bed. His first move was to reach for the light switch by the door and flick it on, illuminating the two matching bedside lamps, which together created a broad pool of yellow light at the center of the bed. Then he stepped inside. "How do you feel?" he asked.

"Not too great."

He nodded, tossed his blazer onto the rocking chair in one corner and approached the bed. He didn't sit on it until Susan gave him a meek nod, and he positioned himself as far from Susan as the mattress allowed. "I knew you had called in sick for the past few days, but I assumed that if you were truly ill you would have gotten in touch with me to cancel our date."

"I did," she said. "I left a message for you with one of the personnel secretaries today."

"Beatrice," he guessed, smiling wryly. "She's a charming lady, but she's dreadful about passing along messages. I checked in at the office just before I left the conference this afternoon, and nobody mentioned that you called." His eyes met Susan's, luminous yet brimming with worry. "I also telephoned you yesterday, to see how you were feeling. No one answered, though. I figured that if you were well enough to get out, you must be well enough to have dinner with me."

"You phoned? Here?" Susan was startled. "I don't remember giving you my number."

Chris laughed. "Susan, I work in personnel. We've got your telephone number on file."

Susan suffered a quick stab of panic. Of course personnel had her telephone number on file—and a whole lot more. What else did Chris know about her?

She shot him a fearful glance, which he evidently had little trouble interpreting. "Please don't tell me you're angry that I read through your file," he implored her, still smiling. "There's nothing in it for you to be ashamed of. Your performance evaluations are glowing."

"There's more in it than evaluations," she mumbled dubiously.

"Oh, yes. Your blood type, if I recall correctly, is A-positive, and you're thirty years old. Your father is listed as your only next of kin, you signed up for the H.M.O. health plan, and you're maxed out in contributions to the 401-K sheltered investment plan. And you're single, which I must say pleases me immensely."

His complimentary remark about her marital status should have warmed her. But she was in no mood to be courted. She lowered her eyes to her lap and fidgeted with the flaps of her robe, drawing them more tightly around her legs.

"Speaking of health coverage, have you called a doctor?" he asked.

"No."

"Susan . . . forgive me if I'm speaking out of turn, but is this your way of freaking out on me?"

Her head jerked up. "What?"

"You warned me on Monday, when I asked you to have dinner with me, that you might freak out on me again. You look awfully worn out, and pretty damned dismal, but you don't look sick."

" 'Sick' is a relative term," she pointed out.

"Granted, you're not in top form. But I think it would be a good idea for you to throw on some clothes and join me in a meal. Where I come from, food has always been considered the first line of defense against all the miseries of the world."

"Chris—"

"We don't have to do it fancy it you don't feel like it. Dairy Queen makes a decent hamburger." He stood and backed toward the door. "Of course, if you'd rather do it fancy, that's fine with me, too. I made reservations at the Yankee Silversmith. Whatever you'd prefer."

He was already in the hall, closing her door, before she spoke. "I don't think I'm up to the Yankee Silversmith."

"Dairy Queen it is," he said, casting her a cryptic smile and then shutting the door.

It didn't take Susan long to slip on a pair of white cotton slacks, a blue boat-neck jersey and her sandals. Nor did she waste much time trying to repair the ravages the last several days had inflicted on her face. She brushed her hair back from her cheeks, slicked her lips with a tinted gloss and then turned her back on her mirror. If Chris felt at all negative about being seen in public with a woman who looked worn out and dismal, he wouldn't have insisted that she have dinner with him.

Dressing didn't take long, but sorting her thoughts did. That Chris didn't mind taking her out even though she was in such a funk was sweet—but his sentiments obviously went beyond merely not minding. He *wanted* to take her out. Regardless of her horrid disposition, regardless of her attempt to head him off with Lorraine's assistance, Chris had forced his way into her home, her room, her life. She had freaked out on him again, and instead of running for cover, as any sane man would, he was going to drag her to the Dairy Queen and feed her a hamburger.

She didn't understand him. But she appreciated his attention, his concern, his refusal to give up. Eventually he *would* give up, if she continued behaving so terribly around him. She didn't want him to reach that point, though. She hoped she'd be able to come to some resolutions about her job crisis before Chris's patience ran out.

He was waiting for her in the living room downstairs. "Nice place," he said, scanning the off-white wall-to-wall carpeting, the rose-and-gray upholstery of the couch and matching chairs, the custom-made draperies and tasteful knickknacks. "Emma would love it."

"Oh?"

"It's very... womanly," he explained.

Susan wasn't sure exactly what his comment meant. Before she could ask him to elaborate, he crossed the room to her and cupped his hand lightly around her elbow to guide her to the door. There was nothing overly possessive about his clasp, nothing coercive about it. Maybe that was what made his touch so oddly seductive, Susan mused, remembering the way she'd felt when he'd held her during her crying jag a week ago. He had a talent for behaving protectively toward her without making her feel helpless or dependent.

Theoretically, an independent, self-sufficient woman like Susan ought to have balked at Chris's protectiveness, but in reality she liked it. At least she did right now. She liked the fact that Chris was going to feed her an actual meal when she lacked the intelligence to feed herself anything more substantial than herbal tea, and that he was going to drag her out into the world instead of letting her continue to wallow in confusion and fear as she'd been doing all week. She liked the fact that Chris was willing to help her regain her sense of her own humanity.

"What's in it for you?" she asked, once they were seated inside his station wagon and heading out of the condominium complex. Because the car lacked air conditioning, he had rolled down both front door windows. Hot air whisked across the seat, rapidly undermining Susan's efforts with her hairbrush and making her hair resemble a tangled brown mop.

Chris glanced at her briefly, then turned his attention back to the road. The wind mussed his hair, too, and the rosy traces of evening sunlight slanting through the windshield captured streaks of gold and red in its tawny depths.

She hadn't intended to sound so cynical, but the question popped out before she could find a more discreet phrasing. At Chris's perplexed silence, she clarified herself. "You said it yourself: I'm worn out and dismal, and not in top form. Why didn't you just leave when Lorraine told you I didn't want to see you?"

His bewilderment momentarily increased, and then his mouth relaxed into a knowing smile. "Your friend must have gotten the message mixed up, Susan. That wasn't even close to what she told me."

Susan cringed. "What did she tell you?"

"That something serious was bugging you, that she had no idea what it was but that maybe a visit with me would perk you up."

Susan clamped her lips shut to keep from swearing. She contemplated various tortures, decided that they weren't nearly gruesome enough to compensate for Lorraine's indiscretion, and then, in a rush of generosity, decided to forgive her. After all, Chris's company *was* perking her up.

But Lorraine's duplicity didn't explain everything. "Why are you so interested in perking me up?" she inquired.

He shot her another sidelong glance. "In other words, why, when you've sent me a few negative signals, haven't I taken the hint?" Reflecting on his answer, he steered into the Dairy Queen lot and pulled into an empty parking space. He shut off the engine and twisted to face Susan. "For one thing," he said slowly, giving Susan the opportunity to absorb each word, "I happen to like complicated women. For another, I don't scare easily. For another..." He lifted an errant lock of hair from her cheek and tucked it behind her ear, affording himself a better view of her face. His voice dropped to a murmur when he concluded, "You are one hell of a sexy-looking lady. And yes, I do hope there's something in it for me."

His blunt statement should have alarmed her. That it didn't told her something about her own feelings, her own hopes. Whatever existed between her and Chris was strong, and it pulled both ways. She considered him one hell of a sexy-looking man.

She wasn't about to deny her attraction to him, but she wasn't certain she was going to follow through on it, either. "I really am a wreck, you know," she warned him.

He let out a soft, rumbling chuckle and swung open his door. "We all have our bad days, Susan."

Ten minutes later, they were seated side by side at one of the outdoor picnic tables in front of the eatery, munching on hamburgers, french fries and milkshakes and watching the Route 10 traffic cruise past them. "Not exactly what you had in mind for tonight," Susan noted contritely.

"We'll go to an elegant restaurant some other time," Chris responded, leaving no doubt that he intended to continue dating Susan. "Eating burgers at a joint like this reminds me of my carefree youth." Indeed, judging from the people occupying the other picnic tables, Susan estimated that she and Chris were older than all the other Dairy Queen patrons by at least a decade.

"Did you grow up in Tulsa?"

He shook his head. "Bartlesville. But we had similar hamburger joints there. Good, hot, greasy food at a rock-bottom price." He smiled nostalgically. "It didn't really matter what I was eating. What I loved was ordering for me and a date, carrying our food outside and eating in the twilight. Just like we're doing now. Twilight is the best time of day, don't you think?"

Susan gazed out at the vista before them: the constant flow of cars, the sprawling shopping center across the road, the silhouetted trees behind the shopping center and, above them, the sky, a lemony shade close to the horizon, changing to pink and then lavender, then a dark blue to the east. Even in this congested neon-lit environment, she had to agree with Chris that twilight was a special time.

"How's your burger?" he asked as he unwrapped his second sandwich.

"Cooked to perfection," Susan joked. She hadn't realized how hungry she was until she bit into the sandwich. All the tea she'd consumed hadn't offered much in the way of nutrition.

"And the *sauce des tomates extraordinaire*?" He waved a foil packet of ketchup at her.

"A gourmet's dream come true," she said with a laugh.

"There's always a bright side, Susan," he asserted, his smile waning slightly. "All you've got to do is find it. I don't know what's bothering you, and as long as you don't want to tell me I don't really want to know. But whatever it is, it can't be all that bad."

"Not when there's such good, hot, greasy food to be had at a rock-bottom price," she concurred, maintaining a light tone.

"At least things are going well for you at work," Chris noted, reaching for his milkshake. He took a long sip through the straw, then set it down. "I hear you've been recommended for a promotion."

Susan lowered her hamburger and stared at the cars coasting past them on Route 10. The sky had grown darker, and most of the drivers had turned on their headlights. Twilight was a beautiful time, she meditated, but ... The trouble with twilight was, it inexorably led to darkness.

"In fact," Chris went on when Susan didn't speak, "I was beginning to wonder whether the reason you called in sick all week was so that you could celebrate your promotion. After all, when I tried to reach you, you weren't home."

"I was at the library," she said quietly.

"The library! Some celebration." He chewed on a french fry. "Maybe we ought to celebrate tonight. I don't suppose they sell champagne here, but—"

"I don't want to celebrate my promotion, Chris," she silenced him.

He was clearly surprised. "Why not?"

Her head began to pound, and she felt the now familiar tension gathering around her lips, in her throat, in her gut. She wanted to scream, to shout to the world the truth about the Pentagon kickbacks. For a few minutes she had been able to forget, to relax... and now, the whole horror of the past week was threatening to loom up again. "Please," she implored him, fighting off the urge to weep. "Let's not talk about it."

Chris sized her up. He had to know from her reaction that work was specifically what *wasn't* going well for her, that work was what had sent her into such a tailspin. Any normal person would be bursting with curiosity, but Chris didn't pry. "All right, Susan," he said softly. "We won't talk about it." And then, apparently sensing that she was on the verge of tears, he arched his arm around her and cushioned her head against his shoulder.

She didn't cry. Chris's respect for her privacy astonished her, and she took strength from it. He cared for her, cared enough not to ask all the questions he must be harboring. He cared enough to pursue her on her own terms, without letting the complications scare him away.

Chris cared about her in a way nobody ever had before. Realizing that if it weren't for the disaster her life had lately turned into she never would have gotten to know him, Susan acknowledged that there might just be a bright side to the entire mess, after all.

Chapter Four

Long after she slid out from under his arm, sat up and ran her fingers through her hair to straighten it, he was still savoring the way she'd felt, the nearly fragile slenderness of her shoulder blades against his upper arm, the weight and shape of her head as she'd tucked it into the hollow where his neck met his shoulder, the dark, silky strands of her hair tickling his chin. Once again he was reminded of how little he understood women, how utterly incomprehensible they were.

He had thought Susan Duvall was a hotshot go-getter at Schenk. Indeed, he had thought she was so eager to excel at work that she'd engaged in an affair with her boss. Chris had been wrong about that, and now he was coming to realize that he might be wrong about the rest. If Susan wanted to advance in her career, why was she so rattled by his mention of her promotion?

He suffered a fleeting twinge of guilt about snooping through her records in the personnel office. He hadn't learned anything that reflected badly on her, and he'd candidly admitted to her that he had investigated her file. What disconcerted him, however, wasn't anything in the file itself, but rather the fact that everything in the file indicated that Susan was on the fast track, shooting for success with a capital *S*. If she was, she should have been overjoyed about her promotion. Not only wasn't she overjoyed, but she seemed downright depressed about it.

He wished she would explain herself to him. If he was patient, maybe eventually she would. In the meantime, he supposed he ought to be thankful that she hadn't shoved him away in anger for having raised the subject.

"Would you like some dessert?" he asked, gesturing toward the crumpled food wrappers spread out before them on the picnic table. "They sell a mean hot-fudge sundae here."

"I don't like to eat mean food," Susan said.

Chris smiled. Susan's effort to make a joke implied that her mood was on the mend. "How about a plain ice-cream cone?" he suggested. "I understand they're as amiable as all get out."

"Thanks, Chris, but no. Really." Susan shook her head for emphasis. "I haven't eaten this much in days."

As soon as the words were out she seemed to regret them. They implied, once again, that she was suffering from some profound difficulty. What could be so terrible about a promotion at work that it would drive away a woman's appetite?

He had promised her they wouldn't talk about whatever was bothering her, and he had every intention of keeping his promise. So, instead of accosting her with his many questions, he helped her to gather up the trash and discard it in the nearest garbage bin. When their table was clear, Chris took her hand and led her back to his car, wondering what was supposed to happen next.

This hadn't been the dinner date he'd planned. In his fantasy scenario, Susan was supposed to have been dressed to the nines when he arrived at her town house, and ready to waltz off with him to the Yankee Silversmith, where they were to have sat at a secluded table for two and dined on a superbly prepared gourmet feast. Over dessert, or after-dinner cordials, Susan's legs and Chris's were somehow supposed to have touched each other under the tablecloth, their knees rubbing, teasing. Perhaps Susan would have slipped off her shoe and run her bare toes along his shin, while her breathtakingly beautiful light brown eyes flashed an intimate message to him, a hint of delights to come...

Chris hadn't allowed his imagination to extend beyond that point. But now he had no idea how to proceed. Susan hadn't run her toes up his leg, nor had her eyes flashed any sensual messages to him. On the other hand, she *had* snuggled up to him and let him put his arm around her.

He wanted to kiss her. Instead, he busied himself settling into the driver's seat, turning on the ignition, backing out of the parking space and joining the steady stream of traffic on Route 10.

"Do you have plans for tomorrow?" he asked her.

She turned to him, and although he couldn't allow his gaze to stray from the road for more than an instant, he detected the glow of pleasure in her eyes and the gentle curve of her lower lip as she smiled. "I'm not sure, Chris," she said. "What are *your* plans?"

"Just hanging out with the kids," he answered. "Nothing special. Weather permitting, we'll probably take the canoe out on the pond, swim a bit and roast up some wieners on the grill for supper. I'd love for you to join us."

"Really?"

He wondered why she seemed so startled. Maybe she'd never dated a father before. Chris was aware that his situation wasn't typical; in most divorces, the mother won custody of the children. Possibly it had never occurred to Susan that a custodial father spent his weekends much as a custodial mother would: in the company of his children.

Chris suspected that once the school year started, Emma and Newt would be busy with their friends and wouldn't want to spend their weekends with him. Although he liked to grumble good-naturedly about his children, he adored them, and he was secretly pleased that he had them all to himself for the summer. Of course, if the thought of spending a day with his kids scared Susan off, or if his kids rejected her, he might very well wish that he *didn't* have Emma and Newt to himself. The kids had never minded his dating in the past, though.

Susan's lengthening silence discomfited him. "What's the problem?" he asked bravely. "Don't you like barbecues?"

"It isn't that," Susan replied, then faltered. She laughed meekly. "It just—it sounds like such a *family* type day."

Chris smiled. "Family and friends. For all I know, Emma may invite a couple of sisters she's gotten to know who live down the road from us, and Newt is likely to invite a few toads. I believe I'm entitled to invite a guest of my choice, too."

"I'm glad to hear I'm as welcome as toads," Susan muttered, although she was grinning. Abruptly she grew solemn. "Are you sure you don't want to spend the day just with your children?"

Chris tossed her a quick glance. "I'm sure I want you there," he insisted. At her hesitancy, he added, "If you're worried about Emma and Newt, don't be. I call them beasts, but they're actually very nice. Not always tame, mind you, but they've had all their shots.''

Susan chuckled briefly. ''I'm not worried about them,'' she swore, then offered Chris a shy smile. ''All right. I'll come over after lunch.''

Chris tempered his own smile in an effort not to look too victorious. While he provided Susan with directions to his house, his sense of victory was supplanted by other concerns. He wondered whether Susan thought that his invitation to spend the day with his family signified something serious, whether his decision to introduce her to his children could be equated with a woman's bringing a gentleman home to meet her parents. He wondered whether she thought it was a prelude to some sort of major commitment.

If that was, in fact, how Susan interpreted the invitation, Chris couldn't really blame her. He wanted to assure her that it had been issued casually, that an afternoon of canoeing and sunbathing with his children implied nothing more than what it was. Yet such assurances wouldn't be completely true. He wasn't certain of specifically what he wanted with Susan, but he *was* certain he wanted more than a casual relationship. His interest in her went well beyond the strong physical attraction he'd felt for her ever since their first meeting a couple of months ago. He was intrigued by Susan. He was tantalized by her complexity.

Maybe most women were mysterious. Chris was no Sherlock Holmes, and he suffered no compulsion to unravel most mysteries. But Susan... She was definitely a puzzle he wanted to solve. She was a woman he intended to know fully. He couldn't explain why, but he suspected that knowing her, understanding her, could be one of the most rewarding undertakings of his life—and that failing to understand her could be one of the most disappointing.

They had reached her neighborhood, and Chris navigated the winding roads to the lot outside her town house. After parking, he got out of the car and strode around to her side. He took her hand as she stood, and she wove her slim fingers through his and ambled with him at a leisurely pace up the slate walk to her door.

"I hope I'll be able to find your house tomorrow," she said. "It sounds a bit confusing. I don't know that part of town too well."

"Would you like me to draw you a map?" he asked.

"No, that's all right." She unlocked her door and ushered him into the foyer. "Why don't you just jot down your telephone number for me, so I can call you if I get lost."

He followed her to the kitchen, accepted the pen and paper she presented to him, and wrote down his phone number and address. Then he set the pen on the counter, straightened up, stared into her eyes and wondered all over again what was supposed to happen next.

"Thanks for dinner," she said quietly.

"My pleasure," he returned.

"No . . . I mean . . ." She averted her gaze and ran her tongue nervously over her lips. Just as nervously, she lifted her eyes to his again. "I mean, thank you for coercing me into leaving the house for a while."

"Was it coercion?" he asked, mildly concerned. He didn't want her thinking that he'd forced her into anything.

"Whatever it was . . . I haven't felt this human in days. I'm glad you don't scare easily."

He studied her face. The amber light from the Tiffany-style lamp above the breakfast table seemed to add

texture to her features, delineating her delicate cheekbones and the hollows below them, the surprising length
of her unadorned eyelashes, the tempting slope of her
jaw. He recalled the moment when he had warned her he
didn't scare easily: in his car outside the Dairy Queen,
just before he'd informed her that he desired her.

Suddenly, Chris knew exactly what was supposed to
happen next.

SHE HADN'T INVITED HIM inside her home for this. She
needed his telephone number, that was all. Yet the moment he slid his index finger beneath her chin and guided
her mouth to his, she recognized how much she wanted
him to kiss her.

Just this one kiss, though, she vowed as her lips responded to the light pressure of his. Just a simple thank-
you-and-good-night kiss, because they were adults and
they'd just gone on something that resembled a date and
they were going to see each other again tomorrow.

His lips brushed hers again, but this time they lingered, moving with tender warmth on hers. His thumb
sketched a trail to the corner of her mouth, stroking,
coaxing. Instinctively, her hands rose to his shoulders,
and he slid his arm around her waist and pulled her more
snugly to himself.

His body seemed a perfect match for hers. She didn't
have to stretch up to kiss him; he didn't have to lean over.
Her hips nearly reached his, and her breasts molded
comfortably to the solid muscles of his chest. It seemed
so easy to hold him, so natural to lift her hands to his
head, to thread her fingers into the auburn depths of his
hair, to allow her lips to part for him as his thumb continued to trace a mesmerizing pattern at the corner of her
mouth.

The powerful thrusting motion of his tongue robbed her of breath, of thought. Her vague notion about a simple good-night kiss dissolved in an astonishing burst of hunger for him. Her fingers fisted at the back of his head as her tongue met the invasion of his, parrying his every advance, sliding forward to the edge of his mouth when he momentarily relented.

He welcomed her aggression with a hushed groan. Angling his head, he lured her tongue past his teeth, which grazed gently over her lips. Then he returned to her mouth, surging deep, gentleness replaced by greed. His fingertips dug into the feminine curve of her hip, urging her closer to him, allowing her to feel his building arousal.

Kisses were not supposed to be this exciting. But then, Susan comprehended that it wasn't just Chris's kiss that was exciting her. It was Chris himself, his warmth, his virile body, the strength of his embrace. He was a sublime kisser, but Susan's response transcended the mere interplay of their lips and tongues. It arose from the mingling of her breath with his, the capture of her spirit by his. A fresh wave of heat swept down through her, gathering in her breasts, her belly, her thighs, pushing everything from her mind but a crazy, helpless yearning for Chris's love.

"Susan..." Gasping for air, he drew his mouth from hers. His lids were heavy, his eyes uncannily bright beneath them as he peered at her. The multicolored clarity of his irises left her with the uneasy impression that, once again, Chris had seen too much, that he had glimpsed her soul and discovered her secrets. Right now her secrets had nothing to do with work and everything to do with passion, but she was no less anxious to keep them hidden.

She tried to pull away, but he cupped his hands around her cheeks and steered her face back to his. For several seconds, neither of them spoke. They both struggled to compose themselves. Their lungs labored in tandem and their gazes fused, neither of them flinching or daring to glance away. Then Chris's mouth spread in a slow, lazy smile. "Well," he whispered. "That was definitely one of the highlights of my life."

Susan would have laughed at his overstatement if she'd been sure that it *was* an overstatement. For her part, the past few minutes had shattered her composure, leaving her severely shaken. "I'm not..." Her voice emerged hoarse and tremulous, and she swallowed and tried again. "I'm not going to invite you to stay."

His smile faded, his lips flexing as he considered her announcement. His eyes remained resolutely on hers, and his thumb—the thumb that had sketched its bewitching designs on the edge of her lip—now stroked her cheek soothingly, rising as far as her temple and curling through the soft brown tendrils he found there. "You'll have to let me stay at least a minute, darlin'," he murmured. "If I left right now I'd scandalize your neighbors."

Susan cringed and let her hands drop to her sides. She felt unspeakably guilty for denying Chris fulfillment after having excited him to such a degree. During the few awkward facts-of-life conversations her father had had with her when she was a teenager, he had indoctrinated her to believe that arousing a man and then turning him away was the gravest cruelty a woman could commit. The point he had hoped to make, of course, was not that Susan should satisfy the man in question but that she should never let him become so aroused in the first place.

It was hard for a young girl to learn about sex from a distant, uncommunicative father. By the time Susan had reached her mid-twenties, she'd managed to unlearn some of what her father had taught her. But certain lessons lingered. "I'm so sorry, Chris," she mumbled, attempting unsuccessfully to break out of the enclosure of his arms. "I didn't mean for everything to get so out of control."

Chris started to chuckle. Susan glanced up anxiously, seeking reassurance that his laughter was genuine and that he didn't loathe her. "Oh, Susan... Sometimes things are meant to get out of control," he argued. "And sometimes when they do, we ought to count our blessings."

"I'm not sure I agree," she muttered. Now wasn't a particularly good time to embark on a theoretical debate with Chris, but she was afraid that if she let his statement stand unchallenged, she would soon wind up out of control with him again. Admittedly, that possibility had enormous appeal, but Susan wasn't going to chance it. "All I meant—" she struggled to clarify herself "—was that I thought we were only going to kiss good-night."

"That's exactly what we did," Chris remarked, apparently vastly amused. "And now I'll go home and dream erotic thoughts about you. I'll see you tomorrow, Susan."

He touched his lips to her brow, then turned and strolled out of the kitchen, not waiting for her to escort him to the front door. As it was, she could barely maintain her balance, let alone attempt anything as physically demanding as walking. The sound of the front door closing behind him snapped her out of her daze, and she made her way to the window in time to see him climb into his car, start the engine and flick on the headlights.

She remained at the window until Chris had driven away. She stared out at the night, the sky now a rich dark blue embellished with a smattering of stars and a narrow sliver of moon. The ornamental streetlights lining the road were illuminated, and the windows of neighboring town houses spilled rectangles of light across the plush lawn.

One of the well-lit town houses belonged to Doris Kenner. Susan knew that Lorraine would still be there, snickering with the other guests over the frilly, filmy lingerie on display on Doris's coffee table. Susan could barge into Doris's living room, grab Lorraine by the arm, tug her into a private corner and whisper, "Thank you! Thank you for not showing Chris the door this evening."

She had had a valid reason for wanting Lorraine to get rid of Chris, and she tried valiantly to remember what it was. Something about the mess at work, her inner conflict concerning how to handle it, the anguish that had driven her to dig herself in and hide from the world. Something about not wanting to deal with anyone else until she'd figured out how to deal with herself and her own dilemma. Something about not having the energy or the perspective to handle a new relationship.

Yet she felt more energized now than she had in a week. She felt her perspective returning, her sense of proportion realigning itself. Losing herself to nightmares hadn't accomplished anything but to make her miserable; opening her mind to others and entertaining new possibilities might give her the strength and the will she needed to reach the proper conclusions.

All of which was irrelevant, she contemplated with a giddy smile. She could hardly think about conclusions and proportions at the moment. She could hardly think at all. Her body was humming with the reality of Chris, his clean male fragrance, the power of his arms around her, the taste of him, the ache of wanting him. Simply thinking about him caused that ache to intensify, an implacable pulsing deep inside her, wanting.

Susan wasn't remarkably experienced with men. She had been in love once, but the affair had ended years ago with her move to Connecticut. She had dated a few men since then, but she'd never felt with any of them what she felt with Chris. She'd never felt so out of control.

It was frightening, in a way, but also enticing. And if Chris was courageous—or foolish—enough not to be scared off by Susan, she was going to match him in courage and foolishness. She wasn't going to be scared off, either.

IT WASN'T UNTIL one-thirty the following afternoon, when she found herself in her car bouncing along a twisting back road sorely in need of repaving, that apprehension set in. Talking to Chris over hamburgers at the Dairy Queen had cheered her up considerably, and kissing him had been marvelous. But spending the entire afternoon with his children? What if they despised her? What if they snubbed her? What if Newt—good Lord, would she even be able to say his name with a straight face?—what if Newt threw a toad down the back of her shirt? What if Emma was enmeshed in some Freudian complex with her father and viewed Susan as a rival for his affection? What if they were obnoxious brats?

Susan had no idea how one was supposed to talk to prepubescent youngsters. She had no siblings, no nieces or nephews, and her own childhood was ancient history, her memory of it dulled by the years. She recalled spending much of her adolescence generally sullen and withdrawn, mooning over unattainable upperclassmen and studying diligently in the hope of winning a rare nod of approval from her father.

Surely Chris's children wouldn't care to discuss schoolwork in August. Nor, Susan suspected, would they care to discuss their unrequited loves. What did that leave? Rock stars? Movies? Toads?

She turned onto the street leading to Chris's house. The road ended at Chris's driveway, which led past the heavily treed front yard to a detached garage. Swinging open the car door, she spotted Chris and a boy leaning on the railing of a broad porch abutting an updated version of a log cabin. "Did you have any trouble finding the place?" Chris called to her.

"No," Susan said, pulling her canvas tote bag from the back seat. She was wearing a swimsuit under her shorts and blouse, and she'd brought some dry clothes to change into.

"Hi," the boy shouted to her as she strolled up the hill to the house. He was clad in swimming trunks and a bright red T-shirt bearing the words "Life's a Beach".

Susan recognized him from the photograph on Chris's desk at work. "You must be Newt," she said politely. "I'm Susan Duvall."

Chris extended his hand to her as she climbed the two steps to the porch. When his fingers closed around hers, she watched nervously for the boy's reaction. She sensed nothing at all; Newt didn't even seem to notice. He straddled the porch railing, dismounted onto the grass, and announced, in a drawl slightly more pronounced than Chris's, "I'm gonna go and see if Emma'll help me get the canoe ready." He sprinted through the trees behind the house and down the slope to the pond.

Chris gazed after his son for a minute, then turned to Susan and kissed her cheek in a friendly greeting. "See?"

he teased. "He doesn't bite, he doesn't growl, and usually he doesn't jump on strangers."

"He talks funny," Susan countered with a laugh. "Just like his dad."

"I keep telling you, Susan, it's you Connecticut folks who talk funny." Chris took her tote bag from her and surveyed her outfit. "Do you want to change? Emma's already down by the water, and I've promised to take Newt for a ride in the canoe. I'd love to take you out in the boat, too," he added, "but I'd strongly advise that you wear a bathing suit for that."

He himself had on a pair of denim cutoffs, canvas sneakers and a loose-fitting polo shirt. Susan wondered whether he was going to follow his own advice and put on a bathing suit. His legs were long and sinewy, the tan skin covered by a sparse dusting of light brown hair. Remembering the way his chest had felt pressed against hers when he'd kissed her last night, Susan imagined that he would look spectacular in swim wear.

"I've got my suit on under my clothes," she told him. "All I need is a towel."

"Don't go away," Chris said. He vanished through the screen door and into the house with Susan's tote, then returned after a minute carrying two large yellow towels. Taking her hand again, he led her off the porch and guided her along a descending flagstone path to the water's edge.

A slim blond girl lay on the pebbly shore, her eyes shut against the sun and her body cushioned by a thick oversize beach towel. Her golden skin glistened from a recent application of suntan oil. The wet-look brown bikini she had on wasn't the skimpiest Susan had ever seen, but she could see how it might alarm a protective father, even if what it exposed was a figure that had scarcely begun to develop curves.

"Emma? I'd like you to meet my friend Susan," said Chris.

The girl opened her eyes and shielded them with her arm. "Hello," she said emotionlessly. Then she squinted in the direction of her father. "Why don't you row Newt to the other side of the lake and leave him there? He's being such a pest."

Chris glanced toward the water to discover his son standing with one foot planted on the pebbles and one inside a beached aluminum canoe, a paddle gripped firmly in his hand. He turned back to Susan.

"Go ahead, take Newt out," she said generously. "I've got to get undressed, anyway."

Something sparked in Chris's eyes when she said the word "undressed," and she realized with some embarrassment that Chris was probably as curious to see her in her swimsuit as she was to see him in his. Her cheeks grew warm, and even warmer as she absorbed the mischievous smile he tossed her way before turning and jogging across the pebbled beach to the canoe. "Emma says you're being a pest, Newt," he reported. "I've been asked to remove you from the premises."

"All right!" Newt hooted, tossing his paddle into the boat's bow and climbing in after it.

Susan tried not to be obvious as she observed Chris stripping off his polo shirt. He had his back to her, and she admired the streamlined contours of it, the lean muscles tapering to his waist, the rounded ridges of his shoulders and the taut curves of his biceps. When he pivoted to throw his shirt onto a dry rock near Emma, Susan caught a glimpse of his chest. It, too, was leanly muscled and limber, the skin smooth and sun drenched, unadorned by hair. Simply looking at Chris's torso revived the pulsing longing she had felt when he'd kissed her, and she conceded that being able to make conversation with Chris's children might well turn out to be the least of her concerns that afternoon.

Seemingly unaware of Susan's surreptitious ogling, Chris kicked off his sneakers, grabbed the second paddle, shoved the canoe into the water and climbed in. Susan didn't dare to slide off her shorts and unbutton her blouse until he and Newt were well on their way to the center of the lake.

Emma inspected the conservative maillot Susan had on, deemed it worthy of a haughty sniff and rolled over to toast her back. Susan considered sitting on the rock where Chris had discarded his shirt, then chose a rock closer to Emma, who continued to watch her, her head resting on her folded arms. Emma's eyes were large and gray, her lips shaped in a self-conscious pout.

"Do you like canoeing?" Susan asked.

Emma shrugged. "It's all right. I'm not going out today, though."

"Oh? Why not?"

"I'm just not," Emma said. She twisted her head to examine a rough edge on one of her fingernails.

Susan knew she was under no obligation to keep the dialogue alive, but she saw it as a useful diversion. Better to chat with Emma than to dwell on Chris's physique. "Do you like to swim?" she asked.

"I'm pretty good at it," Emma granted matter-of-factly.

"Why don't we take a dip now, while the guys are in the boat?"

"Can't," Emma said, then abandoned her chipped nail and balanced her chin on her forearms.

"Why not?"

Emma peeked over her shoulder at the now distant canoe sharing the small lake with a sunfish and two rowboats. Satisfied that her father and brother were well out of earshot, she shifted back to face Susan. "I've got my *friend*," she confided in a whisper.

Susan was momentarily at a loss. Then she smiled, remembering that "friend" was one of the euphemisms she used to use for menstruation when she was Emma's age. Susan also remembered how mortified she used to be whenever she had to talk about it with her father. Chris seemed much more open and accessible than Susan's father, but even so, she imagined that Emma must sometimes feel as awkward as she herself used to feel, and as hungry for a female companion with whom to discuss such matters.

"You can go into the water if you use tampons," Susan noted.

Emma rolled her eyes. "Dad won't let me. He says I'm too young."

Susan laughed out loud. Seeing Emma's hurt look, she explained herself. "That's exactly what my father told me when I was your age. I used to have to sneak to a friend's house and use hers."

"Didn't your mother take your side?" Emma asked.

"My mother passed away when I was nine."

"Really?" Emma lifted her head, propping it in her hand, and studied Susan curiously. "What'd she die of?"

"Diabetes," Susan told her.

"Wow. That's sad." Emma shook her head grimly. "My mom might as well be dead. She lives in California."

"Oh, come now," Susan teased. "California isn't that bad."

Emma remained solemn, failing to catch her unintentional joke. "If she was here, I bet she'd let me use tampons. She's a lot cooler than my dad, you know? Like, she lives with this guy, and they're not even married. He makes records, at least I think that's what he does. You know, like he produces them. She lived with this other guy for a while, he was into rock music, too. She's real cool."

Assuming that Emma was telling the truth, Susan thought Chris's ex-wife sounded like a first-class flake. "Do you see her often?" she asked.

"Uh-uh." Emma shook her head again. "I've never seen her since she left. I'd like to, though. I bet she's beautiful, and she'd probably let me do anything I wanna do. Like, I could wear lipstick and everything."

Susan took a moment to recover from Emma's revelation. That Chris had custody of his children was unusual, even in this liberated age. But for their mother never to have seen them since the divorce... Whose fault was that? The mother's? Or Chris's?

She couldn't believe Chris would prevent his children from seeing their own mother. On the other hand, she couldn't believe Chris had once been married to a woman who wouldn't want to see her own children.

The canoe was floating toward the shore on its return trip, the sounds of Newt's high-pitched laughter and Chris's answering chuckle distorted by the water. "It looks like your father forgot to leave Newt at the other side of the lake," Susan alerted Emma.

Emma cast her brother a supercilious look. "I bet you're gonna want to go out in the boat with Dad. Then I'll be stuck with Newt. He's so gross sometimes."

"We won't be gone for long," Susan promised, rising to her feet as Chris leaped out of the boat and dragged it onto the pebbles.

"The water's great!" Newt shouted. "Wanna come in, Emma?"

"Not today," she said, sighing dramatically.

"How come?"

"Mind your own business, Newt." She closed her eyes, deliberately shutting out her brother.

Newt looked hopefully to his father, but Chris's attention was fixed on Susan. Sighing as well, Newt mumbled something about being starving. He headed up to the house, pausing more than once to investigate a mushroom, a lichen-coated log or a tiny, scampering animal of some sort—Susan was happy not to know precisely what species.

"How about a spin around the lake?" Chris asked her.

"I'd love it," she accepted. "But we'll have to make it a quick one. I promised Emma we wouldn't strand her with Newt for long."

Chris laughed, took Susan's hand and helped her into the boat. He shoved off, climbed in and passed her a paddle.

The sun was hot on her shoulders and arms as she stroked through the water. She was sorry to be seated in the bow, unable to see Chris. But maybe it was just as well that he was out of sight, she mused, concentrating on the eddies created by the flat surface of her paddle as it cut through the clear, still water. If she could see him, she'd undoubtedly start ogling him again.

"Should I apologize for leaving you alone with Emma so soon after you got here?" Chris called to her.

"Of course not. We had a terrific time."

"Did you?" Chris sounded surprised. "What did you talk about?"

Your ex-wife, Susan almost blurted out. She wanted to ask Chris about his divorce, about the woman who, according to Emma, had abandoned her children to live with a rock musician—or more than one rock musician. Susan was dying to ask Chris about the woman he had married at such a young age, the mother of his two children, the wife who had walked out on her family and fled to California without a backward look.

But Susan couldn't ask. Not when she wasn't sure she had a right to know the answers.

His question hung in the air, and she had to come up with a reply. "We talked about tampons," she said.

His silence prompted her to twist around and view him. Her gaze lingered for an instant on his chest, which glistened under a thin layer of perspiration, and then lifted to his face. The reason he hadn't spoken, she realized, was that he was wrestling with his laughter. He lost the struggle and yielded to a loud guffaw. "Tampons! Are you kidding?"

Susan experienced a surge of indignation, an unexpected protectiveness toward Emma. "It isn't funny," she snapped. "You ought to let her wear them."

"What, has she recruited you to her side in the father-daughter wars?" he asked between laughs. "Are you her new comrade in arms?"

"It's obvious she needs one," Susan retorted.

"Tampons are hardly worth skirmishing over, Susan. If you're going to be Emma's ally, you might tell her to save her ammunition for the big ones."

"What big ones? Maybe I'm being presumptuous here, Chris, but I think this *is* a big one to Emma."

"Come on," he scoffed in disbelief.

"Chris," Susan scolded him. "Stop making fun of her. You can't begin to know what it's like to be a thirteen-year-old girl without a woman to talk to about these things. Well, I *do* know what it's like. It's lousy."

He stopped laughing. He also stopped paddling, set his paddle down and reached for Susan's arm. "Turn around," he implored her. "You're right, I'm wrong. Please turn around."

She did, carefully swinging one leg and then the other over the seat, gripping the sides of the canoe to keep it from rocking.

Chris gathered her hands in his and gazed intently into her eyes. "I'm sorry I laughed," he confessed, running his fingertips lightly over the delicate ridge of bones that shaped the backs of her hands. "I didn't realize your mother died when you were so young."

"How did you know she died at all?" Susan asked, astounded.

"There's a note in your personnel file, part of your health record."

Susan nodded, acknowledging once again that in his position Chris had access to a lot of information about her. He already knew her blood type and the details of her pension plan. Why shouldn't he also know that she had lost her mother?

"I wasn't laughing at you," he went on, his expression earnest. "I wasn't laughing at Emma. It's just that . . . well, you took me by surprise. I thought you two were getting to know each other. It never occurred to me that you were talking about . . . well, something like that. It's an odd topic, don't you think?"

"Not if you're a woman," Susan pointed out.

Chris grinned sheepishly. "I suppose you're right. Emma's pretty close to becoming one, and you . . . You are a wonderful, perceptive woman. You were correct to chew me out, Susan. I'm not always sensitive to Emma, although I try to be. Sometimes it's hard on me, too.''

Again, Susan was swamped with questions about Chris's divorce. But she refrained from asking. He was already revealing something personal to her; she had no right to ask for more. ''I'm sure most males would find the subject of tampons hilarious,'' she allowed.

''It would depend on the context, of course,'' he said, his lips hinting at a sensual smile. His gaze swept down the front of Susan's swimsuit, noting the way the clinging fabric displayed the swells of her breasts, the narrowness of her waist, the modest flair of her hips. When his eyes returned to hers, his smile was gone, replaced by a look of blatant longing that stirred a dangerous warmth along her nerve endings, a warmth that had nothing to do with the hot summer sun.

Chris leaned cautiously toward her, running his hand across her cheek and combing his fingers into her hair. His lips touched hers once, lightly, and then again . . . his tongue darting out to tease hers. Before his kiss could register fully on either of them, he settled back onto his bench. ''You are so beautiful,'' he whispered.

Susan couldn't speak. Her only thought was that Chris was beautiful, too, and extremely sensitive about certain things, like recognizing when Susan wanted him to kiss her. She wanted him to kiss her again, but she knew he wouldn't. Not in the middle of a public lake, with his children spying on them from the shore.

He was smiling, and Susan smiled as well. She cleared her throat and plunged her hand into the pond. ''Something tells me you could use a cold shower,'' she mumbled, flinging her hand toward him and spraying water all over his face and shoulders. Howling from the shock of his unexpected baptism, he lunged for her. Before he could knock them both into the water and capsize the boat, she dove in, bobbing to the surface a few feet away.

"Get over here!" Chris hollered, once again convulsed with laughter.

Susan swam to the boat, then treaded water, shaking her hair back from her face. Actually, the water wasn't terribly cold; it was just cool enough to cure her of the effects of Chris's kiss.

Once he had her wrist firmly in his grip he paused before helping her back into the boat. "You aren't going to pull me in, are you?" he asked, eyeing her doubtfully.

"No," she assured him. "If I did, you wouldn't be able to paddle the boat back to shore." Sliding from his grasp, she pushed off, swimming in smooth, graceful strokes toward the beach where Newt and Emma sat sunning themselves.

Susan enjoyed swimming, and the distance she had to travel wouldn't tax her. But the real reason she'd refused to climb back into the boat with Chris was that, if she had climbed in, she wasn't sure she could trust either of them not to kiss each other again, a longer, deeper kiss, one that would rekindle everything they'd felt the night before. And once they started, they might not stop.

Swimming was definitely safer.

Chapter Five

"I don't know why they're so addicted to air-conditioning," Chris remarked. "I usually turn it off the minute I get home from work, and open all the windows. I like breathing real air."

He was seated beside Susan on the porch, gazing at the pond. The sunset sky was streaked with color, pink and violet shadowing the high clouds and a vibrant golden shimmer infusing the western horizon. Susan could easily understand why Chris was so enamored of twilight. That his children would rather shut themselves up in the air-conditioned den with the television instead of enjoying the splendor of a mild August dusk was undoubtedly a result of their immaturity.

Or else it was a result of extraordinary maturity on their part. Perhaps they had declined Chris's invitation to join him and Susan on the porch after dinner because they wanted to give the adults a little privacy.

Susan sipped from her tumbler of iced tea and smiled. Chris had picked some sprigs of wild mint in the backyard and added a few leaves to their tea, giving it a refreshing piquancy. Refreshed—that was the perfect word to describe how she felt. Her hair was still slightly damp from the shower she'd taken before dinner, and her cheeks and shoulders tingled from their extensive exposure to the sun. Her lungs filled again and again with the pine-scented air, her muscles were unwinding from the day's exercise and her mind was at peace. She propped her legs up on the porch railing, took another sip of tea and sighed in contentment.

Much to her amazement, she hadn't had a single thought about kickbacks, John Langers or whistle blowers all afternoon. Not once during her canoe ride, her swim, the somewhat unsettling nature tour Newt had insisted on giving her—"Check out that fungus, Susan! Isn't it gross? This here's a snake hole, by the way. Come on, lemme show you where I caught a one-eyed salamander..." Not once during the feast of barbecued hamburgers and hot dogs Chris had prepared or during her numerous tête-à-têtes with Emma, or during those rare, tranquil interludes like this one, when she and Chris were blessed with a few minutes alone together, did Susan find herself fretting about the professional and moral crossroads at which she was standing.

The obvious explanation for her uncharacteristic serenity was that the Kelso family had offered her a needed distraction from her professional turmoil. But for some reason, Susan didn't buy that explanation. Deep down, she knew the Kelsos were more than just a distraction. They were a *family*, noisy, energetic, demanding...and happy. Susan had had meager experience with genuine families in her life, but after today she appreciated how therapeutic they could be.

A crow took off from the limb of a tree near the water, cawing loudly as it cut a black figure across the sky. Once it flew away, its raucous voice was replaced by the steady, constant chirping of crickets. "Sometimes I think the only reason I bought this house was that the realtor showed it to us in the evening," Chris commented with a laugh. "Show me anything in the twilight, and I'll wind up falling in love with it."

"It's a terrific house, even in the middle of the day," Susan remarked. "It's got a lot of rustic charm."

Chris snorted. "Tell that to Emma."

"Mmm." Susan drank some tea and nodded. "She told me she hates this house."

Chris balanced one ankle on the other knee and shifted in his chair to face Susan. He also had showered before dinner, and had donned a pair of faded blue jeans and a fresh cotton shirt. He'd rolled up the sleeves and left the top two buttons of the shirt undone, but Susan was secretly relieved that once they left the waterfront he'd chosen to cover up his body as much as the warm weather would allow.

As attractive as she found Chris, as enthralled as she was by his kisses, she didn't want to wind up falling for him. Maybe she hadn't thought about her professional crisis all day, but it still existed. Until she came to some conclusions about how to resolve the situation, she simply couldn't get involved with Chris. Building a new relationship took more time, effort and commitment than Susan could devote to Chris right now.

She liked him. She liked him a lot. But it was only fair, both to Chris and herself, that she untangle the mess at work before she tangled herself up with him.

"What else did Emma tell you?" he asked. "She was really chewing your ear off this afternoon."

Susan traced her finger through the mist that had formed on the outer surface of her glass. She and Emma had talked about many things, but Susan wasn't sure Emma wanted her repeating them to Chris. "We talked about shopping," she said, figuring that was a safe answer. "She complained that there weren't many good clothing stores in Cheshire. She said you took her to the mall in Meriden once, but you weren't any fun to shop with."

"She's right about that," Chris confessed with a grin. "To me, shopping is something you do when you have to, not something you do for the fun of it. You need shoes, you go to the store, choose a pair, pay your money and leave. Emma seems to think that trying on clothing is an end in itself. She can visit more fitting rooms in one day than I hope to see in a lifetime."

Susan chuckled, but a part of her commiserated with Emma. Susan might not know much about what made teenagers tick these days, but she knew that most thirteen-year-old girls were compulsive about trying on new clothes. Whether it was to playact at being high-fashion models, to get an idea of what styles became them, or possibly to answer some unknown biological imperative, they simply had to try things on.

Chris couldn't be expected to understand that. When Susan was thirteen, her father hadn't understood it, either. But at least when she was thirteen, her father hadn't uprooted her and moved halfway across the country with her. She'd had longtime friends in her comfortable Long Island community, her friends' mothers, an aunt living two towns away.

"Maybe I could take her up to the mall sometime," Susan offered. "I bet she's going to want to buy some clothes for the fall—she'll be starting at a new school, and she might want to have some new outfits. Would you mind terribly if I made a shopping date with her?"

"Mind?" Chris's face beamed with gratitude. "I'd be delighted! Would you really want to do that?"

"I wouldn't have suggested it if I didn't."

"Emma can be difficult," he warned. "She always gets into a foul mood when we go shopping."

"That's because you aren't any fun." Susan had reached an age where shopping no longer seemed like much fun to her, either, but she would exert herself to make her outing with Emma as much fun as possible. Motherless daughters had to look out for one another. "We . . . we talked about your wife," she said abruptly.

Chris's eyebrows twitched up, then settled back into their normal curves. He drank some iced tea and nodded slightly, apparently waiting for Susan to say something more.

The truth was, she and Emma had talked about the woman more than anything else that afternoon. No matter what the initial subject—tampons, clothing, popular music or the unusual house Chris had chosen to move his family into—Emma found a way to steer the discussion around to her mother: "My mom lives in a real neat house," Emma had asserted. "She's got an indoor grill, a food disposal, a trash compactor, everything. Like, the guy she lives with, this record producer, he's so rich he can buy her anything she wants. She'd never live in a weird house like this." Or: "You know how some ladies get all fat after they have kids? Not my mom. She's real thin and pretty."

Susan wondered how Emma could know so much about a woman she hadn't seen or heard from in years. She wondered whether Emma talked this compulsively about her mother to Chris—and how he felt about it. Most of all, she wondered about the woman herself: what she was like, why Chris had married her, why she had left.

She still wasn't certain she had the right to question Chris about his divorce. But if he honestly wanted to know what Emma had been chewing her ear off about, she wasn't going to lie.

He continued to stare at Susan for a minute, then turned away and gazed toward the pond. "Emma goes through these phases every now and then," he said. "She'll go on and on about Elysse, fantasizing about her, imagining all manner of things about her. Then, all of a sudden, she won't mention her mother for months at a time, for years. And then she'll start in again." He ran his finger in a circle around the rim of his glass, meditating. Then he shrugged. "I tried to make it as easy on Emma as I could, but I don't suppose it's ever easy to accept your parents' divorce."

"How old was Emma when it happened?" Susan asked cautiously.

"Four. Newt was just a baby."

"Why…" Susan paused, still unsure of how deeply she ought to probe. Assuming Chris would change the subject if he felt uncomfortable, she took a deep breath and forged ahead. "Why hasn't your ex-wife seen the children since the divorce?"

Chris eyed her curiously. "Did Emma tell you that?" Susan nodded.

A poignant smile twisted his lips. "It's the truth," he confirmed. "Elysse has no interest in the kids at all. Well, she pretends to have some," he allowed. "Her mother used to come up to Tulsa from Dallas once a year to see the kids. She'd always say Elysse asked after them, and requested some photographs of them and intended to visit them as soon as she could work it out. If she truly wanted to visit them, I suppose she could have worked it out by now."

"Is she really living with a record producer? That's what Emma said."

"Elysse's mother claims that she is. There's no reason she'd want to lie about it."

"A record producer? It sounds so—so glittery, Chris. Like something out of *Entertainment Tonight*."

Chris issued a short laugh. "Doesn't it? But that's the way Elysse was. When she left, it was because she yearned for excitement. Glamor. Something big and glorious and daring. She hooked up with a rock band that was playing in town, and when they left to try their luck in Los Angeles she left with them. She had a fine singing voice, although I think she lacked the discipline to succeed as a musician."

"Why on earth did you marry her?" Susan couldn't imagine Chris paired with a flighty groupie-type woman. He seemed so solid, so stable and family oriented.

Chris laughed again, a fuller, warmer laugh. "Why? I was madly in love with her, of course."

Of course? Well, yes, Susan supposed that, as solid and stable as Chris was, he would never have married someone he wasn't madly in love with.

"We met in college," he said, his eyes still glinting with humor, "and it was pure chemistry. We couldn't get enough of each other. We were both too young, naturally, and it takes more than mutual desire to sustain a marriage, but at the time it seemed like a swell idea." He set down his glass and reached for Susan's hand. "If Elysse and I came face to face now, we wouldn't know what to say to each other. Not that we ever talked too much then. Ah, but the chemistry... When you're twenty-one years old, chemistry matters more than anything else."

When Susan had been twenty-one, what had mattered more than anything else was getting accepted into a prestigious business school. But then, she had never experienced the kind of "chemistry" Chris was describing.

"Why—?" she began, then cut herself off.

"Why what?"

She mulled over her thoughts. Her eyes dropped to their hands, Chris's strong fingers laced through hers, his thumb stroking the inside of her wrist. She was astonished that she could be so aroused by a mere handclasp—especially given the topic of their conversation. Maybe she was experiencing a little of that "chemistry," after all.

"Why don't you seem bitter about it?" she completed the question.

"I'm *not* bitter," he told her, his smile becoming wistful. "Elysse had needs I couldn't answer. Motherhood made demands on her that she couldn't cope with. She left. It happened. What's the point of getting bitter?"

"If someone walked out on me like that, I'd be bitter," Susan said.

Chris shook his head. "Elysse and I had a few wonderful years together. She bore me two children whom I love half to death. The kids and I had some hard times after she left, but we adjusted. We've got one another and we've grown up together, and we're making out all right. I have no grounds for bitterness, Susan. I happen to think I'm pretty lucky."

Susan happened to think so, too. What made Chris lucky was not only that he and his children were making out all right, but more importantly that he had the ability to overcome what would have destroyed a weaker man. "It must have been some adjustment," she commented. "How did you manage with two small children?"

"How does anybody manage?" He propped his legs up on the railing next to hers and lifted her hand onto his lap, sandwiching it between his palms. "In college, I had dreamed of becoming a high school English teacher. I'd begun a graduate program in education, but then Elysse became pregnant, and I knew I'd never earn much money teaching. So I took a job in the personnel office at Schenk's Tulsa plant. You'd be astounded by how many English majors wind up in personnel." He shot her a playful smile, then continued. "When Elysse left, I panicked for, oh, about ten minutes. Then I phoned Bartlesville and begged my mother to come and stay with the kids until I could hire a babysitter. The company was good to me, too. They gave me time off when Emma got the chicken pox, and when Newt fell off his tricycle and broke his arm. And they paid my way through a master's degree in personnel administration. It took a lot of flexibility and juggling—just as it does when a divorced woman receives custody of her children. But you do it," he concluded philosophically. "You do what has to be done, and you roll with the punches."

"You're incredible," Susan murmured, awed by his calm acceptance of his circumstances. No, she disputed herself, it was more than just acceptance. Chris had triumphed over his circumstances. He had constructed a triumph out of them. "Any woman who'd leave a guy like you must be playing with half a deck," she asserted.

Chris's eyes met hers. "In that case, I hope you're playing with a full fifty-two," he whispered before leaning over and covering her mouth with his.

Susan briefly succumbed to his kiss, then pulled back. There was no point in getting carried away when Chris's children were just inside the house. If she continued to kiss him now, she knew intuitively that she'd learn more about "chemistry" than she could handle. And she couldn't very well cool herself off by jumping into the pond, as she had earlier.

Chris accepted her withdrawal without comment. He looped his arm around her shoulders and pulled her snugly to himself. After dropping a light kiss on the crown of her head, he directed his gaze to the pond. The water's surface appeared nearly black, reflecting the darkening sky above. "I've really enjoyed having you here today," he said.

"I've enjoyed being here," Susan murmured, resting her head against his shoulder.

He twirled his fingers idly through the clipped ends of her hair. "I can't believe it took so long for us to get to know each other."

"So long?" she blurted out with a laugh. "Chris, you've only lived in Cheshire since June."

"That's two months," he pointed out. "Which is an awfully long time, when you consider that I wanted to kiss you the first time I laid eyes on you."

"You did?" she exclaimed, twisting to peer up at him. His gaze remained on the water, affording her a view of his rugged profile. "Why didn't you?" she asked, then hastened to clarify herself. "I mean, why didn't you say something? Why didn't you ask me out?"

He glanced down at her, smiling enigmatically. "I thought you were having an affair with John Langers."

Susan expected to tense up reflexively at the mere mention of John's name, but she didn't. She was feeling too comfortable with Chris, too serene. "That's such a ridiculous idea," she scoffed.

"You and John do spend a lot of time together," Chris pointed out.

"Of course we do. He's my boss."

"Outside work, too, rumor has it."

Susan was only mildly surprised to learn that she was the subject of office gossip. Such was the nature of the corporate world, she supposed. "A lot of it is work related," she told Chris. "John tried to teach me racquetball because he thought it would help me professionally. He made sure I attended social events where I could connect with important people. He's been a mentor and a friend to me, Chris. And beyond that, well..." She grinned. "He's practically old enough to be my father."

"Some women like older men," Chris noted.

"And he's married."

"Some women like married men."

Susan shook her head. "*This* woman happens to like John's wife. Margaret's a sweetheart. When I first moved to Cheshire, she actually used to bring me casseroles. She was a one-woman Welcome Wagon. And she and John are very happily married—they've been together for something like thirty years, and in all that time I don't think John has ever even looked at another woman. And they've got three lovely daughters..."

"All right, all right, I'm convinced," Chris silenced her, chuckling. "It's obvious you adore the man. Forgive me for thinking that your adoration extended beyond the bounds of propriety."

Susan bit her lip, aware of why she'd gone on at such length about John's respectability and character. It wasn't Chris she wanted to convince, but herself. She was desperate to remember what a good, decent man John was—a man too good and decent to have committed a crime.

But John *had* committed a crime, and the tension she'd been free of all day suddenly seized her, causing her hands to grow clammy and her stomach to clench. John

Langers, her friend and advisor, a dedicated husband and father, had broken the law.

Chris clearly sensed the emotional chill that overtook Susan. His fingers tightened around hers and he shifted in his chair to confront her. "Why don't you tell me about it?"

She closed her eyes, unable to meet his concerned gaze. "I wish I could, Chris, but I can't."

"It has something to do with work, doesn't it?"

She nodded, her eyes still closed. "Please don't ask me, okay? If I could talk about it I would, but I can't." In particular, she couldn't talk about it with someone from Schenk. If she told Chris, he might feel obliged to report John's illicit activity to the company officers, even if Susan ultimately decided that John shouldn't be reported. Until she decided whether she wished to go public with her knowledge of the kickbacks, there was no way she could tell Chris about what John had done.

Slowly she opened her eyes, almost afraid of what she would see. She found Chris scrutinizing her, his eyes radiant in the descending shadows, his lips pressed together in a grim line. He didn't look disapproving, but rather quizzical, compassionate and maybe a bit disappointed that Susan refused to confide in him. "You promised you wouldn't ask," she reminded him.

"That's right. I did." He loosened his hold on her, forced a smile and swung his legs off the railing. "It's getting late," he remarked, rising to his feet. "I think I'd better do something about getting the beasts ready for bed."

HE LEFT by the back door, clad in his jeans, shirtless and barefoot. It was close to midnight; the kids had been asleep for hours. He himself had undressed and gotten into bed over an hour ago. He'd stretched out across the sheet in the unair-conditioned darkness of his downstairs bedroom, a warm gust entering through the open windows to dance across his skin, and stared at the ceiling, waiting for the restlessness to pass. It didn't.

He wasn't going to swim tonight. He'd swum enough during the day, racing Newt to the raft a neighbor had anchored fifty feet from the shore, and then accompanying Susan on a second trip to the raft. She was a good swimmer, her strokes powerful, her body slender and athletic. In her business suits she always looked somehow dainty, but when she'd stripped down to her swimsuit Chris had seen the well-toned shape of her upper arms, the smooth lines of her thighs, the graceful economy of her body.

When she'd hoisted herself up onto the raft next to him, he'd seen more. He'd seen her breasts, firm and round beneath the damp, clinging fabric, her nipples taut, the hollow of her navel faintly visible whenever she exhaled, the smooth flesh of her hips revealed by the high cut of the suit. He'd seen her hair slicked back from her face, the water darkening it to a shiny black, her long eyelashes beaded with drops of moisture, her throat a smooth, pale arch shimmering until the breeze blew her skin dry. Remembering the way she'd looked on the raft was one of the reasons Chris had found it impossible to fall asleep.

As long as he was sprawled out in bed, however, dreaming about having Susan lying next to him, he wasn't going to be able to think straight. So he picked his way carefully down the narrow path to the water's edge, climbed onto a rock to sit and focused on the shivering reflection of the crescent moon in the pond's rippling surface.

He wanted Susan. Arrogant as it might seem, he was reasonably confident that he could have her. It hadn't required much persuasion on his part to wrest from her a promise that she would return tomorrow for another day of boating and swimming. She enjoyed his company, she welcomed his physical displays of affection—a gentle kiss, a captured hand, an arm around her shoulders. He believed that in the not too distant future he could find that ravishing body of hers next to his in his bed.

She responded to him. At times, she seemed to respond to him at least as powerfully as he responded to her. Trying to explain the physical bond that had drawn him and Elysse together so many years ago, Chris had almost said to Susan, "It was like this, like what happened when you and I kissed last night, what happens whenever we look into each other's eyes, whenever our lips touch."

He hadn't felt anything so awesome since his marriage fell apart—until last night. Until he'd kissed Susan.

But, as he'd implied to Susan, chemistry alone could never be enough. It took more than chemistry to build a relationship. And that was what he wanted with Susan— a relationship. He wasn't going to surrender to the gratification of loving her and then watch her walk out of his life. He'd rebounded reasonably well from his divorce, but he had no desire to go through anything like that again.

With Susan there would have to be more. There would have to be honesty, faith, complete trust. Sharing. He would gladly tell her whatever she wanted to know about him. But she would have to reciprocate. She would have to be open with him.

She obviously wasn't ready to open up yet. Whatever difficulties were currently besetting her, she wasn't ready to fill Chris in about them. He could respect her reticence... for now. He could wait until she was willing to accept the kind of commitment Chris was looking for, until she was willing to love him, not just with passion but with trust. He could wait.

As long as he was waiting, he wasn't going to let lust overtake him. For the first time in nine years, he sensed that he was onto something real with a woman, something real and full and total. He wasn't going to aim for an easy victory with Susan, an episode of rapturous pleasure utterly lacking in soul, without an aftermath or an afterthought.

This time he would be patient. He would have to be. Patience, he knew, was the price he'd have to pay to win Susan's trust.

Chapter Six

"Okay," Lorraine called from the kitchen. "The salad's ready, the table's set and the quiche'll be done in about fifteen minutes." She swung through the doorway to the living room, where Susan was running a dust rag one last time over the coffee table.

Susan turned and gave her friend a grateful smile. "I really appreciate this, Lorraine. Racing home, changing my clothes and straightening up the house in a half hour—I couldn't have handled fixing dinner, too."

"I don't mind," Lorraine assured her. "You should've gone into banking, Susan. Much better hours. Anyway, I love making quiche, but there's a limit to how often I want to eat it."

"Do you think Emma will like it?" Susan asked.

"Why wouldn't she like it? It's like a pie. It *is* a pie."

"It's so...so vegetarian," Susan noted dubiously. "Chris is always feeding her and her brother hamburgers. Oklahoma is cattle territory, isn't it?"

"Real women eat quiche," Lorraine insisted. "Quiche and salad make the perfect meal for a ladies' night. Emma's going to feel so sophisticated—she'll love it."

Not entirely convinced, Susan gave the living room a critical inspection. "Do you think I ought to vacuum?"

"Only if you're planning to perform surgery in here," Lorraine answered sarcastically, pulling the dust rag from Susan's hands and marching back to the kitchen with it. "The place looks fine, Susan. As if a thirteen-year-old girl is going to be handing out points for neatness."

"I just want her to have a good time, that's all," Susan insisted, detouring to the downstairs bathroom to check her appearance before she joined Lorraine in the kitchen. She smoothed out her hair with her hands, adjusted the neckline of her loose-fitting short-sleeved sweater and hiked the waistband of her pleated beige slacks a fraction of an inch higher. She had chosen her clothing with the aim of projecting an image combining maturity and "coolness"—cool enough that Emma would feel comfortable with her, and mature enough that Chris would feel comfortable about leaving Emma in her care for an evening. In addition to looking cool and mature, she wanted to convey an aura of casualness and easiness, a conviction that Emma was, for this one evening, the sole focus of Susan's universe.

Work had not gone well today, nor had it gone well yesterday, her first day back at Schenk after her prolonged absence. Virtually from the moment she'd entered the building, she was assailed by a continuous chorus of "How are you feeling?" and "Take it easy today!" from her associates, which made her feel guilty about having called in sick four days in a row. Many of her colleagues treated her as if she were an invalid in need of drastic pampering.

Whenever Susan's co-workers weren't being cloyingly solicitous of her health, they were congratulating her on her promotion. Naturally, that didn't sit well with her, either. And John, who'd have to be an idiot not to realize that Susan's absence the previous week had nothing to do with illness, treated her with an aloofness so chilly it hurt. She understood that no matter what she ultimately decided to do about her boss, their closeness wasn't going to survive. But the actual experience of being cold-shouldered by someone she'd once considered a good friend was painful.

In fact, the only time Susan had felt happy at work was Monday at lunch, when she met Chris for a sandwich in the dining room. For those forty-five blessed minutes she was able to forget the hassles, forget the crisis, forget everything but the wonderful weekend she'd spent with him and his family.

Forgetting was delightful, but whenever Susan began to succumb to the temptation to put the whole mess out of her mind forever, she sternly yanked herself back to reality. Forgetting was a luxury she simply couldn't allow herself.

Yet, as she gazed at her reflection in the mirror above the sink, she detected no strain in her expression, no hint of the pressure under which she was functioning. She discerned a touch of nervousness about how her evening with Emma would go, but no real tension. For some reason, she genuinely believed that tonight Emma *was* the focus of her universe. And that was as it should be.

Satisfied with her appearance, Susan left the powder room for the kitchen, where she found Lorraine shaking a cruet of salad dressing. "I probably should have vacuumed," Susan muttered, sublimating that urge by sponging down the already spotless counters. "Chris's house was unbelievably tidy. He told me he's hired someone to come in once a week and clean it. But even so...he's got two kids and his house looks much neater than mine. Emma's going to think I'm a slob."

"Maybe her idea of a great time is playing soccer with dustballs," Lorraine remarked with a laugh. "Mellow out, Susan. I know you want to make a good impression on the kid, but you don't need her falling in love with you. Her father, yes. Her, no."

"I don't need him falling in love with me, either," Susan argued, managing a lame smile. "All I want from him at the moment is his friendship."

"Since when have you been the sort to set your sights so low?" Lorraine glanced out the window, then started toward the front door. "His rusty chariot approaches. I'm on my way. Have fun, Susan. Loosen up and enjoy yourself."

"Thanks again for everything," Susan said, accompanying Lorraine through the living room to the foyer. "I really couldn't have pulled off this dinner without you."

"Well, when you told me you were planning to take her to Burger King for supper, I had to butt in and set you straight. Burger King!" Wrinkling her nose in disgust, Lorraine opened the door in time to see Chris and his daughter emerging from the brown station wagon. "Hi, Chris!" she shouted, waving to him and then beaming a smile at the petite blond girl he was escorting up the paved front walk.

Susan was surprised by the familiarity of Lorraine's greeting, until she noticed the meaningful look that passed between Chris and her neighbor. They were more than brief acquaintances, after all; they had been co-conspirators in a plot to roust Susan from her lethargy last Friday evening. Susan wondered whether Chris was as thankful as she was for Lorraine's meddling.

"Hello, Lorraine," he said, returning her smile. "Are you going to participate in this hen party, too?"

"Afraid not. Susan and your daughter are going to have to make do without me. So long, Susan," Lorraine said, patting her friend's shoulder before heading across the lawn to her own town house. "Oh, by the way," she hollered over her shoulder, "I left something for you upstairs."

Although Susan's curiosity was piqued, she wasn't about to ignore Chris and Emma just to race upstairs and find out what it was Lorraine had left. Probably a gag bill for her services. Lorraine's sense of humor was bizarre—not only was she the sort to scramble a message deliberately so that a gentleman caller would wind up inside Susan's bedroom instead of in his car driving home, but she was also the sort to leave behind a jokey itemized list for the cost of the eggs, cheese, pie crust, spinach, mushrooms and labor.

Bill or no, Susan was enormously indebted to Lorraine for having helped her to prepare a nice dinner for Emma. When Susan had called Lorraine Sunday night to fill her in on the two days she'd spent with Chris and his family, she'd mentioned that she and Emma had made a date to spend Tuesday evening having dinner and then shopping at the mall in Meriden. All she'd done was to mumble something in passing about take-out hamburgers, and Lorraine had intervened, describing various menus and recipes and volunteering to help in the preparations. "If the kid is looking for a substitute mother, you can't just shove some fast food down her throat," Lorraine had reproached Susan. "You ought to make it a meal she'll never forget." According to Lorraine, her mushroom quiche was guaranteed unforgettable, and when she offered to make it, Susan wasn't foolish enough to say no.

"I've got to run," Chris said after kissing Susan's cheek. "Newt and I made our own plans for tonight."

"A Little League baseball game," Emma reported, curling her lip. "Dairy Queen and then some dumb baseball game. Yuck."

"To each his own, Emma," Chris said before lifting his gaze to Susan. "What time will you have her home?"

"It isn't like it's a school night, Dad," Emma protested.

"Nine-thirty, ten o'clock," Susan promised. "The stores will be closed by then." She glanced down at Emma, pleased to be able to claim, "No Dairy Queen for us, Emma. We've got a delicious meal waiting for us inside."

"Hmm. I wish I could stay," Chris murmured, shooting Susan an unexpectedly sexy grin.

Her answering smile was teasing. "Unfortunately, you weren't invited. This is a ladies-only night, Chris. Come on, Emma," she said, planting her hand on the girl's shoulder and guiding her up the front steps and into the foyer. "Let's go open the wine."

"Wine?" Chris shouted after them. "You're serving her wine? She's just a child—"

Susan turned and winked at Chris, then shut the door, effectively stifling his paternal admonition.

"Are we really going to have wine?" Emma asked, drifting into the living room and gazing around her. "Oh, wow. This is nice."

"Do you think so?" Susan asked. She had always liked her home's decor well enough, but seeing it through Emma's eyes made her appreciate it even more.

"White carpeting," Emma observed in an awe-filled voice. "We could never have white carpeting. Newt would destroy it in a minute. Besides, it sure would look stupid in a log cabin. Are we really going to have wine with dinner, Susan?''

Susan smiled and shook her head. "It's a bad idea to drink wine before you go shopping," she explained, careful not to insult Emma by implying that she was too young for liquor. "You don't want to be addled. A woman needs her wits about her when she sets out to conquer the mall. Come keep me company in the kitchen, Emma. Everything should be just about ready."

Susan's kitchen didn't dazzle Emma as much as the living room had. "You haven't got a microwave," she noted disapprovingly as she flopped onto one of the chairs at the breakfast table and plucked a mushroom from the salad bowl to nibble on.

"No, I haven't," Susan confirmed, opening the oven and examining the quiche. "To tell you the truth, Emma, I don't trust them. I heard a horrible story about microwave ovens a few years ago."

"What story?" Emma asked, intrigued.

"Now, I know it's too silly to be true, but . . . well, I heard that some woman accidentally put her pet dog inside her microwave—"

"No kidding? Did that story make the rounds here? In Tulsa it was a pet cat." Emma nonchalantly flicked a long lock of blond hair back from her face and fished another mushroom out of the salad bowl. "Everyone was talking about it at school, like how the cat got heated up and expanded from the inside out and—"

"Please!" Susan cut her off. "I don't want to hear it."

"Yeah, well, like you said, it isn't true. I want a microwave."

"Do you cook a lot?" Susan asked, slicing two wedges of the eggy pie, arranging them on plates and carrying them to the table.

"Nah," Emma said, staring skeptically at the food before her. "But with a microwave, we could do all those frozen dinners in five minutes flat. Everybody has a microwave these days. I just think we ought to have one, too. What is this stuff?" She jabbed at the quiche with the tines of her fork.

"Quiche."

"I've never had it before."

"It's like an omelet inside a pie crust," Susan described it. "It's very good." At Emma's dubious glance, she recalled Lorraine's words and added, "It's considered sophisticated."

Emma promptly tasted it. "Not bad," she decided after swallowing. "I bet Newt would hate it. I bet," she went on after swallowing another mouthful, "my mother eats stuff like this in Los Angeles all the time."

"COME ON, Dad," Newt commanded, climbing over the seat to sit beside his father in front, then reaching into the back again for his baseball mitt. "The game starts at six-thirty, and I'm starving to death."

Chris tore his eyes from Susan's door and ignited the engine. That saucy wink she'd tossed him... He knew that she'd intended it only to communicate that he needn't worry about her corrupting Emma with alcohol. So why had it turned him on?

Because everything Susan did had the power to turn him on, that was why. She hadn't looked totally confident; he'd noticed a slight panic pinching her lips when her friend Lorraine had abandoned her, jogging across the lawn and vanishing into one of the other town houses. But, confident or not, Susan was being a damned good sport about this dinner and shopping expedition with Emma. Susan was doing it because she knew it would mean a lot to Emma. Her willingness to go to such a great effort for his daughter was yet another thing that turned him on.

But if he spent the evening thinking about that, he wouldn't be much company for Newt. "I can see you're starving to death, son," he taunted the boy beside him. "Don't bend your arm too fast—if you do, your bones might poke right through the skin at your elbow."

Newt ignored his father's teasing. "I like Susan," he announced.

"You'd like anyone who got your sister off your back for a couple of hours," Chris commented.

"Maybe." Newt slipped his mitt onto his hand and punched the pocket a few times. "I think she's pretty, too, for a lady."

"Given that limitation, yes, I agree. She's pretty," Chris said with a straight face.

"Do you like her?" Newt asked.

"Yes, I do."

"As much as you liked Addie Ferguson?"

Chris cast Newt a quick glance, then turned his attention to the traffic on Route 10. He had dated Addie Ferguson for close to three years back in Tulsa. It hadn't been an exclusive affair for either of them, but it had been a relationship of long enough duration that his children got used to having Addie around. Every now and then she accompanied the family on outings; she frequently appeared at the breakfast table Sunday mornings. She was a bright, cheerful woman, attractive and effervescent. She and Chris had enjoyed each other, and liked each other. But something between them had failed to gel, and when Addie accepted a job in Denver and moved away, neither of them was heartbroken.

"I like different people in different ways," Chris said carefully. "I haven't known Susan as long as I knew Addie. Both of them are fine women. I hope that someday Susan will be as good a friend as Addie was."

"You think she's going to spend the night?" Newt asked, undermining Chris's noble attempt at tact.

Chris searched the Dairy Queen parking lot for an empty space, using the time to formulate a proper response. Fifth-graders today knew a great deal about male-female sleeping arrangements—especially fifth-graders whose fathers happened to be divorced and possessed of a healthy sex drive. Although Chris willingly answered Newt's occasional questions and explained to him the rudiments of procreation, they had never discussed in any detail the reason Addie Ferguson ate breakfast with the Kelsos every now and then.

"Susan might spend the night sometime," he finally said as he shut off the engine. He wasn't going to lie to his son.

Newt bounded out of the car and joined Chris at the front bumper. "You know what I 'specially like about Susan? She wasn't too...I can't think of the word, Dad, but you know, like whenever I show that snake hole to Emma and she always screams and gags and says I'm gross and stuff?"

"Squeamish," Chris suggested.

"Yeah, that's it. Susan wasn't too squeamish. If you want to marry her or something, Dad, it's all right with me."

Chris laughed and held the door open for Newt. Awfully generous of the kid to grant his permission. Although, Chris pondered, his laughter fading, the fact that Susan had won Newt's approval couldn't hurt. Not that Chris was on the verge of proposing to Susan, not that he even allowed himself any expectations along those lines, but sure, he wanted her to spend the night sometime—sometime soon. As soon as he was certain that she trusted him, that their relationship was real and solid...and if it was, why not marry her, too?

For crying out loud—how had Newt managed to turn his mind in this direction? Chris hardly knew Susan. They'd spent a few days together, frolicking in the pond, wolfing down barbecued food, talking...looking into each other's eyes and reading in them the secrets of each other's souls, their mutual attraction, their desire.

Lord, he wanted her. He wanted her to spend the night, the day, whenever. But he wasn't going to blow it by rushing things. He was going to take his time, exercise willpower, make sure that their love had depth and could endure.

Depth and endurance...it sounded a hell of a lot like marriage, Chris conceded. He glanced down at the boy beside him, a pint-size red-haired version of himself, bellying up to the counter and ordering a cheeseburger and a chocolate malt in his booming high-pitched voice. Newt might be young, but he was unnervingly perceptive when it came to his father's feelings. He had figured out before Chris did that marrying Susan was an idea worth considering.

SUSAN HAD TO BE one of the oldest shoppers in the entire mall. Here and there she spotted a senior citizen relaxing on a bench in the air-conditioned arcade, munching on an ice-cream cone, sipping a soft drink or lighting a pipe. But the vast majority of the mall's patrons that evening were teenagers. They loitered in pairs and clusters; they swarmed around the record shops, the clothing stores and the mall's decorative fountains like

ants around a crumb of bread; they huddled near their
pals and cast coquettish looks at members of the opposite sex. Boys strutted; girls preened. Susan felt as if she'd
taken a wrong turn somewhere and gotten trapped inside a high school dance.

Emma was in her element, however. Susan's presence
dampened her ability to flirt, but she feasted her eyes on
the swaggering boys and compared her appearance to the
coy girls. "Okay, like, see how they've got pink streaks
in their hair?" Emma whispered, pointing out a gaggle
of girls lining up to buy Italian ices. "How do you think
I'd look if I did that?"

"Do you want to know the truth?" Susan responded.
"I think you'd look stupid. I think *they* look stupid."

Emma scowled. "I bet my mother would let me streak
my hair. She's blond like me. Maybe she streaks hers."

"If she does," Susan remarked dryly, "she probably
looks stupid, too."

Emma had managed to introduce the topic of her
mother several times during the evening. Susan didn't
exactly mind; she didn't feel competitive with the woman,
or anxious about any lasting heartache the woman might
have inflicted on Chris. On the other hand, she was concerned about the way Emma seemed able, without any
encouragement whatsoever, to invent myths regarding
her mother.

By Emma's estimation, Chris's ex-wife not only was
knowledgeable about all manner of epicurean delights
but cooked well enough to be in a position to teach Julia
Child a thing or two. Emma asserted that her mother had
three holes pierced into each ear, and that each hole was
filled with a diamond stud. She maintained that her
mother had a face like Belinda Carlisle's, a body like
Madonna's, a voice like Cyndi Lauper's and a wardrobe

like Susanna Hoff's. Susan had to ask Emma to identify these personages to her. "They're lady rock stars," Emma explained. "And I bet none of them has as much talent as my mom. The only difference is, she doesn't want to push herself. Like, she's happy just living with this record producer."

Maybe using the word "stupid" in reference to Emma's mother was undiplomatic, but Susan meant what she said. Whatever mousses and dyes the woman might or might not apply to her hair, Emma ought to face the reality of the situation. Chris's ex-wife was selfish, she was irresponsible—and she was gone.

"How about a lemonade?" Susan asked, hoping to soften her harsh assessment of Emma's mother.

Emma's stony expression thawed slightly. "Nah. What I'd really like is, okay, see that denim miniskirt?" She pointed to a mannequin in a showcase window. "I'd like to try one on."

"All right," Susan said, trailing her into the store.

The skirt bore an eerie resemblance to a skirt Susan had owned in junior high school. It looked spectacular on Emma, who was thin enough—and young enough—to be able to display her long legs to great advantage. "Can you see my underpants when I bend over?" Emma asked, twirling in front of the three-way mirror outside the fitting room.

"Not if you bend from the knees instead of the waist," Susan advised her. "Minis take some getting used to, but once you get the hang of it, you'll be fine."

"I bet you used to wear minis all the time," Emma said.

"When I was your age, I did."

"You're too old now?" Emma half asked.

"I think so," Susan answered honestly, refusing to take offense. She *was* too old—if not chronologically, then emotionally. She was a businesswoman now, independent, self-supporting, professional, eager to be treated as an equal to men. Miniskirts were designed for females who wanted to live their lives as if their most pressing concern was whether their underpants stuck out.

Emma scrutinized her reflection in the mirror for a few more seconds, then bounded back into the fitting room. She emerged several minutes later, dressed in her own jeans. "I'm going to buy this skirt," she declared. "You think my dad's going to hit the ceiling?"

Susan grinned. "He might."

"If he does, are you going to take his side or mine?" Emma asked as she carried the skirt to the cashier's counter.

"Yours," Susan promised.

Emma handed the cashier some money, then eyed Susan quizzically. "You're not going to win his heart that way," she warned.

"What makes you think I want to win his heart?" Susan asked, hoping she didn't appear as shocked as she was by Emma's indiscreet observation.

"You're not his first girlfriend, you know," Emma said, stuffing her change into her purse and gathering up the bag containing her new purchase. "They all think they've got to go out of their way to win Newt and me over. You don't have to, though. As Dad would say, when it comes to his social life, we get one vote a piece and he gets three. He invited this one creepy lady over once—" she marched out of the store, Susan at her heels "—and she spent like half the evening gushing all over Newt and me, telling us how nice we were and all, and

Dad never saw her again. She tried too hard, you know? Like, it wasn't real.''

Again, Susan needed a moment to recover. On the rare occasions Susan's father had introduced her to his dates when she was young, she had never spoken so candidly with any of them. She'd been shy, demure and mildly resentful, but she would never have dared to express her feelings aloud. "Is that why you think we're doing this tonight?" she asked Emma. "Is that why you think I took you shopping?"

"I'm just saying, okay, if that's what you've got in mind, don't bother. It won't work."

"What I've got in mind..."

Susan tapered off as Emma's gaze followed a muscular young man in a body-hugging T-shirt. He sauntered past them, favoring Emma with a lingering stare and a smug smirk, and then vanished into a pizza shop. Emma reluctantly turned her attention back to Susan.

"I wanted to go shopping with you because your father's a man and he doesn't understand some things," Susan explained. "He doesn't think shopping is fun, and I do, so I thought I'd take you. That's the only reason."

Emma looked incredulous, but all she said was, "I'll take you up on that lemonade now."

They strolled along the arcade until they found a snack bar selling soft drinks. Susan bought two large lemonades, then located an empty bench for her and Emma to sit on. Emma took a long slurp of lemonade through the straw. Then she lifted her face to Susan. "How do you think I'd look in lipstick?"

"Minnie Mouse," Susan replied. By now she was beginning to grow accustomed to Emma's tendency to zigzag through topics of conversation: a five-second report about her absent mother's ostensible behavior, a request for woman-to-woman advice, a passing caveat about her father, another request for woman-to-woman advice. It was rather like watching a jai alai game, Susan pondered—fast-paced, dizzying, hard to follow but never boring.

"What do you mean, Minnie Mouse?"

Susan smiled. "You know how Minnie Mouse looks, with those spindly little legs, and then those big high-heeled shoes? She looks like she's wearing someone else's shoes, like she's a little girl playing grown-up."

"And that's how I'd look in lipstick?"

"I'm afraid so," Susan said before sipping her drink. "You have a natural look, Emma. I don't think you ought to cover it up with cosmetics."

"Natural," she snorted. "I look like an Okie." She spun her straw through her cup, creating a rattling noise with the crushed ice. "Back in Tulsa I tried putting on lipstick, but it came out looking awful. I mean, like, how do you learn how to put on makeup if you haven't got a mother to teach you? How did *you* learn, Susan?"

"My aunt," Susan recalled. "And friends. And practice. I'm sure I looked like a clown through most of high school—and my father used to scream bloody murder whenever he caught me with mascara on. Fortunately, he didn't get home from work until six or six-thirty, so I had plenty of time to scrub my face before he saw me."

Emma drank thoughtfully. "How..." She hesitated, exercising uncharacteristic courtesy. "How did you feel when your mother died? Was it awful?"

It was at moments like this, Susan acknowledged, that she was glad she'd tolerated all the zigzagging and rude insinuations. When Emma reached out to her, she understood why she was here, now, with this girl. "It was awful," she confirmed.

"How'd she die?"

"She went into insulin shock," Susan related. "She and my father had gone to a party. Maybe she'd had a drink or eaten something she shouldn't have. It's hard to say what set it off. But she went into a coma, and she was rushed to the hospital. A few days later, she passed away." Susan sighed. Her mother's death had occurred long ago, and relating it stimulated only an ache of remembrance. The acute pain of grief had faded over time. "You know," she admitted to Emma, shaping a wistful smile, "I used to imagine all sorts of things about my mother, the same way you imagine things about yours. I used to think about how if she'd lived she would have been much more lenient than my father, much more permissive, much cooler."

"Yeah, well..." Emma shrugged, then drained her glass with a few deep gulps. "The difference is, *my* mother's still alive. So it's not like I'm imagining what she would have been. Like, she *is* all those things."

"Maybe," Susan conceded. "But maybe she's just a sad, sorry woman who missed out on all the joy your father's had raising you and Newt, being a parent and making a family. Your father might not like shopping, Emma, but he's a terrific guy."

"Uh-huh," Emma grunted without much conviction. "But remember, it's not going to work, getting to him through me. How about let's check out some more stores? I want to buy a top to go with this skirt."

Before Susan could finish her drink—before she could even beseech Emma for just one more minute of rest on the bench—Emma was on her feet, darting through the throng in the direction of yet another clothing store. *Did I actually think this would be fun?* Susan wondered, once again feeling substantially older than her years.

But she didn't complain. She tossed her half-full cup of lemonade into the nearest trash can, chased after Emma and smiled, thinking about what a terrific guy Chris truly was.

HE SAW the headlight beams sweep across the tree trunks as her car turned onto the driveway, slowed and stopped in front of the garage. It was nearly ten o'clock, and Newt, while probably not yet asleep, had been in bed for a half hour. As soon as Susan turned off the engine, Chris's ears filled once more with the night songs of crickets and frogs.

He lowered his feet from the railing and stood, trying to catch a glimpse of Susan, to read her expression and brace himself for whatever disasters might have occurred during her evening with Emma. But her face was cast in shadow as she opened her door and climbed out.

Emma's mood was obvious. Burdened by an alarming number of packages and bags, she charged up the hill to the porch, shouting, "Hey, Dad! Wait till you see what I bought! You're gonna hate most of it!"

Chris held his arms open for Emma, but instead of giving him a hug his daughter tossed three bags at him, then pranced into the house with the rest of her purchases. Bemused, he turned to see Susan trailing Emma up the hill, smiling wearily. "I'm not sure," he said, returning her smile, "but I gather the shopping expedition was a success."

"You shouldn't have given her so much cash," Susan scolded him as she joined him on the porch.

He gazed at the packages in his hand. "She wasn't supposed to spend it all."

"I'm afraid she did, and then some."

He ought to have been upset, but he found himself chuckling, instead. "How much do I owe you?" he asked, dumping the parcels onto the lounge chair and digging in the hip pocket of his jeans for his wallet.

Susan touched his arm to stop him. "Forget it," she said. "The only thing she didn't pay for was a pair of feather earrings."

"What?"

"Earrings made of feathers," Susan said, her hand lingering on his wrist, cool and graceful. "I had a pair when I was thirteen, too. I wanted to buy them for her."

Chris knew he should be concerned about his daughter's extravagance, and Susan's. But the feel of her hand on him was too distracting. He slid his arm from her light clasp and wove his fingers through hers, then pulled her to him and kissed her. "You are too much, Susan," he whispered.

"Too much what?" she asked, laughing.

He kissed her again, a longer, deeper kiss. Her tongue moved with his, reaching for him, and he recognized again how easy it would be for them to make love—how easy and how pleasurable. Soon Emma would be in bed like Newt, and Chris could ask Susan to stay. He could lead her off the porch and around the house to his private downstairs entrance, and the children would never have to know. Even if they did know, they probably wouldn't mind. Newt had already gone public with his opinions, and Emma—Chris supposed that a pair of feather earrings was enough to buy her favor.

Too easy, he cautioned himself, abruptly pulling his lips from hers. Making love with Susan shouldn't be so simple. She was a complicated woman, and when Chris finally took her to bed, he wanted all of her—her mind and her heart and her soul—there with him.

He guided her to two side-by-side porch chairs and they sat. Closing her eyes, she rested her head against his shoulder, and he realized he was practically holding her up. "Emma wore you out," he guessed.

"My stamina isn't what it used to be," Susan admitted. "I used to be able to shop for hours at a clip, but not anymore. I must be getting old."

He ran his fingers over the back of her neck in a gentle massage. She felt so good against him, he had to tap his reserves of willpower again, to keep himself from asking her to stay once the children were asleep.

No. He was not going to let Susan become another Addie Ferguson, a familiar face on the weekends, a woman with whom the elements failed to come together. Nor was he going to let her be another Elysse, a woman to whom his passion blinded him, a woman who flew with him to paradise a few times and then dropped him back to earth and floated away.

"How was the ball game?" Susan asked, effectively dragging him out of his reverie.

"Spirited," Chris related. "After the game, Newt and I talked to one of the coaches. There'll be a place for Newt on his team next year, if he's interested. Needless to say, Newt was beside himself with joy. I think the thing he misses most about Tulsa is his old Little League team." He wound his fingers through her hair, savoring its silky texture. "How was shopping? Other than expensive, of course."

"Fun," Susan told him. "Emma is a fascinating girl. You've raised yourself a terrific daughter."

Chris snorted. "I raised my daughter to speak English. Now she seems to spend most of her energy making sure I can't understand her."

"I didn't find her that hard to understand," Susan argued.

"That's because you already speak the language." Grinning, he loosened his hold on Susan. The sleepy timbre of her voice reminded him that, whether or not one understood Emma, the girl had a way of tuckering out sane adults. "I'd better let you go home," he whispered. "You must be beat, and we've got work tomorrow."

"Work," Susan grunted, her eyes fluttering open, flashing with a momentary anguish before clouding over with fatigue.

Chris almost questioned her about the transient flare of panic in those large, lovely eyes of hers. But he didn't. If he did, she would only swear that she couldn't answer, and he would wind up frustrated by her evasiveness.

Instead, he stood, gripped her hands and hoisted her to her feet. Then he arched his arm around her shoulder and escorted her across the yard to her car. "Are you planning to go to the company picnic?" he inquired, then frowned in self-reproach, aware that part of his motivation for asking was to lure her into telling him about her problem at work. Whatever that problem was, it hadn't affected her performance on the job too noticeably during the past two days. When they'd had lunch together on Monday, and whenever he phoned her office to say hello, she seemed composed, her emotions firmly under wraps. But he sensed the torment in her just below her placid surface, the anxiety she refused to explain to him.

"Oh, no," Susan groaned. "The picnic's this Saturday, isn't it. I forgot all about it."

"We folks in personnel never forget about things like that," Chris boasted. Then he grew serious. Half his

motivation for raising the subject might have been to lure
her into talking about her problem, but the other half was
legitimate. "I'd like it a lot if you came with us."

Susan seemed to wrestle with her thoughts. She averted
her face so he could see only the smooth dark strands of
hair dropping to her shoulder. Again he sensed her anguish. He wished to high heaven that she would reveal to
him why the mere mention of going to the company picnic caused a shiver of dread to ripple through her.

But she didn't. She drew in a steady breath and presented Chris with a wry smile. "I'm not sure I'll be going,
Chris. But if I do, I'll go with you."

"It's not just me," Chris pointed out, discreetly
blocking the car door so she couldn't end the conversation by opening it. "Newt asked me this evening whether
you'd come to the picnic with us. And if I'm judging
Emma's mood correctly, I'm sure she'll want you with us,
too. You seem to have won her over in a big way tonight."

"Either it was me or the feather earrings," Susan
joked, her smile losing its forced look.

"I'm sure it was you," Chris claimed. "Knowing her,
she may have forgotten to thank you, but—"

"I don't need to be thanked," Susan insisted. "She
seems to have won me over tonight, too."

She kissed his cheek, and he reluctantly accepted that
as his cue to open her door for her. She folded herself
onto the driver's seat and twisted the ignition switch.

He planted his hands on the seam where the door met
the roof of the car. "Lunch tomorrow?" he asked
through the open window.

"I still haven't caught up on my paperwork from last
week, so I may have to work through lunch," she said.
"But give me a buzz around eleven, and I'll let you

know." She gazed up at him, her smile now encompassing her entire face, eradicating the exhaustion and the tension he'd seen in it just moments ago. "What ever happened to that crazy idea of mine, that it was a bad move to get involved with someone you work with?"

Chris's hands curled into fists against the chrome trim framing the window. *Involved*. Did she honestly think they were involved? The feelings were there, yes, the yearning. The potential for a true involvement. Perhaps on a certain level they *were* involved, but...

But if they really were, why wouldn't she share her troubles with him? Why wouldn't she open up?

He didn't say anything. He only smiled, stepped away from the car, and watched her back down the driveway to the street and drive off. And wondered how it could be that a man who had learned all he needed to know about patience when it came to the rearing of his two beloved, exasperating children still had so much to learn about patience when it came to a woman like Susan.

Chapter Seven

It was black, composed of some sort of translucent fabric with strategically placed insets of lace and satin. Whatever it was, there wasn't much of it.

"I saw this at Doris Kenner's party," Lorraine had scribbled on the pink square of "While You Were Out" message paper Susan found beside the garment, "and thought of you. Try it out on Chris and let me know how it works."

A feeble giggle escaped Susan as she lifted the thing by two satin ribbons which she took to be its shoulder straps. Once she shook it out it resembled a teddy—an extremely skimpy teddy, with a provocative series of satin-trimmed slits running down the front between the two semi-sheer breast cups, and strips of lace bordering the arm holes and leg holes.

Susan had never owned an item of clothing so risqué. When she held it up in front of herself and examined her reflection in the mirror, she decided that it went well beyond risqué and was testing the boundaries of obscene. What, she wondered, was the point of wearing such an article of clothing? It would expose so much of your body, you might as well just go nude.

Dropping the teddy back onto her dresser, where Lorraine had left it for her, Susan lifted the accompanying note and reread it. "Try it out on Chris..."

Her grin vanishing, she placed the note on top of the teddy, drifted across the room to her rocking chair and sat. She was exhausted, and she faced the prospect of another day at Schenk a little more than ten hours from now. She ought to wash, get undressed and hit the sack.

But even if she went to bed, she knew she wouldn't fall asleep. Her mind was whirling, and her nerves bristled. The taste of Chris still lingered on her lips. Her body echoed with emptiness.

Why hadn't he asked her to stay the night? It hadn't been like the previous weekend, when his children played as major a role in Susan's visits and when she and Chris were still feeling their way around each other. Nor had it been like their lunch date in the dining room at headquarters yesterday, when they'd been surrounded by their fellow employees. Tonight was different. Susan was tired, yes, and they both had to go to work in the morning, but... When Chris had kissed her she'd come alive, alive for him alone, alive with desire.

He must have known. He must have felt the immediate surge of energy within her the moment his tongue found hers, the instant his arms closed around her. He must have felt her melting into him, her body fitting itself to his, her pulse racing out of control. He must have heard her faint cry of protest when he unexpectedly pulled away.

However unwise it might be to engage in an affair with him when so much in her life was undecided and unsettled, she honestly believed that tonight she had been ready to act unwisely, to put aside her sensibility and make love with Chris.

Except that he hadn't asked her. He had withdrawn, instead. He'd denied them both the opportunity to behave rashly and recklessly, to immerse themselves in the undeniable passion that bound them together.

"Being the gentleman that I am..." Susan surrendered to an amazed laugh as she recalled what Chris had said the evening they'd first gotten to know each other. He was a gentleman. Just as he had been a gentleman in removing her from a bar when she was making a fool of herself, and in making sure that she was unattached before he asked her on a date, so he was now being a gentleman in not pushing her beyond her limits—even though she would willingly soar with him past those limits if he gave her half a chance. Regardless of their attraction, regardless of the heat that tore through them whenever they kissed, he was holding back, protecting her.

Her father used to call it "saving yourself," a phrase she had always found peculiar. "Susan," he used to lecture, "my advice when it comes to sex is, you ought to save yourself..." He never completed the sentence; he never told her what she was supposed to save herself from—as if she were on an upper floor of a burning building or on the deck of a sinking ship. Sex, she had concluded as a youngster, was a catastrophe from which a woman had to run for her life; she couldn't depend on anyone else to save her.

Chris apparently intended to save Susan, however. Maybe he was saving them both. The temptation to give up, simply to hurl herself into the flames or let a wave sweep over the boat and carry her down into the pulsing current, was strong, very nearly irresistible. But Chris had pulled them back from the brink tonight.

She wondered whether she was supposed to thank him. She also wondered, as she stood, crossed the room to her dresser and fingered the comically lewd scrap of lingerie Lorraine had left for her, whether Chris was too much of a gentleman to succumb to the allure of black lace. The teddy was so scant Susan could fold it into a tiny wad and hide it in her purse. And the next time she felt the way she'd felt in Chris's arms tonight, she could slip it on, fling herself upon him and say, "*Don't* save us."

If she had the nerve, of course.

"WHY CAN'T WE RIDE to the picnic in Susan's car?" Emma asked, screwing her face into a pout as Chris swung the back door of the station wagon open for her. Susan started to say she had no objection to driving, but before she could utter a word Chris stifled her with a sharp glance.

She had received a hasty, cryptic telephone call from him fifteen minutes ago, informing her that Emma still wasn't dressed, so, in the interest of saving time, Susan might wish to drive over to the Kelso house instead of waiting for the Kelsos to pick her up. What she'd inferred from his disgruntled tone of voice was that Emma was deliberately moving at a snail's pace that morning, doing her utmost to aggravate him. Evidently, her latest sulk was just one small battle in their ongoing war.

"We're taking our car," Chris drawled, "because I said so and I get three votes. Now move your carcass." He nudged Emma onto the back seat, slammed the door and then held open the front door for Susan.

It was a muggy, overcast day, and Emma's mutinous gray eyes matched the menacing clouds overhead. After buckling her seat belt, she kicked aside some of the debris on the floor of the station wagon and folded her arms sullenly across her chest. "This picnic's gonna be a drag," she decided.

Newt disputed her dire prediction. "It's gonna be great," he said enthusiastically, bouncing on the seat beside his sister. "Remember how great the Schenk picnics used to be in Tulsa?"

"We knew people there," Emma whined. "We don't know anyone in Cheshire."

"We know Susan," Newt pointed out.

Susan shaped a tenuous smile. She wasn't in as ghastly a mood as Emma, but she, too, was suffering misgivings about attending the company picnic. It was one thing to avoid John Langers at work, and to exercise a frosty cordiality with him when she absolutely couldn't avoid him. But the annual company picnic was an event where people let their hair down, where the president played volleyball with the secretaries and the person slobbering over a juicy wedge of watermelon next to you might turn out to be a department head—or his sticky six-year-old child. The corporate hierarchy was inoperative at the picnic, and animosities dissolved.

Susan doubted that her animosity with John was going to dissolve, though. She'd just have to be vigilant when he was around, and keep her mouth shut.

"Do I turn right or left here?" Chris asked as they reached the Route 10 intersection.

"Left," Susan told him.

"This car is so grungy," Emma groused. "We're gonna drive up to the picnic in this grungy old car, and all these people who don't even know us are gonna think we're trash or something."

Susan eyed Chris, whose jaw tensed slightly in response to Emma's carping. With admirable restraint, he refused to let her rile him. Dressed in a pale blue polo

shirt and jeans, his tawny hair tossed back from his brow
by the hot breeze whipping through the open window at
his side, he looked wonderful to Susan, so wonderful she
forgot her apprehension about having to socialize with
John at the picnic.

"What I think," Emma declared, "is that we ought to
buy a new car. This car is just asking to die."

"*You're* asking to die, babe," Chris muttered under
his breath, barely loud enough for Susan to overhear. He
cast her a quick look, and when his eyes met hers he
chuckled. "Emma," he called over his shoulder. "If you
honestly care to know why we haven't bought a new car,
I'll be happy to explain it to you. Number one, we just
bought a new house—"

"A shack," Emma quibbled.

"A *house*," Chris overruled her, "in Connecticut,
where houses are damned expensive, and we sold our
house in Tulsa, where property values are currently depressed. A little basic arithmetic might indicate that we
didn't exactly clean up on that deal. And then, being that
I'm your father, I have this strange habit of thinking
about such things as what college tuitions are going to
cost a few years down the road, and I get these notions
about how I'd better set aside some money for that."

"I'm willing to skip college," Emma offered magnan-
imously. "Anything to get us a new car."

"I like this car," Newt piped up.

"It's a mess," Emma snapped. "Your junk is all over
the place."

"Yeah?" Newt challenged her. "Whose barrette is
this, huh? Whose mirror is this, Emma? It surely isn't
mine."

"Whose empty Milk Duds box is this?" Emma shot
back. "Whose Dave Winfield baseball card?"

"Whose lipstick?"

"Whose dried-up Silly Putty? That's not lipstick, it's lip gloss," Emma corrected Newt before firing another salvo. "Whose paper-clip chain? Whose Crackerjack prize? Whose pink plastic dinosaur is this, Newt?"

"Whose 'Love' postage stamp? Whose magazine photo of Eddie Van Halen?"

Chris and Susan exchanged another look. She was glad he was driving; she was laughing too hard to focus on the road. "Beasts," Chris whispered. "Definitely a few rungs down from human beings on the evolutionary ladder."

The parking lot of the private country club where Schenk held its yearly picnic was already fairly full by the time they arrived. The clouds had parted around the glaring white sun, and Susan pulled a pair of sunglasses from her bag and put them on before slinging the strap of the bag onto her shoulder and climbing out of the car. She was wearing shorts of a slightly more modest length than Emma's, a gauzy white blouse and sandals, but the steamy heat wrapped its fingers around her and squeezed. "Next year, they ought to consider holding the picnic in January," she groaned, wiping the perspiration from her forehead.

"It's not that bad," Chris argued, locking the car once Emma and Newt had gotten out. He watched them scamper ahead and inside an open-sided pavilion filled with picnic tables for eating at and buffet tables arrayed with food. "Summers are much hotter in Tulsa," he added, taking Susan's hand and ambling with her across the lot to the pavilion.

As if on cue, Chris was halted by Richard and Dave, the Bobbsey Twins of the purchasing department, just outside the entrance to the pavilion. "Hey, Kelso!" Dave hollered. "What's this I hear about them sending you back to Tulsa?"

The simple question struck Susan with the force of a blow to her gut. Back to Tulsa? Was Chris going to be transferred back? He'd only just gotten here, she'd only just gotten to know him... And why was Richard gaping at her? Why, specifically, was he gaping at her hand, which was securely tucked within Chris's? It dawned on her that, even though she and Chris had had a couple of lunches with each other in the dining room this week, the picnic was the first time their co-workers were actually going to see them together in a social context.

The truth was, she didn't mind people thinking of her and Chris as a couple. All her qualms about the questionability of developing a relationship with a professional associate were nonsense—at least when it came to Chris. Indeed, the jolt she felt at the possibility of his leaving Cheshire to return to Tulsa illustrated her feelings perfectly. She wanted Chris to stay, she wanted to be with him and she didn't care who knew it.

"Nothing definite," he was saying. "But probably I'll be flying down for a couple of days at the end of the month."

"A couple of days" registered on Susan's brain, and she began to relax. "A business trip?" she asked him once he'd extricated himself from Dave's clutches and ushered her to the bar set up at one end of the pavilion.

"Two beers, please," he requested before responding to Susan's question. "That's right," he said, grinning broadly. "Last winter, when I was head of personnel down there, I got saddled with the dismal chore of handing out a lot of pink slips. Some fine folks were laid off, friends of mine. Well, now that Schenk's got the Pentagon contract in its pocket—" he accepted two paper cups of beer from the bartender and handed one to Susan "—the Tulsa plant's going to be rehiring. Headquarters is sending me down for a few days to oversee the adjustments in staffing."

Susan hoped her uneasiness at his mention of the Pentagon contract wasn't visible. She hid behind her cup, taking a long sip of the tepid beer and using the time to compose herself. At last she lowered the cup and manufactured a limp smile. "I guess you must be very happy, knowing your friends are going to get their jobs back," she noted. "How come you didn't tell me about the trip?"

"I only found out about it yesterday afternoon. There's a possibility that Richard will be going to Tulsa, too, on some other business related to the new production quotas. That's how come he and Dave knew about it. I haven't even mentioned it to Newt and Emma yet. I'd like to figure out a way to take them along with me. I know they'd love to see their friends."

Susan absorbed his comments superficially. The bulk of her thoughts were directed toward what Chris had said about having had to lay off so many people, including his friends. The Pentagon contract, no matter how it had been achieved, meant that Chris's friends at the Tulsa plant would be able to return to work.

And yet... She wouldn't deny that his friends deserved employment, but that couldn't justify what John had done to obtain the contract.

"There's Newt," Chris remarked as they strolled out of the pavilion to one of the baseball diamonds, where teams were being chosen for a children's softball game. "Let's go watch."

Susan followed Chris through the throngs of people to the bleachers, clutching her cup of beer tightly to keep from spilling it. "Where's Emma?" she asked as they climbed up several rows of seats.

Chris shrugged, unconcerned. "Emma, in case you haven't noticed, is being contrary today. If I asked her to come watch the game with us, she'd run the other way. If I *don't* ask her, she might just venture over on her own."

"Is it just today?" Susan asked. She took a seat beside Chris on the splintery wooden bench and watched as the teams sorted themselves out on the field. Newt seemed oblivious to his father's presence in the audience. One of the game's adult organizers was distributing baseball caps with green-and-white Schenk logos on them. Newt donned his and solemnly punched the pocket of his mitt into shape as he waited to be assigned a position. One word Susan would never use to describe him was "contrary." He seemed like an unusually easy-going boy.

"What do you mean, is it just today?" Chris sipped some beer and then recaptured Susan's hand. "If you're referring to Emma's charming disposition... I'm afraid this latest snit of hers has been in effect for a long time."

"It isn't my fault, is it?" Susan asked nervously.

Chris turned to her. His eyes were steady and piercing, somehow penetrating the dark lenses of her sunglasses. "Why would it be your fault?"

Susan shrugged. "I don't know. Maybe I spoiled her when we went shopping the other evening."

"Feather earrings—bizarre though they may be—aren't going to spoil her, Susan."

"I bought her more than the earrings," Susan confessed. "I bought her a lemonade, and one of those giant chocolate-chip cookies—"

"Leading her down the road to ruin, are you?" Chris laughed. "Maybe it was the wine you served her at dinner."

"I'm serious, Chris. She spent an evening with me, and now she's giving you a hard time. What do you suppose it means?"

Chris squeezed her hand. "What it means is that Emma derives inordinate pleasure from giving me a hard time. I don't mean to prick your balloon, darlin', but I really don't think Emma's mood has anything to do with you."

"That's quite all right with me," Susan said, although she wasn't sure she believed him. She didn't doubt that Emma liked her, or that Emma had enjoyed their "ladies' night" as much as Susan had. But her occasional comments about how Susan shouldn't think that entertaining Emma was the way to Chris's heart gave Susan the impression that Emma wasn't ready to accept her.

"Maybe I'll just see if I can find her, and make sure she's okay," Susan suggested.

"She'll hate you forever if you do," Chris warned. "Emma hates thinking that someone's checking up on her. She views herself as such an independent adult." He offered Susan an ironic smile, then turned back to the field in time to see the first batter ground a ball to Newt, who had managed to get himself assigned to shortstop. He made an accurate throw to first, and Chris bellowed his approval.

"You aren't one of those demented Little League fathers, are you?" Susan asked once he'd subsided in his seat.

"What's demented?" he defended himself. "When my kids do something fantastic, I cheer. I'm happy to say they give me a lot to cheer about. Even Emma, when she isn't being a crab.''

Susan continued to watch the game until Newt had his first turn at bat. He hit a fly ball that carried a long way before being caught by the outfielder. After Chris shouted a few words of encouragement to his dejected son, Susan slipped her hand from his. "I'm going to go get a refill," she said, lifting her cup and angling it so he wouldn't notice that it was nearly half full.

"Uh-huh," Chris grunted, his eyes never leaving the field.

Susan edged past the knees of the seated fans until she reached the end of the bleachers, where she could leap the short distance to the ground. Then she set out in search of Emma. She supposed that Chris was right about Emma's not wanting to think anyone was checking up on her, but if Susan was discreet, if she merely located the girl and made certain that she was all right, Emma wouldn't even have to know about it.

She reentered the pavilion. Rock music belched from speakers at the far end of the enclosure, and Susan wove surreptitiously among the picnic tables, searching the crowd of teenagers gathered around the speakers. It didn't take her long to spot Emma seated on one of the benches. A boy with dark stringy hair and an ersatz shark's tooth on a braided leather rope around his neck sat next to her, regaling her with a long, involved story. Emma appeared rapt, although not so rapt that she didn't remember to show off her legs by crossing and uncrossing them, and to call attention to her striking blond hair by giving her head a languorous toss every now and then.

Susan grinned. Whatever Emma's baffling adolescent disposition might be, plant her beside a good-looking guy and she'd be cured. Although whether the guy in question was actually good-looking was debatable...but Emma clearly thought he was. He himself did, too, Susan surmised from the cocky angle of his head and the way he positioned himself on the bench to display his body.

Satisfied that Emma was having a good time, Susan strode across the pavilion to the bar and handed the bartender her cup. "This was warm," she complained. "Have you got any cold beer?"

He eyed her blandly, dumped the contents of her cup down a sink drain and refilled it from the tap. Susan took a sip. It was just as warm as the last cup had been.

Sighing, she rotated to find herself face to face with a round-cheeked, button-nosed woman dressed in a stylish turquoise jumpsuit, with short, frosted blond hair and an explosive smile. "Susan!" roared Margaret Langers. "It's so good to see you!"

The force of Margaret's greeting drove Susan backward a step. She swallowed, then did her best to return the megawatt smile of her boss's wife. Susan had fretted so much about having to deal with John at the picnic, she'd all but forgotten that she would also have to deal with Margaret.

"Good to see you, too," she managed. "Don't bother getting any beer. It's warm."

"Is it? That's how they drink it in England. If you want to know the truth, I was really planning to get some food. Come keep me company." Margaret curled her fingers around Susan's elbow and ushered her over to one of the buffet tables, where she piled a paper plate high with fried chicken, coleslaw and an ear of corn. "We haven't seen each other or spoken in so long," she prattled, adding two pickle spears to her plate. "You can catch me up on your life while I eat. I'm famished, Susan. I skipped breakfast this morning because I knew they'd be serving a feast here. Are you going to eat anything?"

"Not right now," Susan mumbled, trying to invent some credible news with which to entertain Margaret while the woman gorged herself.

They found an empty picnic table and sat. The air inside the pavilion was even stuffier than the air outside, despite the structure's vaulted roof and the open stretches where outer walls were supposed to be. The humid heat didn't seem to put a dent in Margaret's appetite, however. She smeared butter all over her corn, then bit off a row of kernels.

"How are your kids?" Susan asked.

"I'm in shock," Margaret replied, lowering the ear of corn and wiping her greasy fingers on a napkin. "Shelley is pregnant. Can you believe it? Me, a grandmother. I don't think I can handle it."

"That's wonderful!" Susan exclaimed, genuinely pleased. "Congratulations! Of course you can handle it, Margaret. All you have to do is volunteer to babysit a lot, and spoil the child and lug around a hundred photographs that you show to anyone who stands still long enough. Isn't that what grandmothers do?"

"That's what I figured," Margaret concurred, grinning conspiratorially. "As long as I don't *look* like a grandmother, I have every intention of playing the part to the hilt."

"Say, is that you, Duvall?" a male voice interrupted them.

Susan twisted around to see who had called to her. "Hi, Stuart," she greeted the man, whose office in the acquisitions department was down the hall from hers.

He loped to the table, his crisp tennis outfit nearly blinding her with its bleached whiteness. "Say, I heard you were under the weather a couple of weeks ago. I was out of town, you know, checking out that specialty chemicals place in San Diego, but I heard you missed a whole week, almost. How are you doing?"

"Oh—I'm all better, thank you," Susan said hastily. She'd already had this conversation with most of the people she knew from work. It was certainly not a conversation she cared to have in front of Margaret Langers.

Too late. "Were you sick?" Margaret asked as soon as Stuart had departed. "I'm so sorry, Susan. What was wrong?"

"Nothing," Susan mumbled.

"It must have been *something*," Margaret insisted. "You never miss work."

"Well..." Susan drank some of her beer and tried not to gag on it. If they truly did drink beer this warm in England, it was no wonder their empire had collapsed. "Some bug laid me low for a few days. But I'm all better now. Really."

"So there you are." Another male voice, this one instantly identifiable, reached Susan's ears from behind her back, causing the hairs at the nape of her neck to stand up. "I've been looking all over for you, Margaret. I should have known I'd find you eating..." John's voice drifted off as he neared the table and noticed his wife's companion.

"Hello, John," Susan said rigidly.

"Hello, Susan."

Margaret didn't seem aware of the uncharacteristic iciness in their curt greetings. She turned on her husband and scolded, "Why didn't you tell me Susan was sick?"

John peered down his undersized nose at Susan, his gaze flat and unrevealing. "Sick? Was she sick?"

"She missed a week of work, John."

"Not a whole week," Susan equivocated. "Stuart exaggerated—"

"She wasn't sick," John said, his eyes narrowing on Susan as he circled the table to sit beside Margaret. "There's going to be a horseshoe throwing tournament in ten minutes, Margaret. Don't you want to see me take the prize?"

Margaret's bewildered gaze shuttled between her husband and Susan. "Come on, you two," she goaded them, laughing. "What's going on, here? Were you or weren't you sick, Susan?"

"I was," Susan said.

"She wasn't," John said simultaneously. "If you'd like, Margaret, you can bring your food with you out to the lawn. There's no need to sit in here, where it's so muggy, and listen to Susan's tales of hypochondria—"

"Hypochondria!" The only reason Susan had lied to Margaret about her health was to save John's skin, to spare his wife from having to learn about her husband's crimes. But Susan could no longer think about preserving Margaret's feelings. Her tension erupted in a spurt of rage directed fully at John. "How dare you imply that I'm a hypochondriac! I'm not, John, and you know it! You know damned well why I called in sick, so don't give me any of your bull—"

"Susan, honey, swearing will get you nowhere," he cut her off, smiling unctuously. "If you were suffering from anything a couple of weeks ago, it was from a case of the dithers. I've never seen anyone dither so much about something so trivial—or at least I've never seen anyone with a good head on her shoulders—''

"Don't patronize me," Susan retorted. "Don't talk to me about having a good head on my shoulders. What I've got is an honest heart and a clean soul. Can you say the same, John?"

"Honest heart?" Margaret interjected, floundering. "Clean soul? What on earth are you talking about, Susan?"

"Nothing," she grunted, turning away.

John reached across the table and gripped Susan's upper arm, hauling her back to himself. "Nothing, is it?" he goaded her. "Nothing's bothering you, Miss Sanctimonious? You don't want to dirty your hands with real life, Susan—well, that's your business. But face the facts, lady. If you can't hack it, then clear out. Use the pot or get off."

"I would," she shot back, meeting his fierce glare and realizing that his rage rivaled hers in enormity. "I would, but I'm trying to decide whether to flush you down first."

"Don't do me any favors," John muttered through clenched teeth. "You want to stab me in the back? After everything I've done for you? Well, go ahead, Susan. Be my guest. You'll find out that what they say about dull knives is true—whenever you use them, you're likely to cut your own fingers." He released Susan, hoisted his wife up off the bench, and dragged her out of the pavilion to the horseshoe courtyard across the lawn.

It wasn't until they were gone that Susan became conscious of the small audience that had gathered to eavesdrop on her fight with John. Arguments between colleagues weren't so uncommon that they deserved this much attention—except that Susan and John weren't just colleagues. They were friends, allies, partners. And theirs hadn't been a mere argument. It had been much too bitter, much too nasty to go unnoticed.

Among those who had noticed was Chris. Susan saw him near the buffet table, watching her while Newt, his cap pushed back on his head and his baseball mitt dangling off his belt above his hip, helped himself to a couple of hot dogs. As soon as Susan's gaze collided with Chris's, he gave her a slight nod, then strolled over to Newt, whispered something in his ear, and abandoned him for Susan.

He sat across from her at the table and glowered at the onlookers until they drifted away. Then he leaned across the table. "Are you all right?" he asked her, his voice muted.

"Of course I'm all right," she retorted sharply. She took a deep, calming breath and said, more gently, "I'm fine, Chris."

Chris glanced beyond her, and when she swiveled on the bench she saw that he was following Newt with his eyes. Newt flopped onto a bench at another table with two of his teammates from the softball game. The three boys took turns energetically smearing their frankfurters with mustard.

Susan twisted back to Chris, whose gaze had returned to her. "How was the ball game?"

"Newt's team lost, but he went two for four at bat." His eyes remained on her, their kaleidoscopic flecks of green and gray performing a kind of magic, soothing her. "Why…" He hesitated, searching her face, then pressed ahead. "Why would you want to stab John Langers in the back?"

"I don't want to," she admitted, swallowing the catch in her voice.

"Then why would he accuse you of wanting to?"

Susan sighed. She wished Chris's magnificent eyes could hypnotize her completely. She wished she could lose herself in them, lose touch with the world, dive in and never emerge, never have to face her problems again.

"Oh, Chris..." Her voice cracked again. She folded her arms on the table and rested her head in them, her eyes closed against the mesmerizing power of his. Much as she wanted to lose herself to Chris, she knew that wouldn't solve anything.

He waited for several minutes, but she remained silent. "Are you going to cry, Susan?" he asked. "Are you going to freak out on me?"

"No," she promised, opening her eyes again.

He smiled tentatively. "John Langers is a good man," he said. "I don't know him as well as you do, of course, but he strikes me as a decent sort—and damned good at what he does. Friends are allowed to blow up at one another, Susan. It doesn't mean much in the long run. You'll make up."

"No," she said, softly but firmly. "We won't make up. I can't forgive him."

"What can't you forgive him for?"

Susan raised her eyes fully to Chris's face. He looked not nosy but concerned. It touched her to know that he appreciated the pain she suffered from losing a close friend, that he sympathized with her even though he didn't understand what had happened between her and John.

She wanted to tell him. She wanted to unburden herself, and she could think of no one she'd rather unburden herself to than Chris. But... No, she couldn't. She couldn't tell anyone, not yet.

Maybe she should have spent the past week meditating on her dilemma at work, rather than trying to analyze Chris's refusal to seduce her. She should have followed her initial plan and steered clear of Chris until she'd resolved her professional crisis. Instead, she'd done the opposite. She'd permitted herself to get detoured. She'd devoted her thoughts to Chris instead of contracts and kickbacks.

And if she'd had it to do all over again, she honestly believed she would have done everything exactly the same.

"You know something?" she said, extending her arms across the table and gathering his hands in hers.

"What?"

She smiled crookedly. "If somebody told me I was on the verge of falling in love with you, I don't think I'd argue the point."

Chris seemed startled by her non sequitur—startled and enormously pleased, pleased enough not to ask her why she was changing the subject. "How big is that verge?" he asked, presenting her with a dazzlingly dimpled smile. "Any chance you'll go over it soon?"

"I'd say," she murmured, "that there's an excellent chance of that."

Chapter Eight

"That was a great picnic," Newt summed up with a hearty yawn. "I ate so much, I'm probably gonna throw up the minute we get home."

Susan grinned, by now immune to his grossness. She agreed that the picnic was great, and while she hadn't eaten as much as Newt—as far as she could tell, *nobody* had—she was sated, deliciously tired and utterly mellow.

Chris grinned, too. He was behind the wheel, manually clicking the windshield wipers on and off to clear from the windshield what was either a very fine drizzle or a very thick mist. The air held the ominous, slightly sour scent of an impending summer storm. But whenever the precipitation was going to strike, it had mercifully held off until the festivities at the country club had wound to a close.

"I was really good at the three-legged race, wasn't I?" Newt boasted.

"Stop bragging," Emma criticized, although her tone was low and forgiving. "Just because you won your age division doesn't mean you were so good. It just means everybody else was bad. And anyway, I bet the only reason you won was on account of your partner."

"Three-legged races are teamwork," Newt maintained. "Bruce and I coordinated well. He's a neat guy, Dad. Can we maybe get together sometime?"

"Of course you can," Chris answered. "I'll find out where he lives from his mother at work on Monday, and you and he can make a plan."

"Yeah. You know what I think is neat? That they gave us *both* a prize." The award Newt had received for his victory in the race was an unassembled balsa wood airplane. The organizers seemed to have a prize for every child who participated in one of the races—big prizes like the airplane for the winners, and smaller prizes for the other young contestants.

Emma hadn't entered any of the races. But even though she wasn't in possession of a prize, she was obviously pleased with the way the afternoon had progressed. Glancing over her shoulder, Susan glimpsed Emma's vague, dopey smile and faraway gaze and contemplated what a heady combination it was to be thirteen and infatuated.

Emma noticed Susan spying on her, and her cheeks darkened to a deep pink shade. "How far away is North Haven, Susan?" she asked ingenuously.

"It depends on where in North Haven you mean. It's a pretty big town."

"Okay, like, is it a local telephone call?"

"Yes."

Emma's smile expanded. She lapsed back into her dream state for a minute, then turned to Chris. "Can you drive any faster, Dad?"

Although he remained facing forward, Chris frowned. "Not without breaking the law. Why are you in such a hurry?"

"I'm not in such a hurry," she fibbed. "It's just, I might be getting a call tonight."

"What makes you think he's going to call you tonight?" Chris challenged her, knowing full well who it was Emma expected to hear from. He clearly wasn't thrilled by the fact that his daughter had spent most of the day making goo-goo eyes at the stringy-haired youth in the shark's-tooth necklace. "You didn't give him our phone number, did you?"

"Well...he asked me for it," Emma defended herself.

Chris grimaced. "How old is he, anyway?"

"Old enough," she replied.

"That means he's too old," Chris grumbled. "What was his name?"

"Dean."

Chris grimaced again. "Dean," he muttered, his voice soft enough to reach no farther than Susan's ears. "Why couldn't he have been named Egbert, or Melvin?"

"Oh, come on," Susan whispered in a gentle reproach. "I'm sure he's harmless."

"No one named Dean could possibly be harmless," Chris maintained.

Susan laughed. She was glad Newt and Emma had had such a good time at the picnic. Much to her amazement, she, too, had had a good time. Her argument with John had been painful—and poorly timed, given that Margaret had to witness it—but afterward, after Susan and Chris had talked and she'd unwound from her bitter exchange with John, she'd felt somehow cleansed, purged of anger. Maybe what had released her from her anxiety about her boss was acknowledging how strongly she felt about Chris, accepting her feelings, understanding that he was more important to her than solving her professional difficulties.

Maybe it was something as simple as being in love.

Chris switched the wipers on and off again, then rested his elbow on the ledge of his open window. In spite of the oppressive humidity, he seemed comfortable, his hair tossed back and his collar open to expose a sliver of his sun-bronzed chest. Susan recalled the first time she'd seen his chest, and the way she'd responded to its lean, virile proportions. She recalled the first time she'd felt his chest, when he'd drawn her against himself in the bar, and the way she'd responded to his strength and to the paradoxical gentleness with which he'd comforted her.

That was Chris—strong, gentle . . . and virile. All afternoon she'd watched him in his role as a proud, concerned father, cheering Newt on in the sports contests and stealing furtive glances at Emma as she fell victim to Dean's dubious charms. When Chris hadn't been overseeing his children he'd been with Susan, holding her hand and grinning almost defiantly at the curious stares of their fellow employees. It had been a declaration on his part: *Yes, Susan and I are here together, as a couple, and you may as well get used to it.*

She thought about Chris's behavior today, and his behavior a few nights ago, when he'd politely sent her home with little more than a good-night kiss. She thought about the lingerie Lorraine had given her and wondered whether she would require more assistance from her neighbor in order to seduce Chris.

"Dairy Queen, anyone?" he asked as the fast-food joint's red-and-white sign loomed into view on Route 10.

"Ugh!" Emma groaned, clutching her belly.

"Newt?" Chris asked.

Despite his claim that he intended to throw up, he gave his father's suggestion lengthy contemplation before saying, "Nah. I ate three ice-cream cones at the picnic, Dad. Two chocolate and one vanilla. And an orange creamsicle. I reckon that's enough for one day."

"It's enough for one lifetime," Emma drawled.

Chris cast Susan an inquiring look, and she shook her head. According to her wristwatch it was a few minutes past six, but she had no appetite.

"Home it is, then," Chris resolved, cruising past the Dairy Queen and taking the turnoff that led to his house.

As soon as he coasted up the driveway, swerving around Susan's car, and then pulled into the garage, the children spilled out of the car and raced up the hill to the house, Emma yelling that she had first dibs on the shower and Newt yelling that he didn't need a shower—which was far from the truth, in Susan's opinion. She waited outside the garage near her car while Chris locked up. "You're not leaving, are you?" he asked once he'd lowered the garage door into place.

"I...I don't know." It was one thing to admit to herself that she wanted to make love with Chris, and quite another to do something about it. "Do you want me to stay?" she asked cautiously, listening to the sliding sounds of Emma shutting the house's windows as a prelude to turning on the air conditioner, and trying to imagine how single parents went about conducting their sex lives—if they even did have sex lives.

Chris pulled her to himself, closing his arms around her and seeking her mouth with his. His kiss answered both her spoken question—yes, he wanted her to stay—and her unspoken one. Of course Chris had a sex life; even the most casual kiss from him was an astonishingly sexual act.

This kiss wasn't casual. It was slow and insinuating, his tongue drawing power from hers, teasing it, stroking it, planting hazy notions in her soul about what the rest of his body could do to her if given the opportunity. By the time he pulled away she felt limp, aching with needs she could scarcely understand. "Chris," she whispered.

A muffled rumble of thunder rolled over them from the far side of the lake. The sky abruptly darkened to a dusk shade as thick slate-colored clouds drifted across the fading evening sun. A cool breeze gusted around her bare legs, causing her to shiver. "Tornado weather," Chris noted, his voice hoarse in the aftermath of their kiss.

Susan leaned back in his arms so she could see his face. His eyelids were drooping lazily, but below them his eyes burned with a fierce energy. "We don't get too many tornadoes around here," she said.

"Yet another reason I'm glad we moved to Connecticut," he murmured, the stunning brilliance of his eyes informing her that he considered Susan a primary reason he was glad to be living in Cheshire. He slid his hands up her back and into her hair, and his thumbs brushed over her temples. "I've wanted to kiss you all day," he confessed. "But there were too many people around."

"Including the two in your house," Susan reminded him.

"I think they could handle us kissing," he told her, bowing to touch his lips to hers again.

"Dad!" Newt bellowed from the porch, causing Susan and Chris to spring apart guiltily. "Emma's blasting the air conditioner, and it's just about freezing in here!"

"Too many people around, indeed," Chris muttered with a wry grin. He slung his arm over Susan's shoulders and strolled with her up the grassy hill and onto the porch. "Well, Newt," he advised, "I reckon that as soon as Emma shuts herself up in the shower, you can reset the temperature and there won't be a hell of a lot she can do about it.''

"Yeah," Newt concurred, his hazel eyes sparkling as vividly as Chris's. "Unless she wants to run down the hall to the thermostat wet and naked."

"Don't get your hopes up, son," Chris warned him with a chuckle before turning to Susan. "Maybe nobody else is hungry around here, but I could sure use a sandwich. Bundle up, darlin', and let's go brave the arctic air."

SOMETIME AROUND EIGHT-THIRTY, Newt fell asleep on the den sofa in front of the television. Chris and Susan were seated at a card table at the opposite end of the room, playing Casino and affectionately calling each other names. Emma had loitered in the den for a while, shooting impatient looks in the direction of the telephone. A half hour ago, though, she'd apparently given up on the possibility that Dean of the shark's-tooth necklace was going to call. She'd announced that she was going upstairs to her bedroom for the night and if "anyone" called for her, he was to be told that she was too busy to come to the phone.

Hearing a snore rise from the couch, Chris set down his cards, tiptoed to the television and turned it off. "Looks like this one's down for the count," he reported in a whisper. "Want to help me get him into bed?"

"Sure," Susan said, stacking the cards and crossing the room. "What should I do?"

Chris bent over, heaved Newt's senseless body over his shoulder, and struggled to straighten up. "Open doors," he gasped, staggering for a minute beneath the boy's weight. "Jeez. How much did Newt eat today, anyway? I think he's gained about fifty pounds."

None of Chris's weaving and wobbling roused Newt, whose arms dangled loosely down his father's back and whose feet collided with Chris's hip every time Chris took a step. Susan raced ahead to open the door at the top of the stairs, and again to open Newt's bedroom door. She clicked on the night-table lamp, and Chris dumped his son unceremoniously at the center of the bed.

"I might be a while," he announced once he'd caught his breath. "I've got to rassle him into his pj's."

"Take your time," Susan said as she started for the door. After a quick survey of the room's stereotypically male decor, with its clutter of model cars, posters of baseball stars taped to the wall above the bed and shelves lined with mysterious glass containers of fungus and dead leaves, she left Newt's bedroom.

She strolled down the hall to the living room and gazed through one of the windows at the sky. It had turned an inky starless black, and thunder still roiled the air with its threatening rumble. But the storm hadn't broken yet. In an odd way, Susan could empathize with the unsettled weather.

In the past several hours, she and Chris had both showered to refresh themselves. They had conversed with the children, played cards and gossiped about the picnic guests. Chris had munched on a peanut butter sandwich and grilled Susan about some of the picnickers whom he knew only superficially from work. "Is Allen Hirsch really married to that blond woman? They make such a strange pair," he'd remarked. "Was it just my imagination or did Gene Bowles elbow everybody out of his way during the volleyball game? Hard to believe he played so aggressively—he's such a mouse at work."

They'd chatted, they'd sipped iced tea, they'd tried to keep Emma from pining over the telephone call that never came. And underlying it all, coursing beneath the small talk and the family activities like a gathering thunderstorm just waiting to explode over the universe, was the passion that Chris had awakened in Susan with his kiss outside the garage.

Was he aware of the sultry heat, the charged atmosphere? Had he sensed the storm's imminence?

She heard footsteps behind her, but when she spun around she found the hall empty. She walked back toward Newt's room, and as she neared it Chris emerged from the bathroom, carrying a glass of water in one hand and a toothbrush topped with toothpaste in the other. "I'm going to try to brush his teeth," he explained in a whisper.

"He's asleep!"

"I know, but after all the junk he's eaten today, I've got to do something to clean some of the sugar off his teeth. I've also got to get my office to do something about the inadequate dental coverage Schenk gives us," he muttered before vanishing through Newt's bedroom door.

Grinning, Susan shook her head. She wondered whether, if she ever became a mother, she would be so fanatical about the condition of her children's teeth. Probably. Probably she'd be fanatical about their health, their moods, the crushes they got on older boys...the very same things Chris was fanatical about.

She ambled back down the hall, but stopped when she heard a muffled sound emerging through Emma's shut door. Glancing down at the crack between the bottom of the door and the carpet, she saw that the light inside was off. She listened, then heard the sound again. It resembled a sob.

"Emma?" She knocked on the door, then inched it open and peered into the dark room. "Are you all right?"

"Go away," Emma retorted in a tremulous voice.

Susan mulled over the girl's command and decided to ignore it. "Are you feeling all right?" she asked.

"Just terrific," Emma said, her tone dripping with sarcasm. "Leave me alone, all right?"

Susan hesitated. "Look," she finally said. "Maybe he'll call tomorrow—"

"Yeah. Right."

"Or maybe he won't call," Susan conceded. "You'll be starting school soon, and you'll meet hundreds of new boys."

"Who cares?" Emma said loftily.

Again Susan hesitated. Then she smiled pensively. "You want to know the truth, Emma? Boys stink. They really do. They tell you they're going to call, and then they don't. Boys used to do that to me all the time."

Emma reflected on Susan's admission for a minute. "Why, Susan?" she asked. "Why do they do it?"

"I wish I knew." Sighing, Susan opened the door a bit wider and leaned against the doorframe. The light spilling into the room from the hall revealed the floral pattern on the spread covering Emma's bed and the menagerie of stuffed animals resting on a shelf above it. Emma's face was cast in shadow, but Susan could imagine the girl's tear-stained cheeks and crestfallen expression. "I always wanted to ask my father why boys made promises they had no intention of keeping," she went on, "but I never knew how to ask him. I think maybe boys do it because they think that's what girls want to hear."

"Why on earth would I want to hear a lie?" Emma wailed. "If he wasn't going to call me, there was no reason for him to tell me he was."

"I know, Emma," Susan commiserated. Like I said, boys stink."

"They sure do," Emma agreed fervently.

"The only thing boys have going for them, if you ask me," Susan confided, "is that a select few of them eventually mature into tolerable men. Most of them are lost causes, I'm afraid."

"Lost causes is right," Emma mumbled with an indignant sniff. "I wish they'd all get lost, and that's the truth. I'm all right, Susan. Really, I am."

"Okay," said Susan, taking the hint. "Good night, Emma." She stepped back into the hall and closed the door behind her.

Turning, she spotted Chris in the living room, balancing on the arm of the sofa, observing her. He was far enough away from the hall that he couldn't have overheard her discussion with Emma. Susan understood that he'd chosen that distance deliberately, so as not to infringe on his daughter's privacy. Obviously, whatever sort of boy Chris had been, he was one of the select few who'd matured into a tolerable man. Much better than tolerable, Susan corrected herself, smiling shyly and joining him in the living room.

"How is she?" he asked.

"Bloodied but unbowed," Susan reported.

He eyed Emma's closed door, then nodded and rose to his feet. "Would you like to go out on the porch?" he suggested. "Even though I've turned down the air-conditioning, it's a bit too chilly for my taste in here."

"The porch is fine," she said, following him outside. Even if it started to rain, the broad overhang of the roof would protect them.

The wind had died down to an occasional breeze that gently rustled the leaves and rippled across the surface of the pond. Pale clouds scudded briskly across the sky, blocking the quarter moon, then revealing it through a soft-focus blur, then blocking it again. Susan found the restless atmosphere curiously exciting, filling her with anticipation. When Chris sat on the lounge chair and guided Susan down beside him, she didn't object.

It was a snug fit, both of them wedged between the redwood arms of the upholstered chair, their legs extended along the cushion and their heads and shoulders nestling into the angled back. To give Susan more room, Chris shifted onto his side and draped his arm across her waist. Two amber shafts of light fell onto the porch through the living room windows, illuminating the planes of Chris's face, highlighting the sharp lines of his nose and jaw, emphasizing his dimples and the lively sparkle in his eyes.

He gazed at Susan, and she tried to interpret his enigmatic expression, tried to find in it evidence that he was as ready for her as she was for him. She wished her courage matched her yearning. She wished she had the guts to cup her hand around his head and pull it down to her, to bring his body onto hers, to give him a kiss as rich with magic as the kiss he'd given her by the garage.

But as soon as he began to speak, she was glad she'd refrained from acting. "Bloodied, hmm," he contemplated. "Is Emma really that upset about the creep?"

If Chris was preoccupied by thoughts of his daughter, he certainly wouldn't be receptive to a seduction attempt. Susan inhaled deeply to compose herself. "She wouldn't have been so hurt if he hadn't asked for her telephone number," she explained, doing her best to keep her voice steady and unemotional.

"Who is this kid, anyway?" Chris asked. "Whose son is he?"

"I don't know."

"How can you not know, Susan? Didn't you recognize him? Wasn't he at the picnic last year?"

Susan chuckled, amused by Chris's doting concern about his daughter. "If he was at the picnic last year, he was probably six inches shorter and a soprano. He's at that age when boys undergo overnight transformations and wake up as men."

"Swell," Chris muttered, disgruntled. "Why did he have to transform into a man with a damned fang dangling on a leather noose around his neck?"

"Is that what's bothering you?" Susan asked, smiling indulgently. "Be grateful he didn't have pierced ears."

"What's bothering me . . ." Chris sighed and lifted his hand to stroke a lock of Susan's hair from her cheek. "What's bothering me is that he's old enough to break Emma's heart. I'm almost glad that he didn't call her—except that by not calling he's broken her heart, too."

"There isn't much you can do to spare her from that kind of heartbreak," Susan pointed out.

"I know," he conceded, brushing his hand lightly over her cheek again. "You're very wise about these matters, Susan. What is it, a woman's intuition? A woman's sensibility?"

"I don't think it has anything to do with intuition or sensibility," Susan noted. "I think it just has to do with being a woman."

"Mmm." Chris's fingers floated across her cheek one last time before lacing into her hair. He leaned forward and kissed her. "No doubt about that—you're definitely a woman." His lips moved over hers again, coaxing, teasing, parting them for the sweet intrusion of his tongue. "Susan," he murmured, lifting his mouth from hers and staring down into her eyes. "Were you serious today when you said you were falling in love with me?"

The power of his gaze, the fiery flecks of gray and green glinting beneath those deceptively sleepy eyelids, demanded honesty from Susan. "Yes," she confessed, her nerves tingling with expectation, with hope and fear and acceptance. "I was serious."

His breath was even, caressing her chin as he continued to study her. "It was so sudden," he said. "Not the feelings, Susan, but . . . it was a brutal fight you had with Langers. And then, to say that to me when you were still recovering from it—"

"I don't want to talk about John," she said cutting him off. She and Chris had talked enough about other people tonight. Now, as the wind picked up a bit and another rumble of thunder shook the atmosphere, Susan wanted to forget everyone else, to concentrate only on Chris, to leap beyond the verge in a glorious free-fall.

Somehow she found the courage to reach for him, to curl her fingers through his lush auburn hair and guide his lips back to hers. With a low, helpless groan he surrendered, crushing her lips with his, thrusting his tongue deep into her mouth, rising higher on the lounge chair and urging her body beneath his. His fingers spun through her hair, groped at the fabric of her shirt, journeyed down her arms to grip her hands. "I'm falling, too," he whispered, sliding his lips from her mouth to graze her cheek, her jaw, her throat. "You know that, don't you?"

Susan hadn't known it, not until that moment. She had hoped for it, suspected it, dreamed of it, but she hadn't known until now. Slipping her hands from his, she wrapped her arms around him and held him tight, wishing he could feel through the sheer strength of her embrace how thrilled she was, how relieved, how thankful, how giddy with joy.

He braced himself on his arms and peered down at her again, a mischievous smile curving his lips. "So, darlin', would you like to tell me about how you don't believe in getting involved with someone you work with?"

"No," Susan answered, her fingers probing the limber muscles of his back through his shirt. "The truth is, getting involved with someone can be a whole lot more important than work."

Chris chuckled, although his breath caught slightly when one of her hands roamed beneath his arm along the arching frame of his ribs, and then ventured forward to explore his chest. "Is this news?" he asked, managing to snare her hand and lifting it to his lips for a kiss. "Something you didn't know before?"

Susan meditated. Her free hand moved of its own volition, riding over the cotton of his shirt to his shoulder, sneaking briefly beneath the collar to stroke his neck, running down his shirt to his belly again and causing him to miss another breath. Yet her mind focused on more than his reaction to her tantalizing caresses. She thought about how Chris had always put love before work. He'd chosen his career not because it was something he'd always planned on, but simply because he was a father and his love for his baby took precedence over his dream of teaching. His top priority had been to take care of his family, to take responsibility for his children. Nobody had ever loved Susan like that, and she'd never loved anyone else like that—until now. Until Chris.

"What I didn't know before..." She trailed off, aware once more of the demand for honesty that blazed in his eyes. "When Dave made that comment about your returning to Tulsa, I thought he meant you were going to leave Cheshire for good and I'd lose you. All I could think of was that I didn't want you to go. No—more than that," she continued, struggling to express herself accurately. "I'd be crushed if you left. I'd be devastated, Chris. And...yes, that was news for me."

"Lovely news," he said, dropping a light kiss onto her chin. "I'd be devastated if I had to leave you, too."

"Then don't leave me," she implored him, letting her hand come to rest at the waistband of his jeans, where she gathered a handful of cloth and tugged his shirt upward, pulling it loose. She slipped her hand beneath the fabric and glided her fingers over the smooth, warm skin of his abdomen.

He closed his eyes and let out a shaky breath. "Susan..."

"Yes."

Bowing, he kissed her again, hungrily, greedily, his hips echoing the surges of his tongue. "I want you," he moaned, his words filling her mouth.

"I want you, too."

He slid lower, brushing his lips along the slender arch of her throat. His fingers curved around her breast, kneading it. At her sharp gasp, he turned his attention to the buttons of her blouse, opening them and pulling back the gauzy material. "You're so beautiful," he murmured, wedging his hands beneath her to undo the clasp of her bra. Once it was open, he pushed it out of his way to expose her firm, pale breasts. "So very beautiful," he groaned before taking one flushed nipple into his mouth.

Susan cried out softly at the sucking motions of his lips, at the dance of his tongue over the inflamed flesh. He was obviously as aroused as she was; she felt his hips strain toward hers, the hard swell of him pressing against her thigh through the thick denim of his jeans. Somewhere, deep within the night or perhaps deep within her soul, she heard the drumming vibration of more thunder, the thickening of the air around her as the storm grew perilously near.

With a tortured sigh Chris released her, turning his head and resting it against the rise of her breast. His hand skimmed across her midriff, sketching an abstract pattern, and he wrestled with his breath. Susan combed his hair back from his face and then cradled his head against her, waiting.

After a long moment, he spoke. "I want all of you, Susan."

"Yes," she said, barely a whisper. She twisted her fingers through his dense, soft hair. "It's all right, Chris." She paused, sensing that something was troubling him, unsure of what it was. "I'm on the pill, if that's what you're worried about."

He closed his eyes and his hand came to rest against her lowest rib, rising and falling as she breathed. "Thank you for telling me," he finally said. "But that isn't—that's not what I'm worried about. I'm not worried," he amended. "But..." He drew in another erratic breath, then let it out. "I want more than just your body, Susan. Do you understand that?"

She took several seconds to absorb his words. Yes, she understood. She understood how rare Chris was, how decent, how very much a gentleman. "You have my love," she swore.

He raised his head. His eyes bore down on her, filled with a strange light. "I want your trust," he said.

She tried to make sense of his cryptic request, of his relentless gaze. "I trust you, Chris. Of course I trust you."

"Not enough," he said, slowly withdrawing from her.

Her heart began to pound, not with desire but with dread. What was happening here? What had gone wrong? Why wasn't Chris at this very moment swearing that he loved Susan, too, that they belonged together, that their commitment was genuine and lasting? "What do you mean?" she asked tensely.

He moved her legs to one side of the cushion and sat up, then folded his hands consolingly around hers. "We're attracted to each other," he said, his voice rough and rasping, as if partially trapped in his throat. "We want each other, maybe we even love each other. But if you trusted me, if you *truly* did..."

He trailed off for a moment, gazing toward the pond. Lightning flashed in the distance, diffused into an eerie strafe of silver by the canopy of clouds. Chris waited for the expected reply of thunder before turning back to Susan. He smiled pensively. "Ah, Susan. I've been waiting and waiting for you to open up to me, to share your burdens with me. You've said you can't, and I can accept that. But if you really trusted me..." He glanced away again, shaking his head, yielding to a short, bittersweet laugh. "If you really trusted me, you wouldn't be keeping secrets from me."

Susan checked the impulse to protest that she *did* trust him, that he was insane to think otherwise. A slow anger began to build inside her, as consuming as the sexual yearning it replaced. What Chris was asking for had nothing to do with trust. It had to do with his need for her to divulge something that was none of his business, for no reason but to prove something to him. Even worse, he was deliberately withholding himself, depriving them both of the love they yearned for until Susan complied. He hadn't restrained himself with her because he was a gentleman; he'd restrained himself because he was waiting for Susan to spill the beans to him about the hot scandal in the marketing department.

She shrank from him, jerking her hands from his and curling into a protective posture against the arm of the lounge chair. "What is this, a test?" she spat out, furious with him, and even more furious with herself for having revealed how much she loved him. "If I could have told you, I would have, Chris. You have no right—"

"You could have told me," he interrupted, his voice as low and controlled as hers was enraged, "because you *can* tell me. You can tell me anything, Susan. Anything. Or at least you could, if you trusted me."

"And if *you* trusted me," she argued, "you wouldn't ask. Trust works both ways, Chris."

Aware of her keen anger, he shook his head again and sighed. "Susan, if you're not ready to tell me now, so be it. I'm willing to wait. But when I make love with you, it's got to be complete, body and soul. I'm willing to wait for that, too."

"Good," she snapped, wriggling out of the chair and fumbling with the fastening of her bra and then the buttons of her shirt. "I'm glad you're willing to wait, Chris, because you've got one hell of a long wait ahead of you."

She stormed inside the house to fetch her purse and keys, then raced back outdoors and off the porch, not giving Chris a chance to stop her, not allowing herself a backward glance to see if he even made an effort to stop her. She swung open the door of her car with such violence she nearly tore it off its hinges, and she slammed it shut with equal force once she was settled on the seat. Without bothering to buckle her seat belt or check her rearview mirror, she careered wildly down the driveway to the street, U-turned and sped away.

Somewhere along one of the gloomy, winding roads, she began to breathe again. Sometime after that first inhalation, she became conscious of the patter of rain on the car's roof, and the droplets obliterating her view of the road. She turned on the windshield wipers, drove a minute longer and then veered onto the shoulder and braked to a halt.

The rain abruptly increased, as if an overloaded cloud just above Susan had split at the seams, spilling torrents down upon her. The hammering staccato of the raindrops resounded loudly through the car's interior, rousing Susan from her daze of fury. Although she was safe and dry inside the car, she felt as if the precipitation dousing her car was also dousing her spirit, quelling the bitterness blazing within her and rinsing her mind clean.

Maybe Chris had been testing her. But maybe not. Maybe his longing for her complete love had been genuine. There was something noble about his refusal to settle for a love handicapped by secrets, whatever they were—something noble and touching and romantic and...yes, gentlemanly. He had answered every question she'd ever asked him, no matter what the subject, no matter how it reflected on him. He'd told her about his ill-fated marriage, confessed his insecurities as a father, shared with her his most personal defeats and victories.

All he was asking from her was the same willingness to share, the same trust.

Susan believed it was still too soon to reveal the sordid details of the Pentagon contract to anyone from work. But if she loved Chris, she ought to be able to trust him with anything, including her professional quandary.

She loved Chris.

Clicking her windshield wipers onto the highest speed against the blinding deluge of rain, she turned the car around and headed back to his house.

Chapter Nine

After a while, Chris ran out of curses. Rain thrashed the earth in glistening sheets, and sporadic gusts of wind whipped across the porch, splattering his jeans with raindrops and inspiring him to repeat a few of the expletives he'd already used. He happened to know an impressive amount of foul language, but he rarely vented it, given that he was a father and had to set a proper example for Newt and Emma. But they were sound asleep now, safely out of range. And Chris's stupidity deserved to be condemned with every unprintable term he could think of.

Spewing invectives wasn't the cathartic exercise he had hoped it would be, however. It didn't erase the fact that, on the brink of living out the fantasy he'd been entertaining ever since he first glimpsed Susan in the dining room at Schenk's corporate headquarters, he had instead sent her packing. Issuing an endless string of curses didn't make him feel any better about what he'd done. It only made him feel verbally inadequate along with desolate.

Sighing, he trudged into the house, locked the porch door and plodded down the stairs. The house's lower level was pleasantly cool, even though he hadn't turned on the air-conditioning downstairs. He checked the open windows to make sure no rain was blowing in through the screens, then shut himself inside his bedroom, stripped off his clothing and dove onto the bed.

"Damn," he muttered. Not the most pungent of oaths, but it seemed to sum up his situation rather neatly. He didn't want to be in this big bed alone, isolated from Susan by the rain, by the miles her car was carrying her, by the chasm he'd opened between her and himself with his self-righteousness and his unreasonable demands. How dare he intrude on her privacy? How dare he claim the prerogative of measuring how much she trusted him and unilaterally deciding that it wasn't enough? She had accused him of testing her, and damn it, she was right. Why couldn't he have taken what she'd offered and been satisfied? She had offered so much, so very much—and, selfish jackass that he was, he'd pressed her for more.

He had been selfish, demanding, unreasonable with Susan, exactly the opposite of the way he used to behave with his wife so many years ago. Elysse had never hidden things from him, though. It had been easy for Chris to understand her, to empathize with her, because she had never held anything back.

She had let him know that she found motherhood overwhelming, boring, trying beyond comprehension. She'd let him know that she needed her own separate existence, a chance to define herself as an individual. It hadn't been enough that Chris loved her, and that Emma and then Newt depended on her for their very lives. Elysse had wanted the adulation of strangers, too. And she'd wanted excitement, change, freedom from responsibility.

She was always so frank about her disappointments and dissatisfactions. She trusted Chris to accommodate her needs, and he did the best he could. He didn't object to her performing at the honky-tonks on "Open Mike" night, and subsequently hooking up with a band. He actually enjoyed spending the evenings alone with his children, concentrating solely on them, bathing them and playing with them and reading to them. The storybook sessions Chris used to share with Emma came as close to teaching English literature as he ever got, and he lived for those special times.

Later, hours later, Elysse would come home. Usually Chris would already be in bed, dozing, but he'd rouse himself as soon as she slid under the blanket next to him. Her baby-fine blond hair would smell of cigarette smoke, her eyes would be smudged with the makeup she hadn't bothered to wipe off, but then she would kiss Chris and fill her arms with him, and her hands, and her body... and he wouldn't care that she had just returned from her other life, a life lived in a world that had no room in it for him and their children.

Transient as it was, he had known a kind of contentment with Elysse. If he'd made love to Susan tonight, he might have known that same contentment with her. But it wouldn't have satisfied him. He wanted more from Susan than he had ever wanted from Elysse. Perhaps it was because he'd grown less tolerant with age, less willing to settle for anything short of perfection. Or perhaps it was simply that Susan was who she was: intelligent, beautiful, ambitious, sensitive, a woman he could think of as an equal, a partner. She was the best thing to happen to him in a long, long time, and... yes—he wanted it all. He wanted perfection.

His brain conjured a picture of her lying half beside him, half beneath him on the lounge chair, her body partially exposed to him, the flavor of her skin on his lips.

Her large brown eyes boring into him, imploring, incandescent. Her slender fingers journeying across his abdomen, arousing him to such an extent he believed for a mindless moment that nothing in the world could be as important as this, nothing could be as important as uniting with her, becoming a part of her, loving her without a thought of anything beyond that instant, that unity.

And how did he go about showing her how important she was to him? By pressuring her, rejecting her, sending her on her way.

Moping in bed did no more to improve his spirits than swearing at the clouds. Chris sat up, pushed a thick shock of hair back from his face and stared out the window at the phalanx of rain-soaked trees standing along the slope to the pond at the rear of the house. There had to be a way to make things better, he ruminated. He could present Susan with flowers—no, too trite. He could call her and beg for forgiveness—but then she'd have the option of hanging up on him.

He could send her a telegram. A singing telegram. He'd write the song himself, a doleful ballad about a lovelorn man who accidentally, stupidly drove his lady away. "Susan, I'm losin'..." he began, then decided it sounded too depressing.

He noticed a passing beam of light slicing the tree trunks beyond the window. At first he thought it was lightning, but upon reflection he realized that it couldn't be. The light had a yellowish cast to it. It hadn't flickered, as lightning would, but, rather, had swept across the woods and then angled off toward the pond.

Headlights. The headlights of a car cruising up the driveway.

A spark of hope ignited inside him, but he quickly extinguished it. If the headlights did belong to Susan's car, she had probably come back only to chew him out. Reaching for his jeans and pulling them on, he rummaged through his supply of curses for a few final profanities, which he uttered in an effort to prepare himself for the worst. Then he padded barefoot out of his room, through the back door and out into the downpour.

The headlights went dark as he turned the corner of the house and neared the garage. He had no trouble identifying the car idling in the driveway. The motor chugged for a minute longer, and the wipers shuttled futilely back and forth. Then Susan killed the engine.

Chris didn't move. He didn't dare to approach. He had already imposed too much on her. If ever he needed to be patient, to wait until she came to him, this was the time.

Rain spilled down onto him, saturating his hair, skittering across his chest, gluing his jeans to his legs and turning the grass-covered ground spongy beneath his feet. Susan stayed behind the wheel, dry and cut off from him. He itched to race to the car, smash his fists through the windshield, drag her out and make love to her, right there, in the driveway, in the rain. "Lunatic," he muttered in self-reproach, and his mouth filled with rain water.

The constant clatter of the precipitation distorted the click of the door latch giving way. Chris remained alert, batting his eyes to keep the water out of them, watching as she slowly climbed out of the car, wishing he could see her face. But it was too dark, too rainy.

She closed the door and picked her way across the grass to him, apparently oblivious of the rain showering down onto her head. Long before she reached him her hair became waterlogged, hanging heavy around her damp face. Her shirt, the shirt Chris had unbuttoned, now clung to her breasts, the breasts he had held and kissed and momentarily lost his mind over. Her long, slim legs, exposed below the cuffs of her drenched shorts, shimmered with moisture. She looked unbelievably sexy.

Perhaps she had come back only to torture him, he thought, swallowing a strangled moan.

At last she was close to him, close enough for him to touch. Willfully keeping his arms at his sides, he lifted his eyes from her body to her face. Drops of water lay scattered like clear pearls across her delicate cheeks and chin, more drops were trapped in her long black lashes, yet more beaded on her soft, full lips. She didn't duck her head, didn't wipe away the dampness, didn't avert her eyes. She simply stood there and let the storm pound down on her as it pounded down on Chris.

"We have to talk," she said. Her voice was laden with promise, a thin thread of human warmth through the descending torrents.

He felt something snap inside him—his control, his rationality, his sense of fairness, his humility. Nothing mattered anymore but Susan. She had come back. That was enough.

"We can talk later," he resolved, extending his arms and dragging her to himself. "Not now." He pressed her body to his, wet cloth to wet skin, mouth to mouth. The stormed raged around them, yet Chris felt flooded by Susan's presence. He drowned in the joy of embracing this wonderful, precious woman whom luck had brought back to him tonight. He kissed her hard, silencing any desire she might have to talk, any desire she might have to do anything other than love him.

From the way her lips took his, and her tongue, from the way her arms circled his neck and her breath melted into his, he realized that she didn't really want to talk right now, either.

SHE KNEW she had to weigh more than Newt. But Chris seemed to have no difficulty hoisting her into his arms and cradling her to his chest. His legs were stable, his hold on her unshakable, and his lips never left hers.

For a minute he remained outdoors with her, supporting her body and kissing her mouth, kissing her with a blazing longing that burned away all the logical conclusions she'd reached in the car, the thoughts that had motivated her to drive back to Chris's house. She *had* come back to talk, but that goal was rapidly fading from her mind.

Refusing to move his lips from hers, he carried her in sure-footed strides down the hill to the house's back door. He ended the kiss only to allow her to turn the door knob for him; once she did, he kicked the door open and hurried inside with her, not stopping until he reached his bed. He laid her across the broad mattress with heartbreaking gentleness, as if she were fragile, something he cherished beyond measure.

His room was cast in shadow, the only light coming from the moon-reflecting clouds outside the open windows. Susan couldn't make out much of her surroundings, but her body told her that the sheets beneath her were rumpled—and that they'd been dry until Chris had put her down. "I'm getting your bed all wet," she whispered.

"I don't care." Chris sat beside her, his jeans leaving a damp imprint on the linens. He worked efficiently to open her blouse, peeled away the soggy material and tackled her bra. In less than a minute he had stripped her naked. He shucked his jeans, not hampered by their clammy stickiness, and tossed them negligently across the room. Then he swung his legs up, slid his body onto hers and caught her mouth with his.

There was something blunt about his motions, something raw and hot and devoid of ritual. Susan didn't mind. She wanted this, not just Chris and not just love, but *this*. No secrets. Absolute trust.

The storm outside matched the storm in her body, wild yet wholly natural, frightening, awesome. Chris's hands streaked across her skin, sometimes rough, sometimes so tender her eyes filled with tears. He caressed her flesh and cajoled it. He explored her quivering body with his mouth, igniting her nerves wherever his lips alighted. Raindrops mingled with sweat, and Susan's and Chris's bodies became slicker and damper as his smooth, hard chest crushed down on her pliant breasts, as his strong legs wove through hers.

She didn't speak. She didn't have to tell him where to touch her, or how. He seemed to know, to anticipate and then to surprise her. A mere turn of her head and his lips conquered the flesh below her earlobe. The slightest shift of her hips and his fingers were there, tracing the angular bone and then massaging the muscle of her thigh.

He didn't speak, either. She relied on his gravelly sighs and her own instincts to direct her. Everything she did seemed to provoke a groan or a delighted gasp from him—tracing the supple contours of his back, following the curve of his buttocks, closing her teeth lightly over the ridge of his shoulder. With her every foray, he shuddered, moaned an inchoate assent, rose and repositioned himself to offer her more—his chest, his stomach, the backs of his knees, his cheeks and chin.

She was scarcely aware of her body adopting a rhythm, rocking toward him in invitation. He responded with his hand, his fingers floating down between her legs, sliding against her. For a mindless instant she submerged herself in that preliminary ecstasy, but before she could lose herself completely he pulled away. Still without speaking, he drew her legs up around him. His tongue plunged into her mouth as his body became one with hers, and then she did lose herself, suddenly, swiftly, closing her eyes and holding her breath as the clamorous pulses tore through her.

She opened her eyes again, abashed at the speed of her response. Locking his elbows to support his body above her, Chris held himself motionless so she could fully savor the release. When his eyes met hers he smiled slightly, then bent to kiss her. This time his kiss was as light as a sigh. His renewed thrusts were equally gentle, a quiet attempt to lure more from her.

She wanted to tell him that she had nothing left to give him, that she was utterly satisfied and wanted only for him to be satisfied, too. But before she could say anything he was proving her wrong. She was astonished to feel a subtle tension building inside her again, but there it was, fed by the skillfully restrained movements of his body against her sensitive flesh.

She watched his face above hers, his eyes shining under his seductively heavy lids, his jaw tightening as his control was gradually eroded by hungry passion. His surges grew harder, deeper, more urgent, allowing nothing short of total surrender.

With a soft cry, she gave herself over to him. Her body arched up, absorbing him, convulsing around him. He threw his head back and squeezed his eyes shut. Every sinew in his body seemed momentarily strung taut, and then he relented, defeated by the power of his climax.

He sucked in a delirious breath, then relaxed and lowered his head to her shoulder. She closed her arms around him and slid her fingers into his thick, damp hair, taking comfort in the cool, slippery texture of it and in the solid weight and firmness of his body on top of hers. She felt his lips brush against her, a kiss commingled with a sigh. "Is it my imagination," he mumbled in a hoarse, barely audible voice, "or did I just die and go to heaven?"

She smiled and cuddled him closer to herself. "Wherever you are, Chris, I'm there, too."

"You are, thank God," he whispered, lifting himself to gaze down at her. "When you left...I never felt so alone in my life." His index finger traced the delicate curve of her lower lip with an almost reverent tenderness. "If you hadn't come back—"

"But I did," Susan said, meeting his piercing stare, trying to remember what had prompted her to flee his house, and then to return. Her mind was a muddle of incoherent thoughts, prominent among them the notion that she must have been deranged to have left this man, and that returning to his arms and to his bed had been the sanest act she'd ever committed.

He bowed to kiss her, then raised himself again. "I shouldn't be thanking anyone but you, Susan. What happened just now was pretty damned incredible."

"Mmm." She sighed as her body reacted to his words with an involuntary spasm of pleasure. "I think I'm supposed to thank you for that, Chris."

"No," he murmured, running his finger over her lip again, and then her chin, her throat, her collarbone. "It wasn't me, darlin', and it wasn't you. It was us. It was chemistry."

Susan nearly protested that it couldn't be chemistry. Chemistry was what Chris had had with his ex-wife, and Susan didn't want him comparing her to another woman, even if he'd loved that other woman enough to marry her. Whatever it was that had exploded between Susan and

Chris didn't resemble anything she'd ever experienced before, and she wanted that to be true for him, as well.

Then she reconsidered. His past was no more relevant than hers. What counted was now, here, this bed, this night. What counted was their love, their shared desire, their own unique, personal chemistry. "You know what?" she said, then started to laugh.

Chris smiled. "What?"

"I have this thing at home . . ." Her laughter increased as she pictured the strange garment Lorraine had given her.

"What thing?"

"It's . . . I thought I was going to wear it to seduce you."

"Oh?" His eyebrows twitched upward, and his smile expanded. "Care to describe it?"

"Well, it's—it's a lacy black teddy."

"Uh-huh." His roving index finger wandered from her collarbone to her breast and described a teasing circle around her nipple, making it swell into a peak. "What's a teddy?"

"Don't you know?" she asked, surprised. "It's ladies' underwear, kind of a one-piece thing—"

"I can't begin to imagine it," he cut her off, grinning slyly. "You'll have to model it for me."

"I haven't got it with me," she told him.

His smile became gentle, hypnotically sweet. "You don't need to wear anything to seduce me, Susan," he assured her, his voice dissolving into another deep sigh as his gaze followed his hand to her breast, and then beyond to the concave stretch of her stomach, the sharp projections of her hips, the dark, downy hair below and between them. "The truth is, the less you wear, the better I like it." He sketched a curving line with his hand down her front to repossess with his fingers what he'd already claimed with his body.

At his galvanizing touch she flinched, then moaned and turned toward him, allowing him to deepen his caress. "Chris—" her voice emerged trembling "—I don't think..." She moaned again, unable to prevent herself from responding, unable to keep her muscles from flexing, contracting, driving her against his fingers.

"Good idea," he whispered into her hair, sliding his free hand under and around her waist, pulling her closer to him. "Don't think."

"It's too much," she pleaded faintly, not even conscious of what she was pleading for.

He nipped her earlobe. His mesmerizing words floated through her hair and sank into her heart. "It's not too much, darlin'. Nothing is too much. This is just for you, because I want to see you crazy with love again."

"I can't..."

"Trust me." The words penetrated her, permeated her, and then she remembered. She remembered that she'd come here not to make love but to prove to Chris that she trusted him.

Yet this, too, was proof of her trust. She couldn't respond to a man she didn't trust—and she couldn't respond so completely to a man she didn't trust completely.

Closing her eyes, burying her face against his shoulder, she abandoned herself to her trust in Chris, to the consummate, consuming love he had awakened within her. It pounded through her weary flesh, draining her, causing her to weep and sink against him in sheer exhaustion.

"You'll stay the night," he murmured.

"Yes," she mouthed through her tears, not bothering to consider the fact that if she remained with him tonight she'd have to face his children tomorrow morning—children old enough to understand what a woman would be doing in their father's bedroom overnight.

She would deal with that eventuality when she had to. Chris would help her deal with it. She trusted him.

"SUN'S OUT," he called to her.

Susan stretched languidly, her legs extending beneath the top sheet and her fisted hands punching upward into two pillows. The realization that this bed was much too large—and much too empty—jolted her awake. Her eyes popped open, then closed again in response to the harsh glare of morning sunlight burning through the windows.

Shoring up her courage, she opened her eyes again, more cautiously this time. Chris was standing at one of the windows, clad in a clean pair of shorts and an unbuttoned shirt. Susan indulged in an appreciative perusal of his virile chest and his long, leanly muscled legs, with their fine dusting of honey-colored hair. Sighing regretfully over the fact that he was across the room from her instead of next to her in bed, she raised her eyes to his face. His square chin was roughened by an overnight growth of beard and his eyes looked sleepy—but then, they always did. Lazy lids notwithstanding, Chris seemed unconscionably wide awake.

"What time is it?" she asked drowsily.

"A little past nine-thirty."

All right, so he was entitled to be wide awake. She pushed herself up to sit, draping the sheet discreetly around her nude body, and surveyed the sunlit bedroom. Chris's furniture was nondescript, the sort of bland modern pieces one might find in a second-rate motel. The floor was covered with a plush carpet of brown, with a pile so deep she imagined she would lose sight of her toes if she stepped on it barefoot. Above the dresser hung a framed, enlarged photograph of Chris and his two children seated on the wooden steps of a farmhouse porch. The picture had obviously been taken a few years ago, when Emma was still more a girl than a woman. All three of them looked happy in the photo, huddling together and grinning affectionately.

Susan liked the photo, and the carpet. And she liked Chris's bed for the simple reason that some unspeakably marvelous things had occurred in it last night. But her thoughts about the night she'd spent with Chris faded as her gaze drifted back to the photograph. Newt and Emma. How was Susan supposed to behave with them now that she was their father's lover?

Buttoning his shirt, Chris crossed the room to the bed and sat. He kissed the tip of her nose and grinned. "Do you always sleep this late?"

"Just on the weekends," she replied, scanning the luxurious expanse of brown carpet and trying to figure out why it, too, elicited a vague panic from her.

Chris provided an indirect answer. "My bathrobe'll be a bit too big on you, darlin', but it's the best I can offer. At least you won't be tripping on it—you're nearly as tall as me."

"Where's my clothing?" she asked, the reason for her panic suddenly obvious. Chris had thrown her clothes onto the floor last night when he'd undressed her. They should be there now, but they weren't.

"Just finishing up the rinse cycle," he told her. "Your stuff was a mess, Susan, all wrinkled and water stained. You wouldn't have wanted to put it on. Don't worry— I've got a dryer, so it should be done in less than an hour."

"Chris." She tried to smother the frantic edge to her voice. "Chris, what am I supposed to do until it's ready?"

He grinned. "I just told you—you'll borrow my robe." He kissed her again, then stood and crossed to a closet. He opened the door, pulled a sashed bathrobe of royal blue terry cloth off a hook and carried it back to the bed.

She eyed the robe, then him. "What about Newt and Emma?"

"What about them? They've got their own bathrobes."

"Chris." She swallowed, wishing she could be as nonchalant as he was about what struck her as a painfully awkward situation. "It isn't a joke, Chris. If they see me in this bathrobe, they're going to know I was here with you all night."

He resumed his seat beside her, scooped up her hand and touched his lips to the knuckles. "If they saw you in the clothes you wore yesterday, they'd reach the same conclusion. You *were* here with me all night, and I for one am pleased as all get out about it." He emphasized the point by planting another kiss on the back of her hand.

"You may be," she grumbled. "But what about your kids?"

"Susan." Lowering her hand to his lap, he ran his thumb over her palm, stroking aimless figure eights over the skin and reminding her that, until she'd confronted the issue of his children, she had also been pleased as all get out about having spent the night with Chris. His tickling caresses sent tiny thrills of pleasure up her arm and into her chest, distracting her. She pulled her hand from his and sternly folded her arms across her chest, leaving no doubt that she considered dealing with his children a matter of extreme gravity. "Newt and Emma know the facts of life," Chris said calmly, respecting her discomfort. "Owing to her seniority, Emma knows a few more facts than Newt, but they both have a handle on it. In fact, Newt and I have already talked about the prospect of seeing your lovely face at our breakfast table."

"What?"

"He brought it up. He asked me if you might be staying the night, and I said I hoped that someday you would."

"Good Lord," Susan muttered. Chris's revelation made her uneasy, but she also found something perversely amusing about it.

"Kids today are a bit more sophisticated than our generation was," Chris went on. "And the children of a divorce tend to be even more sophisticated. I've dated before, Susan. Newt and Emma haven't had much trouble accepting it."

Susan knew Chris was only trying to make her feel better. But thinking about the other women who had awakened in his bed in the past didn't make her feel better at all. "Do you and Newt discuss your sex life often?" she asked sharply.

Chris had little difficulty reading her wounded expression. He cupped his hands over her shoulders and urged her face to his. "To tell you the truth, Susan, no, we don't. He really took me by surprise when he asked about when you were going to stay here overnight. But then, when I thought about it, I realized he was asking because he's awfully fond of you. It was more like a suggestion on his part."

"Great," Susan snapped, unconvinced. "Maybe when he grows up he can become a pimp."

Rather than take offense at her caustic remark, Chris laughed. "Remind me to let you sleep late next weekend, darlin'," he teased. "You're a terror in the morning, aren't you." He placed a kiss on her forehead, then slid the bathrobe over her arms and closed its front flaps around her slim body. "Much too big," he appraised it. "But it covers everything it's got to."

"No it doesn't," Susan argued, tying the sash in a double knot. "I'm not going upstairs without underwear."

Much to her annoyance, he laughed again. "Then you'll have to borrow some of mine," he said, rising and moving to the dresser. "Those panties of yours—tiny though they may be—won't be dry for some time."

"They aren't tiny," she grunted churlishly.

"They're tinier than I'd ever let Emma get away with. Then again, I'd probably ground Emma for a decade if she ever wore a lacy black—what was that thing you were telling me about last night?"

"A teddy," Susan muttered, grabbing the white cotton briefs he handed her and pulling them on. It occurred to her that she'd never seen Chris in underwear—last night, all he'd had on were his jeans. It further occurred to her that he'd probably look breathtakingly sexy in his briefs, and that she felt breathtakingly sexy wearing them. Thinking about the way the smooth elastic waistband and the soft knit fabric would cling to his anatomy caused a dark flush to spread across her cheeks.

Embarrassed, she pulled the bathrobe even tighter around her before emerging from the tangle of sheets. "How do I look?" she asked tensely.

"Gorgeous," he swore, no longer laughing. He enveloped her in his arms and held her snugly to himself. "If you weren't so obviously uptight about the whole thing,

I'd take a peek under the robe. Maybe someday when the kids aren't around, you can give me a whole fashion show—my jockey shorts, your black lace thing . . ."

"Stop it, Chris," she protested, conscious of her cheeks growing warmer. "You're only making me feel worse."

He kissed her hair, then smoothed it out with his hands. "Woman, you feel better than anything I've ever felt before. Give me a smile and let's go upstairs."

Climbing the stairs with Chris, Susan sent a silent prayer heavenward that Emma and Newt had already finished breakfast and were in their bedrooms, or down at the pond rustling up some toads to play with. Luck wasn't with her, however. Both of the Kelso children were seated at the kitchen table, surrounded by sections of the Sunday newspaper. Newt was skimming the comics and shoveling spoonfuls of a nauseatingly pastel-colored cereal into his mouth. Emma was meticulously peeling an orange, her eyes flitting between Ann Landers and the fruit's rind. She was dressed in a baggy T-shirt and short shorts, but Newt still had on his pajamas.

At Chris's and Susan's entrance, they both looked up. Newt's spoon clattered back into the cereal bowl, sending pinkish drops of milk flying across the table. The unintended sprinkling provoked Emma to shriek, "Watch what you're doing, Newt! Yuck! You're such a slob!"

"Good morning to you, too," Chris drawled, abandoning Susan to fend for herself while he glided to a counter and filled the coffee maker with water.

Emma and Newt ignored their father. Their eyes were riveted to Susan in her incriminating outfit. Newt presented her with a toothy grin. "Hey, Susan, did you stay over?"

"Don't be so dumb," Emma answered for Susan. "What do you think, she came here before sunrise, snuck in the back door, put on Dad's bathrobe and came upstairs with him?"

Susan wished she could say that that was precisely what she'd done. Not that her reputation would be greatly enhanced in the children's eyes by such a ridiculous explanation, but it still sounded better to her than admitting that she'd spent the entire night wrapped up in Chris's arms, loving him, giving and taking and going happily mad over him.

Emma's sardonic tone had less of an effect on Newt than on Susan. "Hey, that's great," he said cheerfully. "You want some Frankenberries, Susan?" He gestured toward the garish cereal sloshing around in his bowl.

Chris turned from the coffee maker and smiled at Susan. "I could scramble some eggs," he offered.

Susan had little difficulty making her choice. "Eggs sound delicious," she said, crossing to him. "I'll make them, if you'd like."

Chris's eyebrows arched. "I didn't know you could cook."

"She can't," Emma called over her shoulder. "The night I had dinner with her, her neighbor cooked it."

Traitor, Susan muttered under her breath. It wasn't that she objected to Chris's knowing that Lorraine had made the quiche, but...well, Emma wasn't exactly going out of her way to make Susan feel welcome. "The reason I didn't cook dinner that night," she said, trying to keep her tone free of tension, "was that I'd been at work all day, and I didn't have the time to fix anything special. My neighbor did have time, because her work schedule is different than mine. It isn't always easy to juggle a career and cooking. I'm sure your father can attest to that."

"My dad," Emma volleyed back, "can't cook even when he's got the time."

"I resent that!" Chris said before bursting into laughter.

Susan forced herself to relax. If Chris wasn't going to let Emma put him on the defensive, she wouldn't either. She curved her lips into a weak smile and turned from Emma.

Chris supplied her with a mixing bowl and a carton of eggs. "I'll make some toast," he volunteered after banging a skillet onto the stove for her. "Who wants toast?"

"Me!" Newt hollered.

"Emma?"

Emma shook her head and daintily separated a wedge of orange. "I'm not hungry," she declared before popping the wedge into her mouth.

"Is that all you're eating? It's not enough," Chris scolded.

"Eggs and toast are fattening. I don't want to get fat," she said piously.

"And I don't want you to get anorexic. One slice of dry toast, babe. If you don't eat it, I'll stuff it up your nose."

"Yuck. That's gross," she reproached her father.

Ten minutes later, Chris cleared the newspaper sections from the table and Susan carried over a serving platter of fluffy scrambled eggs and a plate of toast. True to her word, Emma took only a single slice of toast, which she methodically tore into a dozen pieces and dropped onto the mess of orange peel in her plate. In the time it took to make the meal, Newt had wolfed down a second bowl of pink cereal, and he helped himself to a robust mound of eggs and plenty of toast. "This is delicious!" he declared after forking some down. "I don't care what Emma says, Susan—you're a great cook. You oughtta stay over more often so we could have eggs all the time.''

Susan didn't have the nerve to respond to that. She cast a quick glimpse in Chris's direction and found him gazing at her and grinning, as if he agreed wholeheartedly with his son—although Susan had reason to believe that scrambled eggs weren't Chris's main interest when it came to Susan's staying over.

Once she'd demolished her toast, Emma stood. "Excuse me," she said frostily as she carried her plate to the garbage pail and dumped its contents. "Susan, please don't take this the wrong way—I mean, like it's fine with me if you want to hang around here with Dad and all. But as far as making breakfast goes, well, I don't think it's going to work, you know?''

"What the hell does that mean?" Chris roared, his smile gone.

Susan had a good idea what it meant. It meant the same thing Emma had meant when she'd told Susan that taking her shopping at the mall wasn't going to work. Susan had taken Emma shopping because she'd wanted to, and she'd cooked the eggs because she wanted to. She had no ulterior motives.

Her eyes met Emma's, and she was relieved to see no hostility in them. What she saw was confusion, skepticism and an unfocused anger. Her answer was a brave smile. "I won't take it the wrong way, Emma," she vowed.

Emma wrestled with her thoughts for a moment, then conceded with a nebulous smile of her own. "Okay," she said before sidling out of the room.

Chris stared at the empty doorway, scowling. "Isn't it too early for her to be in a snit?" he asked.

"She's just ticked off on account of that Dean dude didn't call her," Newt analyzed. "She's been a grouch all morning. You guys are lucky you missed most of it. Can I please have another piece of toast?"

Chris shoved the plate of toast toward his son, his eyes remaining on the doorway. "You think that's what it is?" he asked Susan. "Disappointment about that creep?"

"Part of it," Susan deduced.

Chris turned to her. "And what's the rest of it?"

"Me," she admitted in a small voice.

Chris glanced at Newt, who, fortunately, was engrossed in smearing butter across his toast, and then back at Susan. He nodded slightly. "So," he addressed his son, recognizing the necessity of changing the subject. "Shall we take the canoe out today?"

For the duration of the meal, Chris and Newt discussed the canoe, the pond, the likelihood that after the previous night's storm the water would be too cold to swim in, and strewn with twigs and leaves knocked off the trees by the wind and the pelting rain. Finally Newt reached his digestive limit and departed from the kitchen, carrying the comics and the sports section with him. "How does he stay so thin?" Susan asked in astonishment, contemplating the enormous quantity of food he'd consumed yesterday at the company picnic and again this morning.

"He's a boy," Chris explained, rising and carrying several plates to the sink. "He burns it up." He filled the sink with dish soap and water while Susan cleared the rest of the breakfast things from the table. "Now," he said, presenting her with a dry dish towel and then plunging his hands into the suds in search of a plate, "tell me why my daughter's in a snit over you."

"Who can say?" Susan shrugged and dried the spotless plate he handed her. "Maybe she's edgy about sex. Maybe she sees me as a rival for your attention." Even as Susan listed those possibilities she discarded them. Emma gave the impression of being normal and matter-of-fact about things, and she didn't seem unduly attached to Chris. "Maybe she's embarrassed that I'm wearing your bathrobe. I know *I'm* embarrassed about that."

"Emma is not easily embarrassed," Chris noted. "And you, darlin', are much too easily embarrassed. Maybe she was just trying to embarrass you further." He considered what he'd said, then shook his head. "I don't think that's it. She likes you, Susan. I've seen the way she relates to you. I should think she'd want to make you feel at home here."

"I do feel at home," Susan let slip, then lowered her eyes to the dripping cereal bowl in her hands. Cooking breakfast in Chris's kitchen had seemed right to Susan; she hardly ever bothered cooking breakfast for herself in her own house, but here, it had seemed appropriate. Helping Chris with the dishes seemed right, too. Even bickering with Emma seemed right.

In fact, as she reflected on it, the last twelve hours had seemed more right to Susan than the rest of the week had—more right than the rest of her life. She used to think she belonged not in a man's bed, not in his kitchen, not shooting the breeze with a couple of sassy kids, but in her office playing the role of the ultimate businesswoman. Lately, however, everything she did at work, every aspect of it, every dirty detail she knew and fretted over, made her feel wrong, out of place, out of her element. Was it possible that she didn't belong there anymore?

The notion caused her mind to spin. She *had* to belong there; she had to belong to her work, her career. She'd geared herself for it, she'd designed her life around it. She'd emulated her father, studied, struggled and made the grade. Just because a highly respected individual broke the law in the company's name didn't mean Susan no longer had a place there.

Chris dropped the sponge onto the counter and rotated to Susan. "What?" he asked, peering into her eyes and trying to make sense of her stunned expression.

She shook her head, then leaned against him and ringed her arms around his waist. "Does that bother you, what I just said?" she asked, unable to look him in the face when she asked.

"That you feel at home here? Not in the least." He assured her, grazing the crown of her head with his lips. "I'd love to hear you say you feel at home in my underwear. You're welcome to sneak into it whenever the urge strikes."

Susan almost chastised him for making fun of her when she was so overwhelmed by her epiphany. But she didn't. A joke was undoubtedly exactly what she needed right now. "Speaking of underwear," she muttered, drawing back, "where's that clothes dryer of yours? Jockey shorts are swell, but—"

"But they aren't made of black lace," Chris agreed, sliding his hands to her bottom and giving it a loving squeeze. "All right, let's take care of your clothes. And then," he added casually, taking her hand and leading her down the stairs, "I believe you mentioned something last night about our having to talk."

Chapter Ten

They didn't have a chance to talk until well after dinner.

By the time Susan had rescued her clothes from the basement laundry room—a chore that took much longer than expected because the minute she and Chris had reached the downstairs hallway leading past his bedroom, he'd assaulted the knot in the bathrobe sash, dragged the robe from Susan's shoulders and found the sight of her clad in nothing but his briefs too erotic to let pass—it was nearly noon.

Afterward, after that impetuous, glorious tussle on his bed, while they lay sated and slowly recovering, with Chris's clothes and those mischief-making briefs heaped about them, Susan was amazed to realize that a few bewitching kisses from him had been enough to make her forget about the proximity of his children upstairs. Indeed, a few bewitching kisses from Chris were enough to make her forget the hour, the sunshine, the reality of the universe that existed beyond his arms.

But the rest of the universe, including but not limited to Newt and Emma, was out there, and Susan and Chris reluctantly got dressed. By the time they emerged from the bedroom, Newt was at the garage, munching on a bologna-and-cheese sandwich and single-handedly trying to drag the canoe outside. Because she didn't have a swimsuit with her, Susan announced that she wouldn't be going out in the boat. As soon as she said that, Emma declared that she wanted to ride in the canoe with Newt and Chris. Smiling apologetically, Chris helped his children on board and paddled out onto the pond, stranding Susan to wait for them on a sunbaked rock near the shoreline.

She felt melancholy sitting in solitude while the Kelsos floated off without her—melancholy yet oddly peaceful. Emma's peculiar behavior made a certain sense to Susan. As a teenager, she had behaved much worse with the few girlfriends her father had introduced her to—which was probably why he had introduced her to so few of them. She had resented them for trying to replace her irreplaceable mother. She couldn't blame Emma for resenting her for the same reason.

Except that Susan's mother had died. She had been a loyal wife and an adoring mother, the source of all the warmth and affection in the Duvall household. When she died, she *had* been irreplaceable, and both Susan and her father knew it. He had dated for social reasons, and for sexual ones, but there had never been a question of his remarrying.

She wondered whether Chris intended to remarry, then chastised herself for allowing her thoughts to travel in that direction. Maybe he would remarry, and maybe his relationship with Susan would develop to the point that he would view her as a woman with whom he might choose to end his bachelor-fatherhood. But their love was still too young for Susan to be thinking along such lines. Just because the man went berserk over her when she was wearing his underwear didn't mean he was ready to make an everlasting commitment to her.

Or she to him. She loved Chris; there was no question in her mind about that. She loved him, she liked him and she felt increasingly comfortable with him. But as he had reminded her, they had to talk. What they had to talk about was John Langers and the Pentagon contract. That mess hadn't miraculously vanished simply because Susan had fallen in love. It was still present, still with her, and before she could even think in terms of romantic commitments, she had to straighten some things out in her own life, in her own mind.

It would be good talking to Chris about the problem, though. It would be good sharing it with him. If anyone would understand her moral qualms, he would. He was so decent, such a gentleman. He would understand—and, she hoped, he would give her the strength she needed to set matters straight and make things right. Anyone who placed such a high value on trust would recognize the need for Susan to take action regarding an untrustworthy colleague.

She hadn't given much intensive thought to the subject recently. She'd been too busy worrying about whether she should allow herself to be distracted by Chris—and then finding herself distracted by him, anyway. But Chris wasn't a distraction anymore. He was a part of her, enriching her, clarifying her thoughts rather than muddying them.

And now that she could think clearly, she realized that preserving her career was no longer the most significant goal in her life. She gazed out at the pond, the canoe drifting parallel to the opposite shore, Emma and Newt using their paddles to splash water onto their father and tree limbs heavy with leaves forming a verdant canopy over them. Watching the Kelsos at play, she understood that, her father's example notwithstanding, there were many things in life more valuable than climbing a corporate ladder. Like love, family, sunlight on a summer afternoon—and trust. And principles. And decency.

"GOD, IT SMELLS GOOD out here," Chris murmured, handing Susan a tumbler of iced tea and dropping onto the porch chair closest to the lounge chair, where Susan was sprawled out. He propped his feet on the edge of the lounge and inhaled deeply, appreciating the air's bracing pine scent, which had been unleashed by the previous night's rain. Contrasting with that scent was the lingering smoky aroma of the barbecue dinner he had served up for Susan and the kids an hour ago.

It had never smelled like this in Oklahoma. Out there, the air carried the perfume of dry grass and dust and, in the city, auto exhaust fumes. It had never occurred to Chris when he'd been working at the Tulsa Schenk plant that Cheshire was such a bucolic village. Whenever he had communicated with headquarters, he had envisioned the cross-country telephone wires connecting him to a glass skyscraper nestled amid countless other glass skyscrapers, like those found in downtown Stamford or Hartford. His first trip to Schenk's headquarters had been a shock. He couldn't for the life of him figure out why anyone would situate a major chemical company's corporate headquarters in an industrial park in the middle of nowhere. But now that he'd been transferred here, he was thrilled by the location.

He liked the fragrance of the evergreens. And he liked the people who lived in Cheshire. One person in particular, he thought, leaning back in his seat and raising his tumbler in a silent toast to the bright-eyed, dark-haired woman on the lounge chair.

"It does smell good," she agreed, turning to gaze at the sun, which had slid low in the sky and taken on a soft peach-colored cast.

By now Chris had learned the rhythms of this region. Soon, he knew, the world would glide completely into darkness. The crickets were waiting for the sun to wax a little pinker and dip a little lower, and then they'd commence with their nighttime symphony. The shadows were beginning to stretch, as if waking from their daytime slumber. Chris recalled how Susan had stretched when she woke up that morning, her arms extended, her toes pointed beneath the sheet and her spine arching with an elastic grace that put him in mind of felines, dancers...and sex.

"Can I talk you into staying again tonight?" he asked. Hearing himself pose the question took him somewhat by surprise. It was one thing to have a woman at the table on Sunday morning, but quite another to have her there on Monday morning. Addie Ferguson had never made a weekday breakfast appearance in his home. Chris had never asked her; she had never suggested it. Theirs hadn't been that kind of relationship.

His relationship with Susan was that kind. Or, if it wasn't, he wanted it to be—the kind that encompassed weekends and weekdays, every day, every night. The kind in which the bathroom adjoining his bedroom would gradually fill up with feminine things, his shaving utensils crowded onto one shelf of the medicine cabinet to make room for her cosmetics and creams, the counter surrounding the sink cluttered with bottles of deodorant and tins of talcum powder, and wet stockings dangling over the shower curtain rod. The kind where her shoes would take over the floor of his closet like an occupying army and his pillows would smell of her, all the time.

"We have work tomorrow," Susan pointed out.

"So we'll go to bed early," he proposed, then grinned slyly. "The earlier, the better."

Susan tore her eyes from the sunset panorama and returned his wicked grin for a moment. Then the corners of her lips fell, settling her mouth into a solemn line. "Chris, we haven't had any time to ourselves all day, but now that the kids are inside watching TV, we really should talk."

He did his best to temper his smile. He wanted to have this talk with Susan—he wanted it so badly he'd felt obliged to remind her of it that morning. All day, however, she had avoided the subject—whatever the hell the subject was. He had been afraid to remind her again, afraid that he was asking for too much.

But now, at last, she would share with him the worry that had been gnawing at her for weeks, that had compelled her to freak out on him and retreat from him. "Okay," he said, nodding and then sipping some tea. "Let's talk."

Susan lowered her eyes to examine the droplets of condensation skittering down the side of her glass, and then looked back up at Chris. "It's about work," she began. "Well, of course, you already know that. It's about work, and it's about John Langers. You know that, too."

He nodded again, not commenting on the inexplicable nervousness that was causing her to babble.

Susan took a deep breath, then smiled edgily, flashing her tiny white teeth at Chris. "You know the rocket fuel contract Schenk just won?"

"Of course I do," he said calmly.

"Well...it was more than just our bid that won us that contract. John..." She drew in another deep breath, then forced out the words. "John paid some people off."

Chris waited for her to elaborate. Given the way Susan had acted, given how agitated she was now, he expected something a bit more earth-shattering than this. "What people?" he asked gently when she remained silent.

"The purchasing agents at the Pentagon."

"Uh-huh," he drawled, still waiting for more.

Susan angled her head, staring at Chris in bemusement. The sun had inched lower in the sky, and was partially hidden behind the spires of the evergreens fringing the horizon. Portions of her pretty face were preyed upon by shadows—one side of her nose, the delicate crease denting her upper lip, the curve below one eyebrow. "Pentagon officers," she finally said. "Federal employees. John bribed them. He arranged for them to pocket kickbacks, in order to guarantee that they'd give the contract to Schenk."

"All right," he said, measuring her, waiting still.

"All right?" she erupted. "Chris, that's against the law!"

"Probably."

"No 'probably' about it," she retorted.

"Okay. No 'probably' about it," he granted. "Even so...I'm sure it isn't the first time in the world somebody bribed the feds to win a bid. It isn't my area of expertise, Susan, but I'm not naïve enough to think it's never been done before."

"Just because it's been done before doesn't mean it's right," she asserted.

"Of course it doesn't. All I'm saying is, when it comes to big contracts like this, with cutthroat competition in the bidding—"

"Kickbacks are illegal," Susan said, succinctly cutting him off. "John Langers committed a crime."

It began to make sense to Chris now. Kickbacks—sure, they were illegal. They offended him. But he'd been working in the corporate world long enough not to get into a lather about certain distasteful business practices. They occurred, they were wrong, you got upset about them... but you didn't freak out.

Not unless the person breaking the law was your idol, your mentor, a man you were so close to that a newcomer to headquarters might mistake you for lovers.

"You assumed Langers was above that kind of thing," Chris surmised.

"Assumed? I *knew* he was," Susan said hotly. She bit her lip, then smiled so poignantly Chris felt something sharp and angry twist inside his gut. God, but it must have hurt her, seeing her hero defile himself that way. He wished he could have protected her from such a ghastly hurt.

"Well, the old boy sure let you down, didn't he," Chris said sympathetically.

Susan seemed suddenly impatient with him. "Chris, you don't seem to realize how serious this is. John broke the law, and I'm the only person who knows about it— other than the Pentagon crooks who took the kickbacks. I know about it, and if I do something about it John's going to lose his job. At the very least," she added grimly.

"Exactly what are you thinking of doing about it?" Chris asked, curious.

"Going public? Reporting him?" Susan's voice rose anxiously after each suggestion, as if she were seeking confirmation from Chris. "I don't know, yet. What he did was wrong, but I don't—I don't know if I can bring myself to destroy his life over it."

"It's a real dilemma," Chris agreed.

Susan's gaze locked with his, imploring him tacitly. Imploring him for what? he wondered. What did she want him to tell her? That she'd imagined the whole thing, that if she closed her eyes and counted to three it would all go away? He wished he could say that, but he couldn't, and she knew it.

"What would you do in my place?" Susan asked.

He had expected the question, but he hadn't yet prepared an answer. He took his time, drinking some tea, studying the orange and purple streaks the sun left in its wake as it disappeared below the earth.

What would he do? Langers wasn't a friend of his, so he wouldn't have a personal problem dealing with the man's transgression. But there was more at stake than Langer's career at Schenk, or even his criminality. As far as Chris was concerned, the most important issue was the contract itself.

He shifted his legs on the end of the lounge chair, extending them and crossing them at the ankles. "Before I started working for Schenk, I was planning to be a teacher—I've told you that. The training included some student teaching." It was his turn to ramble, now, his turn to labor through his thoughts. "I apprenticed with a fine lady," he said. "She gave me a lot of rope in her freshman English class, told me she really wanted me to get a feel for the life of a teacher, and the only way I'd be able to do that was to *be* a teacher. That meant dealing with the kids one-to-one, giving them tests, grading them. They started out as a faceless blur, Susan, but the more I got to know them, the more human they became. They were real people, with real problems. And when I had to flunk a couple of them, I thought it was the most painful job in the whole world."

Susan's impatience grew. "Chris, what does that have to do with—"

"I later found out that it wasn't the most painful job," he continued. "The most painful job, I've learned, is laying people off." He sighed, reminiscing. "I have friends at the plant in Tulsa. I have friends, good friends there who got laid off, and I was the one who had to do it. It was heart wrenching, Susan—these were fine, hard-working people with mortgages to pay and children to feed and a willingness to work. But I had to do it because fuel sales were way down." He paused, reliving the agonizing period of layoffs the Tulsa plant had endured last winter. "Now," he resumed, "along comes John Langers, and he breaks a law...and as a result my friends are going to get their jobs back."

Susan pressed her lips together, appraising Chris. "You're saying I should keep quiet about what John did?"

Chris shook his head. "That's not what I'm saying at all."

"You know that if I report him, there's going to be a major fuss—big headlines, congressional hearings, muckrakers under every rock. The contract is going to be nullified. All your friends are going to wind up back on the unemployment lines."

"That's probably what will happen," Chris concurred.

"I might lose my job, too," she added in a near whisper.

"You might." He frowned, looked away, wished again for some magic word that would make everything better for Susan. But there was no magic word. He couldn't keep Newt from banging and bruising and scraping himself, and he couldn't keep Emma from mooning over insensitive creeps wearing fish teeth on strings around their necks. And he couldn't make Susan's problem go away, either.

"But...but what John did was against the law," she stressed, a strange, broken plea.

"It's a tough one, Susan, it really is," he commiserated. "I can't tell you what to do. However..." He smiled warmly, set his glass down on the plank floor of the porch and let his hand come to rest on her knee. "I'm glad you told me. You trusted me with this, and that means the world to me."

"It doesn't mean much to me," she snapped petulantly. "You haven't been any help at all."

Chris laughed. "What kind of help did you expect? It's a hard call, either way. Langers did something bad, but a lot of good is going to come of it. You're dealing in shades of gray, darlin', not black and white. There's no easy answer." He patted her knee in encouragement. "Here's what I *will* tell you, though. You're one of the smartest, most reasonable, most capable people I've ever known in my life. I've got faith in you, Susan. You'll do what you've got to do, and it will be right for you. And that's the best any of us can hope for."

Susan's eyes fell to his hand on her leg, then shifted away to stare at the pond. A resonant blue darkness was creeping across the sky from the east, throwing her face into even deeper shadow. Although she didn't move her leg from his hand, he knew intuitively that he hadn't told her what she wanted to hear, and that she was annoyed with him for it.

"I'm sorry," he murmured. He meant his apology several ways: he was sorry about her predicament, sorry he couldn't solve it for her... sorry that he was falling short of her needs, even though he couldn't help it.

She said nothing. She only watched the pond, its placid surface reflecting the final, fading traces of daylight in the western sky.

"Susan," Chris coaxed her, suddenly desperate to gain her forgiveness—even though he'd done nothing that required forgiving. "Look at it this way: whatever you choose, you can't go wrong. If you report Langers, you're square with the law. If you don't, you've saved a lot of jobs. Either way, you can't lose."

She twisted back to him, her eyes opaque and her lips taut. "You wouldn't report him, would you," she guessed in a low, accusing voice. "You'd choose to save the jobs."

"I don't know what I'd do," he argued, frustrated by her refusal to accept the situation for what it was. "But it's your choice, not mine. Don't lay it on me, darlin'. You're the one who's going to have to live with the result of it." He exhaled tiredly. His hand tightened on her knee, his palm molding to the smooth, oval bone and his fingertips kneading the skin above it. "I know you'll make the choice that's right for you," he said, his tone now placating, laced with optimism. "The best way to make that choice is without an interference from me or anyone else. I have faith in you, Susan. Have a little faith in yourself."

Her irises seemed to grow flintier and darker as the night expanded to swallow him and Susan. She sighed, and he sensed some of her fury leaving her. "I have faith in myself," she said in a hushed, oddly leaden voice.

"You're right. I shouldn't have expected anything from you."

You can expect plenty from me, he almost cried out. She could expect his love, his respect, his support no matter what decision she reached. But that wasn't what she wanted from him. She wanted him to provide her with a way out, a quick, painless resolution. And he couldn't do that.

"I think..." She sighed again, then shifted her leg the slightest bit—just enough to let him know she wanted him to remove his hand. He obeyed her unspoken command, and as soon as he did he felt an encroaching sense of dread. "I think I'd better go home," she said, completing the thought, shooting him a pensive smile that vanished almost before it could register on him.

"Susan." He smothered the urge to grab her knee again, to grab her body, to hold her prisoner at his house, in his arms. "Susan, you're blowing this thing out of proportion. I mean, we all face professional hassles—"

"Yes," she agreed swiftly, her voice clipped. "Yes, and we face them alone. That's what you're trying to tell me, isn't it?"

"That doesn't mean you've got to run off on me," he maintained, trying to keep his tone free of the desperation building inside him, threatening to tear apart his soul. "Professional hassles are one thing, Susan. What you and I have going is something else."

"Yes," she said again, no longer sounding terse. Her gaze thawed, the hardness in her eyes melting into a shimmering layer of tears. "You're right, Chris," she admitted. "They're two separate things. I thought I could deal with them both simultaneously, but I can't. One of them has to be put on hold."

Me, Chris comprehended. *You're putting me on hold.*

He thought they'd gone beyond this point. He thought that was what last night was about, and this morning and the whole day. He thought they'd reached a place of total trust, knowing they could rely on each other and take strength from each other. Why on earth did she need to compartmentalize herself, to refuse Chris's love until every other detail of her existence was secure? That wasn't what life was all about. What the hell was she afraid of, that by opening her heart she'd lose her ability to think?

He trusted her, and he had finally come to believe that she trusted him. But maybe, just maybe, she didn't trust herself.

She left soon after. The desolation Chris felt at her departure this time was different from what he'd felt last night when she'd driven off. Then, he'd grieved over having come so close to winning her love. Tonight, he grieved over having won her love and then lost it. Who was the great thinker who had claimed that it was better to have loved and lost? he wondered morosely. Tennyson? Good thing Chris hadn't become an English teacher, after all. If he had, he might have spent the school year raving about what a liar Tennyson was.

Chris's only hope was that Susan wasn't lost, but simply on a temporary sabbatical. And yet, how could he love a lady who could turn her love off so easily, who could say, in effect, "I'll get back to you when I'm feeling up to it"?

The truth was, he was furious with her. And with himself. And, just for the hell of it, with John Langers for having placed them all in this intolerable situation.

Exhaling, attempting unsuccessfully to stem the bitterness washing through him, he turned his back on the lakefront vista. Twilight was gone, anyway; night had taken over.

The children didn't give him a hard time about bedtime. Perhaps they could tell that their father was in no mood for back talk. When Chris turned off Newt's bedside lamp and tucked him in, the boy innocently asked how come Susan hadn't said goodbye before leaving, and also when she'd be visiting again. To both questions, Chris answered, "I don't know, Newt. I just don't know."

"I hope soon," Newt remarked.

"So do I. Good night, son."

"'Night, Dad," Newt mumbled, closing his eyes and tumbling instantly into sleep in the way only energetic young boys seemed able to. Chris smiled sadly at his slumbering child. The smile was because he loved Newt, and the sadness was because someday Newt, too, would be faced with the torturous task of trying to make sense of women.

He abandoned Newt's room, closing the door to block out the hall light, and then paused at Emma's doorway. Talk about unfathomable females—he never knew, these days, whether or not he was supposed to tuck his daughter in and kiss her good-night. Sometimes she still wanted to be his little girl, and she sulked if he didn't give her a hug and wish her sweet dreams. Other times she acted haughty and standoffish, as if there were something perverted about a father's wanting to touch his lips to his daughter's forehead.

He peered into her dark room, hoping for a clue of her temperament. "Dad?" she whispered.

He took that as an invitation and crossed the threshold. "What's up, babe?" he asked.

Emma's small, dainty face was framed by the floral-patterned linen slip covering her pillow. Her pale hair was brushed smooth, her eyes were wide and round. She looked like a little girl, but her words implied otherwise. "I heard you and Newt talking, Dad. Well, I know why Susan left without saying goodbye."

Chris wondered whether Emma noticed his flinch of surprise. He almost blurted out that Susan *had* said goodbye—to him, at least, if not to the children. But in a sense, she hadn't said goodbye, not really, not in a way that mattered. And he was desperate for an explanation, the solution to the puzzle of Susan.

"Why?" he asked, his tone hushed, his hand resting on the headboard, balancing him as he leaned over Emma. "Why did she go?"

"It's like this . . . see, she told me, Dad, when she was my age and boys would lie to her, they'd promise they were going to call her and then they wouldn't. She told me they did that to her, Dad. And maybe they did it to my mom, too—I'm not saying you did it to her, Dad, but a long time ago, when she was my age, maybe some boys were rotten to her and lied to her, too. It hurts, Dad. Like Susan said, boys stink."

There was more to the convoluted explanation than Chris could absorb right now, but he clung to Emma's words, clung to the headboard and took as much in as he could. "Not all boys stink, Emma," he argued, thinking only to preserve his daughter's ego. He would analyze the rest later, and try to figure out what Susan—and Elysse—had to do with the admittedly rotten behavior of most adolescent boys.

"It isn't your fault, Dad," Emma reassured him, sounding unnervingly mature. "But when you're a girl . . . things happen when you're young, and you never forget. And then, one day, all that hurt comes back up inside you, like an explosion, and you turn and leave. You remember how those boys hurt you, and you just want to leave. I bet someday I'll leave, too," she concluded, the pain obvious in her eyes even though she managed to conceal it in her voice.

"No," Chris murmured forcefully. "That Dean fellow was a jerk, Emma. Don't let him dictate the rest of your life."

"He won't," Emma said sagely. "He won't be the only one. Other boys are going to hurt me, too. Then, maybe, some nice guy'll come along and I won't know how to be nice back."

"Of course you will," Chris promised her. He cupped his hand around her cheek, touching her with gingerly affection. "You already know how to be nice, Emma, and that's something you don't forget."

"You don't forget the hurts, either," she pointed out.

"Maybe you do. Scars fade."

"I don't know," Emma said dubiously. "Doesn't it hurt when you think about my mom? Don't you ever miss her?"

Chris thought for a minute, then smiled and shook his head. "No. I truly don't, Emma, not anymore."

"Do you miss Susan?"

Susan had been gone only a half hour, yet Chris believed he missed her more than he'd ever missed Elysse. "Yes," he whispered truthfully. "But she'll come back. She has to," he added under his breath, thinking that no betrayal, whether by an unknown snotty boy fifteen years in her past or by a sleazy boss a few weeks ago, could keep Susan out of his life forever.

If it did, if she never came back ... no. Chris believed in hoping for the best. Things had a way of working out. She would come back.

She had to.

"HERE WE GO," said Lorraine, carrying a huge bowl of popcorn into her living room and setting it on the coffee table. "Now let me just put in the tape, and we'll be all set."

Seated on the sofa, Susan stared at the mountain of popcorn before her and tried to will an appetite for herself. For three days, she'd been subsisting on heavily sugared herbal tea and an occasional slice of bread. The last real meal she'd eaten had been the barbecue at Chris's house Sunday night. But every time she thought about that delicious meal—and the conversation that had followed, she lost her appetite again.

"I still don't understand why you rented *The Way We Were*," she muttered, shifting her gaze to Lorraine, who was busily punching various buttons on her VCR. "The movie's on television so often."

"It wasn't on tonight," Lorraine pointed out. "And I thought it was high time for a viewing." The sitcom on the screen was replaced by several seconds of gray snow and then the start of the movie, with its gloriously sentimental song. Grinning, Lorraine turned and surveyed the couch. "Do we need anything else? Kleenex?"

"I'll pass," Susan said, determinedly dry-eyed.

"Playing with fire, aren't you," Lorraine teased, bouncing down onto the plump cushions next to Susan and brushing a springy coil of hair out of her eyes. "Now, let's talk."

"Talk? I thought we were going to watch the movie!"

"That's for background. I put it on to establish the atmosphere, Susan. Now tell me why I haven't seen that rattletrap brown station wagon cruising the parking lot lately."

Susan sighed. She wasn't hungry, but munching on some popcorn seemed like the least obvious way to stall for time.

It had been hard enough avoiding John Langers at work—but it was agony avoiding Chris. Her body ached for him, her heart yearned for him, and yet . . . her logic insisted that she had to keep her distance from him until she was able to cut through what he had appropriately called "shades of gray" with a bright, brutal light. She had to work it out, and he had already told her he wasn't going to help her. Fair enough. That was his choice. She was a grown-up; she would work it out alone.

"I'm mad at him," she said, startling herself.

"Why?" Lorraine tossed a handful of popcorn into her mouth. "He didn't like the teddy I gave you?"

Susan closed her eyes and shuddered. With or without the black lace teddy, she knew Chris liked her, loved her, longed for her—just as much as she longed for him. "The problem isn't—it has nothing to do with that," she said vaguely, opening her eyes and staring at the white puff of popcorn slowly growing soggy in her palm.

"What does it have to do with?"

"I'm . . ." Susan sighed, forced herself to take the popcorn morsel into her mouth, chewed and swallowed. "Somebody at work broke the law," she said quickly, providing Lorraine with an abridged version of the story. "I know about it. I—I sort of turned to Chris for advice."

"And?"

"And he wouldn't give me any," Susan revealed. She smiled faintly, anticipating Lorraine's reaction and cutting her off. "I know, he was showing his respect for my integrity and my independence and all, and yes, that's flattering in a way, but—" She drew in a deep breath, then muttered, "Damn it, I wanted him to say, 'Report the bastard! Turn him in!'"

"And he didn't." Lorraine settled back into the sofa, chomping on popcorn and considering what Susan had told her. "I take it turning the bastard in is what you want to do," she deduced.

"I don't know. I guess so." Susan closed her eyes again and shook her head, partly in frustration and partly in self-disgust. She felt weak, and disappointed in herself. Too cowardly to turn John in without urging, she had been hoping that Chris would inspire her to do the right thing.

But he hadn't. He'd backed off. He'd refused to intervene.

Didn't that make him as much of a coward as Susan?

"I don't know, Lorraine," she reiterated. "I thought Chris was one of the most upstanding men I've ever known. But there he was, going on and on about how maybe what the guy did wasn't so terrible, even if it was against the law. How could Chris say that? Doesn't he know right from wrong?"

"Don't you?" Lorraine asked pointedly. "If you did, you would have turned the guy in by now."

Susan nodded. She stared blankly at the television screen for a moment, watching a remarkably dapper-looking Robert Redford flirting with a remarkably frowsy-looking Barbra Streisand. She knew that in only a few more scenes the characters would be in bed together, making love and pretending that all the differences that stood between them didn't matter.

What were the differences between Chris and Susan? Not that she had a clearer sense of right and wrong than he did; she didn't. As Lorraine said, Susan would have reported John by now if she'd believed that was the only possible way to handle the mess.

No, the difference between Chris and Susan was much simpler than that: she needed his help, and he had refused it. Oh, he'd give her his support, his companionship, his heavenly lovemaking—but not help, not direction, not a guarantee that everyone would live happily ever after.

"There are times..." she murmured, no longer paying attention to the torrid bedroom scene unfolding on the screen. After the weekend she'd spent with Chris, fantasizing about Robert Redford seemed anticlimactic. "There are times," she repeated, slowly, thoughtfully, "when you just want to fall apart and let someone else take care of you. I've been strong all my life, Lorraine. I've been strong and sturdy, the consummate professional woman. I've never expected anyone to take care of me, and I've never asked for it. But...but I wanted Chris to take care of me, just through this crisis. I want him to make it all better for me, and he wouldn't. He said he couldn't."

Lorraine gave her friend an intense examination. "I'll get the Kleenex," she said, making Susan aware for the first time that her cheeks were streaming with tears.

Lorraine rose from the couch and left the living room. Susan curled up in the upholstery, burying her face in her hands, weeping. She wept because she felt helpless, and she wept because she hated feeling helpless. She wept for the loss of her friend John, and for the loss of her lover

Chris. She wept because it felt good, and because she hoped that once she'd run out of tears, she'd find the strength and courage to do what she had known all along she would have to do.

And she'd do it without Chris, damn him. She would do it alone.

THE FOLLOWING DAY, she shut herself into her office at headquarters, refused all calls, skipped lunch. She ignored the files awaiting her attention, the papers requiring her assessment, the clients requesting her ear. She spent eight long, single-minded hours scribbling on a legal pad: a letter to the Chief Executive Officer. A letter to the Senate Armed Services Committee. A letter to the F.B.I. A letter to the editor of every newspaper she could think of.

She wrote each letter, crossing out words, inserting arrows and footnotes, decorating the margins with asterisks. Then she tore each letter from the pad, crumpled it up, tossed it into the garbage pail and began all over again.

It was the toughest workday she'd ever had in her life.

By five o'clock, she still hadn't composed a letter worth saving, but she felt a little bit better about what she'd accomplished. She *could* do this thing alone, she realized. She was still furious with Chris for not being with her in her office, helping her, offering suggestions and phrasings. But if he was going to force her to be tough, she would be tough. so tough she'd never need anyone again, not even him.

The last thing she expected, when she arrived home at five-fifteen, was to have Chris tell her he needed her. She heard her telephone ringing as she fidgeted with the lock on her front door. It was still ringing when she got inside, and she raced into the kitchen and lifted the receiver. And heard his voice, hoarse with panic: "Susan—please, I need you."

She didn't speak. He had buzzed her office a couple of times at work, but she'd asked her secretary to run interference, and the calls had ceased. Was he calling her at home so her secretary wouldn't be able to cut him off?

How could he need her? Why did he, of all people, think she would be willing to help him? Why couldn't he have said, "Susan—please, you need me and I'm here?"

But he didn't say that. What he said, after giving her plenty of time to speak and concluding that she wasn't going to, was: "It's a bad one, Susan, and I need you. Emma's run away."

Chapter Eleven

The police were already at Chris's house by the time Susan arrived. She had to edge her car past the cruiser in the driveway to park by the garage. Through the windshield she saw Chris and Newt on the porch conferring with two uniformed officers.

It was a bad one, all right.

Yet she was somehow cheered by knowing that, in a time of need, Chris was willing to call upon her for help. She would have been justified in refusing to rush to his aid; after all, he had refused to offer her much help in solving her crisis. But she wouldn't deny him her assistance. She couldn't. No matter how much she resented him, she loved him.

Besides, she couldn't shake the notion that she herself was partly to blame for Emma's disappearance. In avoiding Chris, Susan had to cut herself off from his children, as well. Newt was stable and easygoing; he could adjust to not having her around. But Emma... Emma was prickly and temperamental. Sometimes she seemed fiercely determined to reject Susan, but other times she depended on Susan for counsel and support. If Susan wasn't available, whom could Emma turn to for advice about tampons and miniskirts and how to deal with the deceitfulness of young men?

Not wishing to disturb Chris while he huddled with the police officers, Susan got out of her car as inconspicuously as possible. She stood at the edge of the driveway, waiting until Chris acknowledged her arrival before she approached. He was still dressed in his business attire—a white oxford shirt beneath a lightweight suit of pale gray. His tie hung loose, his collar lay open, and his hair was a mess. Susan, too, still had on her silk blouse and skirted linen suit from work. She hadn't wanted to waste time changing into more comfortable clothes.

When she had first driven up, Chris had glanced over his shoulder without really focusing his vision. Now, having concluded his statement to one of the officers, he turned fully to view the driveway, and his gaze met Susan's. She was stunned by the deep lines of worry etched into his handsome face, the grim shadows darkening his eyes and the stoical rigidity of his jaw, the reflexive fisting of his hands at his sides. But the sight of Susan seemed to relax him slightly. His mouth relented, spreading into a shy smile of relief, and his fingers unfurled. "Susan," he said, so softly she had to read his lips to know that he'd called to her.

She strode up the hill to the porch, her gaze shifting from Chris to the uniformed policeman by his side. Behind them, Newt was seated with a policewoman on the lounge chair, chattering away while she took notes.

When Susan reached the porch Chris extended his hands to her. Now was not the time to work out their personal problems, she understood, automatically stepping into his embrace. As her arms closed around him, his tightened about her waist and he sighed brokenly. "Thank you," he whispered. "Thank you for coming."

Her fingers slid consolingly over his back, detecting his tension in the bunched muscles of his shoulders, in the quickness of his breath. No matter what had gone wrong between them last Sunday, Susan treasured the feel of him. Her anger at him was legitimate, and it hadn't miraculously disappeared...but she had missed him. Throughout this long, difficult week, she had missed Chris terribly.

"What happened?" she asked, effecting a deceptively calm tone as she loosened her hold on him. She was as alarmed about Emma as Chris was, but he was counting on her for support. She wouldn't be able to provide much of that if she flew into a frenzy.

He let go of her and raked his hand anxiously through his disheveled hair. "According to Newt, she ran away. A little over an hour ago. She said..." He swallowed and glanced toward his son, who was solemnly describing for the policewoman the outfit Emma had been wearing when she left. "She said," Chris mumbled, "that she wanted to go to Los Angeles to see her mother."

For an instant Susan was surprised. Then she decided that she wasn't surprised at all. Not only because Emma was obsessed with her absent mother—or, at least, obsessed with her concept of what her mother was like, not only because Emma was in dire need of a female adult in her life, but because it was only natural for a daughter to want to see her mother. Even now, twenty-one years after her own mother had passed away, Susan would give anything, anything in the world for a chance to see her mother once more.

"Mr. Kelso?" the policeman broke in, eyeing Susan inquisitively.

Chris turned. "Officer Grimaldi, Susan Duvall," he tersely introduced the two, not bothering to identify Susan further.

"Do you know the missing child?" the policeman asked Susan. "Can you tell us anything about her that might help?"

"I'm sure Chris has told you everything important," she said, then gave the question further thought. There could be more to Emma's running away than simply a curiosity about her missing mother. Susan felt uncomfortable about mentioning it, but she wasn't going to hold back anything that might help the police to find Emma. "I spent the night with Mr. Kelso last weekend," she reported in an admirably level voice. "Emma didn't seem terribly pleased to find me here Sunday morning."

Susan's announcement seemed to astound Chris more than the policeman. "That has nothing to do with this," he argued.

"How do you know that? Emma seems to run hot and cold about me, Chris. Sunday morning, when she realized that we'd spent the night together, she was definitely running cold."

"She's crazy about you," Chris asserted with more passion than Susan expected.

"I don't think—"

"She is," he swore, hushed yet vehement, his tone so heavy with emotion Susan wondered whether he was truly talking about his daughter. "She's been asking all week when you'd be visiting again. I told her," he added, his voice becoming gruffer, "that you wanted some time to yourself."

"And now she's run away," Susan groaned, suffering another surge of guilt.

The policeman was scribbling away on his note pad, apparently finding Susan's comments useful. "Without getting too personal, Mr. Kelso... if there was some sort of upheaval in the family that might have triggered Emma's decision to leave, we need to know about it. Now if Ms.—uh—" He faltered, groping for Susan's name.

"Duvall," she supplied.

"If Ms. Duvall spent the night here, maybe it upset your daughter."

"It didn't," Chris stubbornly insisted.

"And then you two had some sort of a falling out?" the policeman asked Susan, evidently seeing her as more willing than Chris to discuss the subject frankly.

"She missed you," Chris interjected, again leaving Susan to wonder whether he was speaking for his daughter or himself. His gaze burned into Susan, pleading, accusing. She couldn't shake the feeling that what his eyes revealed was far more personal than anything she had told the policeman about her relationship with Chris.

Officer Grimaldi waited for a moment, but when neither Chris nor Susan elaborated further, he changed the subject. "All right. Let's talk about Emma's finances, Mr. Kelso. It would help if we could figure out how much money she might have had access to."

Chris's gaze held Susan for another beat. Then he turned from her to the policeman to calculate how much of her allowance Emma might have saved that summer.

Susan discreetly moved away. She overheard Newt embarking on a long-winded lecture about his fungus collection; the policewoman looked less than captivated by the topic. Susan crossed the porch to him. "Hey, Newt, I bet you're starving," she said, a safe guess. Newt was always starving.

The boy's eyes lit up. "Yeah, let's go get something to eat."

The policewoman cast Susan a grateful smile, then rose from the lounge chair and joined her partner and Chris by the railing. Lifting his eyes from the policeman's note pad, Chris glimpsed Susan taking Newt's hand and heading for the door. He sent her a slight nod of approval.

True to his word, Newt was ravenous. Nothing, not even the disappearance of his sister, could smother his appetite. He made himself a huge, oozing peanut butter and jelly sandwich, poured a glass of milk, grabbed a bag of potato chips from a drawer and settled himself at the table. "I think," Susan said once she'd wiped the dribbles of milk off the counter and found a napkin for him, "I'll go keep your father company."

His mouth stuffed with chips, Newt mumbled something affirmative. Susan left the kitchen.

When she returned to the porch she found Chris alone. His jacket lay in a crumpled heap on a chair, and he'd rolled his shirtsleeves up to his elbows. His hands gripped the railing, his unbent arms propping him up as he watched the officers climb into the cruiser. His shoulders appeared to be knotted with tension beneath the limp cotton cloth of his shirt. The muscles in his forearms and wrists were visibly straining, doing their part in his entire body's effort to keep him under control.

"Chris," Susan said quietly.

He twisted to view her. He had no smile for her this time, not even a smile of relief. For a long moment, Susan wondered whether her presence offered him any solace at all. She had nothing besides comfort to give him. If she couldn't even give him that, she might as well go home.

Except that, before she could think of a reasonable excuse to take her leave, he said, "Come here."

She went to the porch and placed her hands on the railing next to his. His fingers were larger, thicker and browner than hers, and they clung to the railing as if to a lifeline. Raising her eyes from their hands, she saw the policewoman behind the wheel smiling and giving Chris a thumb's-up signal before she backed the cruiser down the driveway.

"What happens now?" Susan asked as the sound of the police car's engine faded in the hot evening air.

"We wait," Chris replied in a low, taut voice. "We wait here by the phone, in case Emma calls."

"And what are they going to do?" she asked, gesturing toward the spot where the cruiser had been parked.

"They're going to investigate," he said, his voice even lower and tauter, his usually glittering eyes devoid of light. "Susan, why did you tell Grimaldi about us?"

He seemed to be asking her something well beyond the simple question he'd uttered. But precisely what that something was, she couldn't guess. "I thought it might help," she answered honestly.

"It probably did," he admitted, turning away. "It's been a damned lousy week around here. Maybe..." He sighed. "I'm not sure I blame Emma for running away."

Again Susan attempted to infer the meaning underlying his words. Had Chris been in a foul mood since Susan's departure? She didn't know he was capable of moods; he was always so optimistic, so mellow. Had he been disturbed enough by Susan's withdrawal from him to become unpleasant with Emma, unpleasant enough to make her want to run away? Or was he shouldering too much of the blame for Emma's departure?

Susan wished she had the guts to wrap her arms around Chris again, to tell him that it was all right to have been in a foul mood, that Emma's departure wasn't his fault. He seemed to be in such desperate need of a hug, but she couldn't dispel the notion that he would recoil from her if she gave him one.

It seemed safer to concentrate on Emma, so that was the direction Susan took. "Do you know what time she left?"

"Newt said around four o'clock. He waited for a few minutes, just in case she came back, and then he telephoned my office. I was at a meeting with Bob DeGraff all afternoon, and . . ." He exhaled bitterly. "I never received the message."

"Beatrice?" Susan guessed, recalling Chris's complaints about the scatterbrained personnel secretary who was always forgetting to pass along phone messages.

He nodded. "Would it shock you to hear me say I'd like to cut that woman to ribbons?"

Susan allowed his death threat to pass without comment. "If Emma left at four, she couldn't have gotten very far," she consoled him.

Chris turned to her, and the raw fear distorting his features shocked her much more than hearing him express the desire to murder his incompetent secretary. "How far does she have to go?" he rasped. "All she has to do is hike out to Route 10 and pick the wrong person to hitch a ride with. She's a girl, damn it, and the world is filled with sick men. You know that."

Yes, Susan knew that. She knew it well enough to have hesitated before getting into a car with Chris the first time she'd ever spoken to him. Was Emma smart enough to refuse a ride from a stranger?

Susan didn't want to think about it, but clearly Chris did. Or, perhaps, he didn't want to think about it but couldn't help himself.

Susan's apprehension, her confusion about the past week, her resentment of Chris for having forced her to face her problem at work without him, without his help...none of it mattered anymore. There would be time to yell and complain and stamp her foot at him later. Right now she had only one course of action: to take him in her arms and hold him.

He returned her hug. The porch railing was no longer his lifeline; Susan was, and he clung to her with a desperation that nearly tore her soul from its mooring. He pressed his forehead to hers, shut his eyes, struggled against the urge to cry, to scream, to curse.

Susan felt the rage, fear and frustration building in him. She remembered her own recent bout with those emotions, the day she had learned that her good friend was a crook. With her, as with Chris, those emotions had been an outgrowth of betrayal and loss. She recalled how she had lost the battle Chris was now fighting, the battle to contain herself and remain poised. She recalled how she'd wept and how he'd held her. If only she could offer Chris now what he'd offered her that evening....

What he'd offered her then was his sanity, his perspective, his steadiness. He had taken action when she'd been unable to. He'd seen her situation, gotten her out of the bar, helped her to clear her head.

Now it was Susan's turn to be the sane, steady one. "Maybe you ought to phone your ex-wife," she suggested.

Chris leaned back to stare at her. For the first time since she'd arrived, she saw a hint of life in his eyes, a spark of animation in their gray-green depths. "The police already mentioned that idea,'' he told her. ''But they felt it would be premature to call her now—it would only frighten her. They don't think Emma's left the area.'' His voice cracked on the final words.

''Listen to me,'' Susan said brusquely, trying to shake him out of his despair. ''Just because they don't think she's left the area doesn't mean they *do* think she's lying in a ditch somewhere. Emma is fine.''

''How do you know that?''

''I don't,'' Susan allowed. ''But you don't know she *isn't* fine, and I happen to think that my ignorant assumption is a lot nicer than yours.''

She perceived his eyes brightening again, glinting with a tiny measure of hope. ''Oh, Susan,'' he drawled in a whisper. ''I don't know what you must think of me right now—''

''I think you're a father,'' she told him earnestly. ''A very devoted, very loving father.''

''A lousy father,'' he refuted her grimly. ''Kids don't run away from happy homes and good parents.''

''I don't think she was running away from you, Chris,'' Susan murmured. ''I think she was going to visit her mother. I think she just wants to see the woman with her own eyes. It seems like a normal thing to want.''

Chris contemplated Susan's explanation, then shook his head and pulled away from her. ''I wish I could believe that,'' he muttered. ''But I—''

He was abruptly silenced by the ringing of the telephone inside the house. With a sharp intake of breath, he sprinted across the porch and grabbed the doorknob. Before he could twist it the ringing stopped.

This time he did curse. A single vile word wrenched itself from his mouth. Then Newt's voice boomed from the kitchen, carrying through the screens in the open windows: "Dad? The cops are on the phone."

Chris went very pale, months of summer sun vanishing from his complexion. He eyed Susan nervously. "What do you think?" he whispered.

"I think," she said gently, "you ought to go inside and talk to them."

He nodded, forced his lips into a pathetic smile, and marched into the house, Susan at his heels.

Newt was slouching against a counter, the receiver in one hand and a half-eaten apple in the other. He thrust the phone at Chris the moment the two adults entered the room. Susan perused Newt's face. If the police were calling with grave news, they had apparently kept that fact hidden from Newt, because he didn't look the least bit worried.

"Christopher Kelso here," Chris addressed the caller. He listened, nodded, listened some more, mumbled a yes. Gradually his shoulders fell into their usual alignment, and his spine sagged. He sank onto a chair, cradled his head in one propped-up hand and said, "Yes. No problem. We'll be there." He lifted his eyes to Susan. They were damp with tears.

After a minute, he dropped the receiver onto the table, indicating that the call was finished. Susan dutifully carried the receiver to the phone and hung it up. She looked back to Chris, waiting for him to collect himself enough to tell her and Newt what the police had said.

For a long time, he only rested his chin in his cupped palms, closed his eyes and mouthed a silent prayer. Then he opened his eyes and sought Susan with them. "She's all right," he reported, his voice weak yet joyful. "They found her at the train station in New Haven. She's all right."

Susan offered to drive down to the city precinct station, and Chris didn't argue. He was obviously too drained to concentrate on driving. He sat beside Susan, staring at his hands in his lap, bending and straightening his fingers, weaving them together and then unweaving them.

In the back seat, Newt entertained Susan with a rambling monologue critiquing her car's air-conditioning system, its four-speaker stereo, its sun roof, its automatic windows and five-speed transmission. "Dad, if you ever decide to trade in the station wagon, these are some of the options we ought to look into," he recommended.

Susan covered up Chris's uncharacteristic silence by feeding Newt questions at the appropriate times. She could tell that Chris was in no mood to discuss automobile options with Newt. "Don't tell me Emma's convinced you that you need a new car, Newt," she said. "I thought you liked the station wagon."

"It is getting old," Newt observed solemnly. "The nice thing about an old car is, nobody cares if you spill something in it. A new car, you can't track mud in it and all. New cars always smell special, though. You know what? I heard there's a spray the car dealers use to make the cars smell new, like an air freshener. Even new cars don't smell like new cars until they spray 'em. Isn't that weird, Susan?"

It took them a half hour to reach the police station across the street from the train depot in downtown New Haven. The sudden stillness of the car as Susan shut off the engine shattered Chris's trance. Newt bounded out onto the sidewalk, but when Susan reached for the lever to open her door Chris grabbed her wrist and forced her around to him. "I'm still pretty scared," he whispered.

"Don't be." Susan rotated her hand to capture his and gave it an encouraging squeeze.

His gaze merged with hers and held it. Once more, his eyes seemed to be saying a great deal, yet Susan couldn't decipher their enigmatic light. She sensed only a jumble of undefined emotions, followed by one she identified as determination. "Let's go," he finally said.

The process of having Emma released into Chris's custody was more complicated than Susan would have imagined. She and Newt waited in a nondescript lounge while Chris was led away down a hall. He was gone over an hour, and although Susan was reasonably certain that Emma was in good health and ready to go home, her mind conjured up all sorts of ghastly possibilities: that Emma was throwing tantrums, refusing to let her father take her home, accusing him of hateful things. Susan wondered whether Emma was at all aware of what a fantastic father she had. She wondered whether Emma could begin to realize how lucky she was to have him.

She held those thoughts at bay by conversing with Newt about television police dramas and feeding quarters into a soda machine for him. He was draining his second can of 7-Up when Chris and Emma finally appeared at the doorway to the lounge. "All set," Chris announced.

Susan zeroed in on Emma. She was dressed in the short denim skirt she'd purchased at the mall, and the blouse she'd bought to go with it. Dangling from her earlobes were the garishly colored feathers Susan had given her. Her mouth was pinched into a miserable pout, and her eyes were impassive. Her long blond hair spilled down her back, giving her a waiflike appearance.

Susan suffered yet another stab of guilt. She was unnerved by the fact that Emma had chosen to run off wearing the apparel Susan had helped her to buy—not to mention the earrings, which Susan herself had picked out. It seemed painfully significant to her, although what it signified was beyond Susan's grasp.

She directed her attention to Chris. He still wasn't smiling, but the lines around his mouth had relaxed discernibly, and the crease lining his brow was no longer in evidence. He was holding Emma's hand, but she wasn't holding his. Her fingers lay inert within his palm; her arm appeared almost boneless.

"Okay," Susan said too brightly, rising from the vinyl couch where she and Newt had been sitting—when he wasn't romping around the room, hitting all the buttons on the sundry vending machines.

Newt inspected his sister and smirked. "Hey, Emma—guess you didn't make it too far, huh."

"Shut up, jerk," Emma snapped. Susan detected a quiver in her voice.

They exited the modern cinder block building and walked down the street to the car. Susan wondered whether the prospect of riding in her car instead of the rattletrap station wagon would boost Emma's spirits. If it did, Emma hid it well. She slumped sullenly in the back seat, jabbing the two halves of her seat belt together and cursing when they didn't mesh instantly.

"Dad!" Newt shrieked. "Did you hear what she said? She said—"

"Hush, Newt," Chris said. "Get in the car and button it, all right?" Newt subsided and did as he was told.

Susan didn't say anything to Chris until both of the children were settled in the back seat. Before Chris could open the front passenger door, she touched his arm to stop him, peered into his eyes and asked, "How are you?"

"Wiped out," he confessed with a sad laugh. "Someday, when Newt isn't around to criticize my language, I'll tell you what I think of social workers. Let's go home."

Let's go home. As if by running this ghastly errand together, they had magically repaired whatever was wrong between them. They hadn't, but for the moment Susan didn't care. The thought that Chris could refer to his house simply as "home"—as if it were hers as much as his—warmed her immeasurably.

Nobody talked as Susan pulled away from the police station and steered toward the highway, heading north to Cheshire. Everyone was steeped in his or her own thoughts. In her rearview mirror, Susan could see Newt pulling on the strap of his seat-belt, testing the spring action. To her right, Chris stared straight ahead, his eyes blank, his focus not on the road but on something deep inside himself, something only he could see. Susan couldn't view Emma without taking her eyes off the traffic, but she suspected that even if she could face the girl, she'd have no idea of what Emma was thinking, unless Emma chose to share her thoughts.

Emma chose to share them somewhere around the New Haven-Hamden town line. "I hate her," she declared, her bitter words fracturing the silence. "I hate her. I don't know why I thought I'd want to see her. I hate her!"

Chris's eyes sharpened, and he twisted in his seat to gaze at his daughter. "You don't have to hate her, babe," he said with such tenderness that Susan's mouth fell open.

"I *do* have to," Emma protested. "She left me, Dad. She just turned her back on me and left. And she left you, and Newt and—and she just ran out on us and acted as if we didn't even exist. She's a cruel, horrible, evil lady and I hate her. I wish she'd die!"

A wrenching sob escaped Emma, then another and another. Chris contorted himself in an effort to reach her. His hand brushed her knee, and he stretched even farther so he could stroke her arm. "Don't wish that on her," he murmured.

"Why shouldn't I?" Emma wailed. "She acts like I'm dead."

Chris shook his head. "She doesn't act like you're dead. She just..." He sighed, searching for the right phrasing. "She just never figured out how to fit us into her life—or how to fit herself into ours."

"But I was so little when she left," Emma choked out, hiccuping through her tears. "I was so little, I don't hardly even remember her. And Newt—he was just a baby, and—and she abandoned us—"

"She abandoned you to me, which wasn't so terrible," Chris pointed out. "I don't mean to sound egotistical, Emma—and maybe I'm not the best dad in the world. But your mother left you to someone who loves you and wants you and believes in you. You could have done worse."

"She was cruel, she was evil—"

"She was selfish," Chris granted. "She was selfish and confused, and she wasn't much of a mother, even when she was with us. She did what she felt she had to do, what she thought would be best for all of us. There's no right or wrong about it, Emma. It wasn't cruel or evil. She left, and that's the fact of it. She left and it hurt. But if she had stayed, feeling as she did, it would have hurt just as badly. Maybe even worse, as time went by."

"Nothing could hurt worse than this," Emma moaned. "My own mother doesn't love me." Hearing Emma's sorrowful words, Susan felt her eyes mist over.

As agonizing as it had been to lose her own mother, at least she had never lost her mother's love.

Chris smiled wistfully. "You've got my love, Emma," he vowed. "I love you, and Newt loves you. Don't you, Newt?"

"Sure," he chimed in. "Even if you're sometimes a creep."

"And Susan—" Chris said reflexively, then hesitated and shot her an inquiring look.

"I love you too, Emma," Susan said at once. She didn't have to think about it; she didn't have to chide Chris for presuming too much. She did love Emma.

Chris continued to gaze at Susan for an extended moment. A sweet warmth emanated from him, tacit but real. For the first time since Susan had arrived at his house that evening, she understood what his eyes were trying to tell her: *Thank you. Thank you for being here, for being you, for helping me.*

He twisted back to his daughter. "Maybe I'm testing the bounds of reality here, Emma," he went on, his voice gently husky, "but I think that in her own way, your mother loves you, too. She loves you enough to let you lead your own life, without having to deal with her selfishness and her insecurities."

"I don't believe that," Emma grumbled.

Chris's smile ebbed slightly, but it didn't disappear. "Whether or not you believe it, babe, that's the way it is. You've got to accept it."

Emma lapsed into silence for a minute. "You're angry with me for trying to see her, aren't you," she said.

"I'm angry with you for taking off the way you did," he explained. "You did something very dangerous, running away like that, and you scared the hell out of me. But as for trying to see your mother—no, Emma, I'm not angry about that. I'm hurting for you, that's all. I'm hurting for you."

They had reached his house. Susan pulled into the driveway, coasted to a halt and turned off the engine. Emma and Newt bolted from the car, and Chris shoved open the door to chase after them. Before Susan could figure out what she was supposed to do, he turned to her, covered her hand with his and said, "Stay." It was half an order, half a plea.

She nodded.

Chris vanished into the house with his children. Susan took her time getting out of the car. She ambled across the lawn to the porch, pulled off her jacket, fluffed her hair away from her neck. Deciding that the comfort of her feet was worth sacrificing a pair of stockings over, she yanked off her high-heeled shoes and padded across the porch to one of the chairs. She sat, propped her legs up on the railing, and ruminated on what Chris had told Emma about her mother's actions.

Sometimes there was no right or wrong answer to a crisis. Sometimes, what answer there was lay in the twilight in between.

Chris's wife hadn't been cruel or evil. She'd done what she thought was best. She had left and it hurt; if she had stayed, it would have hurt...

There was something eerily familiar in those words, and Susan struggled to place it. Something Chris had said to her last Sunday, before she'd left him. She stared out at the dusk-lit pond and willed herself to remember.

"Either way, you can't lose."

He had been discussing her problem with John—she remembered it now. He'd pointed out that whether or not she reported John, something good would come of it. Either way, she couldn't lose.

John wasn't evil or cruel, either. Like Chris's ex-wife, he had done what he thought he had to do. He had committed a crime and created many jobs at Schenk. He'd done something underhanded so people like Chris's friends in Tulsa could return to work.

Life would be a lot easier if things were black and white. But they rarely were. Chris had taught Susan that much.

The sky darkened above her, and the air cooled. Through the open windows, she occasionally heard Emma's voice, occasionally Chris's, once or twice Newt's. She wondered how severe a trauma Emma's stunt had inflicted on the family. In a sense, she felt lonely, isolated on the porch while the three Kelsos barricaded themselves inside to hash things out. She felt like an outsider, just as she'd felt like an outsider last Sunday when Chris and his children sailed off in the canoe and left Susan on the shore.

Yet she could understand their need to close ranks and mend themselves, without interference from others. The three of them had been a team for nine years. They were a family. That was what Susan envied. She was independent, she had a career and a distant father...but she didn't have a family.

She heard the door open behind her. Lowering her feet to the floor, she turned in her chair to discover Chris behind her. He looked sad and tired...but his eyes shone brightly, and his dimples deepened as he neared Susan.

"How is Emma holding up?" Susan asked. She wasn't sure she was ready to talk about Chris and herself yet.

He shrugged and dropped onto the chair next to Susan. "She'll survive. We all will, I reckon." He chuckled faintly. "Have I gone gray?" he asked, tilting his head toward her.

"It's too dark to tell," she said, grinning.

"One more thing to thank the dark for," he mumbled, straightening up and staring at Susan. He paused for a minute, then said, "Well, go ahead. Chew me out. I deserve it."

"What?" Susan scowled. "What you deserve is the Nobel Peace Prize. For starters."

"Susan—"

"You were magnificent, Chris. You handled this thing so beautifully—"

"I made a mess of it," he refuted her. "I was a wreck. I—" A shuddering groan escaped him, and he looked away. "Oh, Susan, I'm such a hypocrite. How can you stand me?"

She gaped at him. Here she'd been, about to lavish praise upon him for his wisdom, and he was all but daring her to walk away from him again. "I love you, Chris," she confessed.

He spun back to her, his gaze hard and skeptical. "I'm a hypocrite," he repeated. "I'm a coward, I'm a two-faced—"

"Chris, what are you talking about?"

"I fell apart here today, Susan. I fell apart, and I reached out to you, and you were there. I couldn't have handled any of this without you. You pulled me through, Susan, and—" He broke off, shaking his head, glancing down as if he couldn't bear to meet her bewildered gaze. "Last week, you asked less of me, so much less, and I refused you. And today...you came. You took charge, you held me together... I wasn't there for you last week when you asked me to help you shoulder your burden. Damn it, I wasn't there for you. But today...you were here for me."

"That's all I was," Susan reminded him in a hushed, earnest voice. "I was here, period. I drove the car. You did everything else."

"You had the guts to tell the police the truth, Susan. I couldn't even face it. At the police station in New Haven..." He groaned again, this time in disgust. "The social worker waltzed us around, trying to uncover any dirty secret she could dig up. I think she was looking for signs of—" He broke off, unable to say the word.

"Abuse?" Susan asked.

He nodded. "I guess they've got to do this, to protect kids who've got a real reason to run away. But...but it was—God, it was offensive, Susan, listening to her hint around like that...and she kept at it until I turned on Emma and asked whether last Sunday had anything to do with her leaving. And...she said it did, Susan. And then the social worker got off our backs."

Susan felt a frisson of dread ripple across her abdomen. "What did Emma say about Sunday?"

"She said..." Chris drifted off, his eyes dropping from Susan's face to her hand. He reached for it, lifted it, curled his fingers slowly around it. "She warned me that night, damn it. She all but declared her intention to run away—for the same reason you ran away."

"But I—"

"You did run away, Susan. And I can't say I blame you. You turned to me, and all I did was to hand you some crap about how I'd support you but you had to deal with Langers yourself. You turned to me, and I said, 'Don't lay it on me.'"

What Chris was saying was true, yet she couldn't bear to see him so hard on himself, not after what he'd just been through. "Chris, I—"

"She said," he continued stubbornly, "that women leave because men hurt them. Like that shark's-tooth fool hurt her. She said that if she was running away from anyone in Cheshire, it was Dean." He cursed. "She made that remark in the social worker's office—and for a minute I couldn't even remember who the hell Dean was. That bastard. He hurt her. Like I hurt you. Men are awful, Susan—we're so damned blind most of the time—"

"Chris." She had to stop this self-defeating speech of his. "Chris—shut up, okay?"

His eyes flashed at her. When he saw the laughter curving her mouth he smiled tentatively.

Susan waited, making certain that he wasn't going to start in again. Then she proceeded. "Chris, you were right Sunday night. You gave me much more than support—only *I* was the one who was blind. I wanted answers you couldn't give me. But you gave me what you could—your faith and your love. That's all I really needed."

"Are you sure?"

"I am now. And as for today, Chris—that's all I gave you. My faith and my love."

"And a drive to New Haven."

"All right," she conceded, laughing. "If it'll make you feel better, you can reimburse me for the gasoline."

"What . . ." Chris leaned forward, gazing steadily at her, his hand snug around hers. "What are you going to do about Langers?"

"I still haven't made up my mind," Susan replied, feeling calmer and more peaceful about that fact than she had in weeks. "What I do know, thanks to you, is that even if I make the wrong choice, it won't be *that* wrong." Her fingers curved around his hand, and she lifted it to her lips for a kiss. "I used to hate twilight," she confessed. "I liked daylight, and nighttime didn't bother me, but that vague period in between, when everything looks hazy and the world loses its shape and color—it used to make me edgy. Not anymore. I know twilight leads to darkness, but—"

"Only half the time, darlin'," Chris pointed out, sharing her smile. "The other half of the time, it leads to sunrise."

"Mmm. Yes, I guess it does."

"Which is why I like it," he murmured, pulling her out of her chair and onto his lap. He folded his arms around her waist and guided her lips down to his. "It can go either way, and either way is fine with me." He kissed her again.

Susan bowed to him, slid her tongue into his mouth and absorbed his contented sigh. She still preferred sunrise to sunset, emerging from the haze into light instead of darkness. She imagined she always would.

But as long as she had Chris beside her, imparting his love and strength and serenity to her, she knew that either way would be fine with her, too.

Epilogue

Night lay tranquil over the pond. The mid-October moon was full, an awesome orange disk pinned to the sky just above the tips of the evergreens bordering the water's edge. Despite the chorus of crickets and frogs churning the atmosphere, Chris felt like the only living creature in the world. Leaning against the porch railing, he stared down the hill toward the road, as if his desire alone could make Susan's car materialize in the driveway.

He felt lonely, but not unhappy. There was something strangely joyful about missing someone so badly, loving her so strongly that her absence for a single day hurt. In his first marriage, spending his evenings alone with the children while Elysse traipsed off with her fellow musicians hadn't bothered Chris, not nearly as much as having to spend this one evening without Susan. It wasn't as if she was out chasing an "open-mike night" dream, either; her trip to New York City had been important, necessary, not a rejection of Chris and the children.

Chris closed his eyes and willed her car to appear. When he opened them, they took in the sight of an empty driveway. He muttered an oath, then laughed. It was marvelous, being so insanely in love.

His laughter ceased the moment he detected the distant rumble of an automobile engine. It grew louder as the car drew nearer, and then a pair of headlights stabbed the garage door as the car turned onto the driveway. Chris let out his breath, vaulted over the railing, and jogged down the hill to greet Susan.

He barely gave her a chance to climb out of the car before he had her enveloped in a crushing bear hug. "What a welcome!" she said breathlessly, folding her arms around his shoulders and tucking her head into the crook of his neck. "I'm bushed."

"It's late," he pointed out, kissing the soft brown wisps of hair at the crown of her head. "I missed you. I was expecting you home much earlier."

Susan nodded and sighed. "Dinner with my father turned out to be something of an ordeal. For some reason, he felt obliged to subject me to a lecture of marathon proportions. He sends his regards, by the way."

She extricated herself from Chris's embrace and leaned across the front seat of the car for her briefcase. Chris beat her to it, lifting the leather case from the seat and then shutting and locking the car door. He looped his arm around Susan, feeling the slender ridge of her shoulders under the slight padding shaping her blazer. It made him think of the sexy curves lurking within her prim suit, the silky warmth of her thighs hidden beneath her straight skirt.

His mental picture of her body compelled him to bypass the porch for the downstairs back door, a shortcut to the master bedroom. She hesitated, glancing up at the porch and the lighted living room windows. "Are the kids in bed already?" she asked.

"Already? It's after ten on a school night," Chris said indignantly. "Of course they're in bed."

Susan looked disappointed. One more reason Chris loved her—as if he needed to count the reasons—was that she was so good to Emma and Newt. No, it wasn't that she was good to them, but that she liked them, genuinely and without reservation. She liked them, and they liked her. "How were they this evening?"

"Fine," Chris reported, holding the door open for Susan and following her inside. "Emma had one of the Dip Sisters and another classmate over for dinner. They were supposed to do their homework afterward, but it sounded like all they were doing was whispering boys' names and giggling. Oh—and Newt's big news is, he auditioned for the school glee club and made it."

"Good for him!"

"Bad for us," Chris cautioned her, grinning. "It means we're going to have to sit through every school assembly the glee club performs at. I've suffered through a few assemblies in Tulsa, and let me tell you, they can be wretched."

Susan laughed.

They entered the bedroom, and Chris placed Susan's briefcase on the floor by the closet. She stepped out of her shoes, and he eased off her blazer for her. Then his fingers worked down the front of her blouse, unbuttoning it.

"Chris—"

He kissed her solidly, his lips fused to hers, smothering her attempt to speak. Her blouse slipped down her arms and onto the carpet, and his fingers worked nimbly on the fastening of her skirt. It dropped to the floor with her blouse, leaving her in her slip and nylons.

It was a pretty slip, made of some slinky beige fabric, and it was shaped in such a way that she didn't require a bra. Chris moved his hands up from her narrow waist to her breasts, and she moaned into his mouth.

"Are you trying to say something?" he drawled, running his thumbs over the tips of her breasts until they stiffened.

"I only thought..." She sighed, trying to steady her voice. "I thought you'd want to hear about what happened in New York."

"Later," he whispered, directing his attention to his own clothing. Without argument, Susan sat on the edge of the bed and removed her stockings while he stripped off his shirt and jeans. Then he returned to her, sliding the ribbon-thin straps of her slip down her arms and kissing the peach-hued skin of her shoulders.

He considered asking her to leave the slip on. Ever since the day he'd seen her in his underwear, he'd been acutely conscious of how erotic certain undergarments could be on Susan. Not just his briefs, or this slip, but that little black teddy thing that Lorraine, bless her heart, had given her...

Right now, however, he wanted only Susan, only her. In a single swift motion, he swept the slip up and over her head. Then he gently pushed Susan down onto the bed and sprawled out beside her. Her flesh was softer than any velvet, smoother than any satin. Sexy lingerie might be fine, but Chris wanted more than fun tonight. He wanted her, her body enveloping his, possessing his. He had missed her all day, all evening, and now he had to prove to himself that she was here, truly home.

As her lips hungrily claimed his, he recalled the first time they'd made love. She had mentioned that she wanted to talk then, too. And he had said, "Later." Not that he didn't love talking to her—but sometimes other needs took precedence.

Her hands skimmed over his chest and he groaned. He twisted to kiss her throat, and she echoed his groan. "I missed you," he said, his voice rough and ragged as his lips grazed down to her breast.

"You already told me that," Susan reminded him, weaving her fingers through the hair at his temple and brushing it back from his face.

"And now I'm telling you again." He touched his tongue to her flushed nipple and watched with fascination as it swelled into a taut nub. Women's bodies were so damned mysterious; too much of what happened to them happened secretly, out of a lover's view. That was one reason Chris adored Susan's breasts; they responded visibly. They let him see what he was doing to her. "And now," he murmured, "I'm showing you how much I missed you."

She groaned again, her back arching to him. Her hand reached down between their bodies, seeking. She found what she was looking for, covered him, stroked him. For an instant he thought he would die from the sheer pleasure of her touch.

Shoring up his willpower, he eased out of her clasp. His hand followed the route hers had taken, down to her, to the place where all her magnificent womanly secrets lay hidden. As soon as his fingers rubbed against her she arched again and cried out softly, giving him a wild sense of power. He wished he could magically dive inside her skin and feel what she was feeling.

He could. He did, rising onto her and joining his body to hers. He thought about how miraculous it was that a man and a woman could experience this, could share a love this extreme, this intense—and could also be dependable, trusting friends. Fifteen years after he'd met Elysse, nine years after she'd left him, he believed that the most important lesson he'd learned was that love bound with trust was infinitely more valuable than love alone.

Learning that—*having* it—had been worth the wait.

Susan wrapped her legs around him, urging him deeper. "I love you," he whispered. He had no desire to talk, except to say that.

She didn't speak, but her lips curved into an enchanting smile. Her eyes, those big warm honey-brown eyes of hers, closed, and she tightened her grip on his back and buried her lips against his shoulder. She gasped, gasped again and trembled. He felt the surging pulses of her climax lifting him, driving him toward ecstasy, storming through him in a consuming rush. He could no longer think, no longer breathe. All he could do was feel, feel Susan, feel himself fill her with his love.

"Will it be like this forever?" she asked, a long time later.

Chris dragged himself back into consciousness. He opened his eyes and found her face a mere inch from his, her hand once again pushing his hair back from his sweat-damp face, her breath mingling with his above the pillow. "Yes," he promised. "It will always be like this."

She rolled onto her side, cuddling up to him. He closed his arms protectively around her. Despite the fact that they were nearly evenly matched in height, she always seemed small to him after they'd made love. Her build was so much more delicate than his, her bones almost fragile and her skin exquisitely fair. Holding her afterward was as blissful as loving her had been—well, *almost* as blissful, he amended, his smile widening.

"Okay, Susan," he said. "Tell me about New York. How did the interview go?"

"So-so." She inched back from him to meet his gaze. "No," she corrected herself. "It went well, for the most part. It went fine."

Her expression contradicted her statement. Her lips, an unnaturally red color in the aftermath of his forceful kisses, were pressed into a ruler-straight line, and though her eyes still glimmered with lingering passion, a shadow hovered over them. Why, Chris wondered in an abrupt surge of anger, was it impossible to make things right for the people you loved? Why did Susan have to pay for someone else's mistake?

Because that was the choice she'd made, he answered himself. Because it was *her* choice, and she'd made it.

"Does the job interest you?" he asked.

"I think I'd do well there," she allowed, then sighed. "I don't know. Maybe they'll make me an offer, but . . . New York City is too far away from Cheshire, Chris. It's over two hours each way. The commute would kill me."

"We could move closer to the city."

Susan shook her head. "I don't want to leave this house. I love it here. And the kids are getting adjusted to their new schools. Now that Emma's made some friends in her classes, and Newt's made the glee club. . ." Susan shook her head. "I don't want to move. I'll try to find a position with a firm closer to Cheshire." A pensive laugh slipped past her lips. "I don't know why I'm even thinking about this firm in New York. They probably won't offer me the job."

"They'd be crazy not to," Chris said encouragingly. "You're smart, talented, ambitious—"

"And out of work," she concluded bitterly. "I blew it again, Chris. I've been on three interviews, and I blew the same question each time. They always ask me why I re-signed from Schenk, and I just don't know how to answer. If I tell them I resigned because my boss broke the law, they're going to wonder why I didn't report him to the authorities. If I tell them I resigned because I couldn't get along with my boss, they'll think I'm an uppity underling, not a team player. If I tell them I resigned for personal reasons, they'll think I'm being evasive.''

"Do you regret resigning?" he asked.

"No," Susan said. "I don't think any other solution would have worked. I couldn't report John, but I couldn't keep quiet about what he did, either. I had to put it in writing, and I had to leave. Now Schenk can decide what they want to do about it. It's up to them—and I think it should be." She sighed again, lowered her eyes to Chris's chin and muttered, "I'm almost sorry I agreed to meet my father in town for dinner after the interview today. He ranted and raved for hours about how I should have kept my mouth shut and stayed on at Schenk, how I sacrificed all my career goals over some trivial lapse on the part of my boss. He said I was lucky I'd hooked up with you. 'Thank goodness Chris is willing to support you,' he said.''

"Aha! I should have known you only married me for my money," Chris teased. He longed to see Susan smile, a real, full-fledged smile. What she gave him was a lame, half-hearted one. "You do regret resigning, don't you," he pressed her.

"Yeah," she admitted. "A little. I don't know how to be unemployed, Chris. I feel like I'm at loose ends."

"You're not at the end of anything," he reassured her, slipping his index finger beneath her chin and tilting her face back to his. He dropped a light kiss on her mouth. "You're in between. Things will get brighter soon."

"Either that, or they'll get darker," she joked glumly. She curled her arms around Chris and held him tight, taking all the comfort he had to give. "Things are already brighter," she whispered. "I've got you, and we've got the kids. I ought to quit while I'm ahead."

"You already quit," Chris playfully reminded her. "Isn't that what we're talking about?"

"We're talking," she asserted, "about priorities, and knowing when to count your blessings."

"And learning to roll with the punches."

"And learning to roll..." With an unexpected burst of energy, Susan shoved Chris onto his back and rolled on top of him. Straddling his waist, she gazed down at him, favoring him with the honest, heartfelt smile he had been longing for. "I love you, too," she whispered, bowing to kiss him.

He framed her face with his hands, held her head to him, sipped the sweetness of her mouth. "Ah, Susan," he said, sighing. "I wish I could make it better."

"You do," she vowed, snuggling her body into his and drawing the blanket up over their bodies. "You make everything better."

She closed her eyes, issued a tiny yawn, and dozed. Chris watched her, taking delight in the peace that settled over her, over them both. He was painfully aware of how transient that peace was. Tomorrow, she would wake up and still be unemployed. Problems like hers didn't disappear overnight.

But the darkness would pass and the sun would rise, and the world would keep turning. Eventually, Susan would find a job she liked. Maybe she would discover, as Chris had so many years ago, that the career she thought she wanted wasn't the only kind of work she was suited for. Maybe, he thought with an ironic grin, she could become a high school English teacher. Or maybe she'd never take another paying job at all. It was her decision to make. He'd back her, whatever she chose.

This problem would disappear—and a new one would arise to take its place. That was the nature of things. The world would keep turning, spinning on its axis, carrying Chris and Susan through darkness and sunshine, through twilight.

They would ride it out together, and their love would light their path and keep them warm. That, too, was the nature of things, he contemplated as he bent to kiss Susan's cheek one last time before turning off the lamp.

The passionate saga
that began with SARAH continues in the compelling,
unforgettable story of

Elizabeth

MAURA SEGER

In the aftermath of the Civil War, a divided nation—and two
tempestuous hearts—struggle to become one.

Coming in April

Harlequin Category Romance Specials!

Look for six new and exciting titles from this mix of two genres.

4 Regencies—lighthearted romances set in England's Regency period (1811-1820)

2 Gothics—romance plus suspense, drama and adventure

Regencies

Daughters Four by Dixie Lee McKeone
She set out to matchmake for her sister, but reckoned without the Earl of Beresford's devilish sense of humor.

Contrary Lovers by Clarice Peters
A secret marriage contract bound her to the most interfering man she'd ever met!

Miss Dalrymple's Virtue by Margaret Westhaven
She needed a wealthy patron—and set out to buy one with the only thing she had of value....

The Parson's Pleasure by Patricia Wynn
Fate was cruel, showing her the ideal man, then making it impossible for her to have him....

Gothics

Shadow over Bright Star by Irene M. Pascoe
Did he want her shares to the silver mine, her love—or her life?

Secret at Orient Point by Patricia Werner
They seemed destined for tragedy despite the attraction between them....

CAT88A-1

PAMELA BROWNING

. . . is fireworks on the green at the Fourth of July and prayers said around the Thanksgiving table. It is the dream of freedom realized in thousands of small towns across this great nation.

But mostly, the Heartland is its people. People who care about and help one another. People who cherish traditional values and give to their children the greatest gift, the gift of love.

American Romance presents HEARTLAND, an emotional trilogy about people whose memories, hopes and dreams are bound up in the acres they farm.

HEARTLAND . . . the story of America.

Don't miss these heartfelt stories: American Romance #237 SIMPLE GIFTS (March), #241 FLY AWAY (April), and #245 HARVEST HOME (May).

Harlequin Intrigue
Adopts a New Cover Story!

**We are proud to present to you
the new Harlequin Intrigue cover design.**

Look for two exciting new stories each month, which
mix a contemporary, sophisticated romance with the
surprising twists and turns of a puzzler . . . romance
with "something more."